Oliver Optic, A. Burnham Shute

Four Young Explorers

Sight-Seeing in the Tropics

Oliver Optic, A. Burnham Shute

Four Young Explorers
Sight-Seeing in the Tropics

ISBN/EAN: 9783337337353

Printed in Europe, USA, Canada, Australia, Japan

Cover: Foto ©berggeist007 / pixelio.de

More available books at **www.hansebooks.com**

FOUR YOUNG EXPLORERS

OR

SIGHT-SEEING IN THE TROPICS

BY

OLIVER OPTIC

AUTHOR OF

"THE ARMY AND NAVY SERIES" "YOUNG AMERICA ABROAD, FIRST AND SECOND SERIES" "THE BOAT-CLUB STORIES" "THE ONWARD AND UPWARD SERIES" "THE GREAT WESTERN SERIES" "THE WOODVILLE STORIES" "THE LAKE SHORE SERIES" "THE YACHT-CLUB SERIES" "THE RIVERDALE STORIES" "THE BOAT-BUILDER SERIES" "THE BLUE AND THE GRAY AFLOAT" "THE BLUE AND THE GRAY—ON LAND" "THE STARRY FLAG SERIES" "ALL-OVER-THE-WORLD LIBRARY, FIRST SECOND AND THIRD SERIES" COMPRISING "A MISSING MILLION" "A MILLIONAIRE AT SIXTEEN" "A YOUNG KNIGHT-ERRANT" "STRANGE SIGHTS ABROAD" "AMERICAN BOYS AFLOAT" "THE YOUNG NAVIGATORS" "UP AND DOWN THE NILE" "ASIATIC BREEZES" "ACROSS INDIA" "HALF ROUND THE WORLD" ETC., ETC., ETC.

BOSTON
LEE AND SHEPARD PUBLISHERS
10 MILK STREET
1896

TO

MY APPRECIATIVE AND VALUED FRIEND

FREDERICK D. RUGGLES, ESQ.

RESIDING ON A HISTORIC HILL IN
HARDWICK, MASS.

This Volume

IS RESPECTFULLY AND CORDIALLY
DEDICATED.

PREFACE

"FOUR YOUNG EXPLORERS" is the third volume of the third series of the "All-Over-the-World Library." When the young millionaire and his three companions of about his own age, with a chosen list of near and dear friends, had made the voyage "Half Round the World," the volume with this title left them all at Sarawak in the island of Borneo. The four young explorers, as they became, were permitted to spend three weeks there hunting, fishing, and ascending some of the rivers, while the rest of the party proceeded in the Guardian-Mother to Siam. The younger members of the ship's company believed they had seen enough of temples, palaces, and fine gardens in the great cities of the East, and desired to live a wilder life for a brief period.

They were provided with a steam-launch, prepared for long trips; and they ascended the Sarawak, the Sadong, and the Simujan Rivers, and had all the hunting, fishing, and exploring they desired. They visited the villages of the Sea and Hill Dyaks, and learned what they could of their manners and customs, penetrating the island from the sea to the mountains. They studied the flora and the fauna of the forests, and were exceedingly interested in their occupation for about a week, when they came to the conclusion that "too much of a good thing" became wearisome; and, more from the love of adventure than for any other reason, they decided to proceed to Bangkok, and to make the voyage of nine hundred miles in the Blanchita, as they had named the steam-launch, which voyage was accomplished without accident.

After the young explorers had looked over the capital of Siam, the Guardian-Mother and her consort made the voyage to Saigon, the capital of French Cochin-China, where the visit of the tourists was a general frolic, with "lots of fun," as the young people expressed it; and then, crossing the China Sea, made the port of Manila, the capital of the Philippine Islands, where they explored the city, and made a trip up the Pasig to the Lake of the Bay. From this city they made the voyage to Hong-Kong, listening to a very long lecture on the way in explanation of the history, manners, and customs, and the peculiarities of the people of China. They were still within the tropics, and devoted themselves to the business of sight-seeing with the same vigor and interest as before. But most of them had read so much about China, as nearly every American has, that many of the sights soon began to seem like an old story to them.

Passing out of the Torrid Zone, the two steamers proceeded to the north, obtaining a long view of Formosa, and hearing a lecture about it. Their next port of call was Shang-hai, reached by ascending the Woo-Sung. From this port they made an excursion up the Yang-tse-Chiang, which was an exceedingly interesting trip to them. The ships then made the voyage to Tien-tsin, from which they ascended by river in the steam-launch to a point thirteen miles from Pekin, going from there to the capital by the various modes of conveyance in use in China. They visited the sights of the great city under the guidance of a mandarin, educated at Yale College. Some of the party made the trip to the loop-wall, near Pekin. Returning to Tien-tsin, with the diplomatic mandarin, who had accepted an invitation to go to Japan in the Guardian-Mother, they sailed for that interesting country, where the next volume of the series will take them.

It may be necessary to say that the Guardian-Mother, now eighteen months from New York, and half round the world, reached Tien-tsin May 25, 1893; and therefore nothing relating to the late war between China and Japan is to be found in this volume. Possibly the four young explorers would have found more sights to see, and more adventures to enjoy, if they had struck either of the belligerent nations during the war; but the ship sailed for the United States before hostilities were begun.

Of course the writer has been compelled to consult many volumes in writing this book; and he takes great pleasure in mentioning among them the very interesting and valuable work of Mr. W. T. Hornaday, the accomplished traveller and scientist, " Two Years in the Jungle." This book contains all that one need know about Borneo, to say nothing of the writer's trip in India among the elephants. His researches in regard to the orang-outang appear to have exhausted the subject; though I do not believe he has found the " missing link," if he is looking for it. Professor Legge contributed several articles to " Chambers's Encyclopædia," which contain the most interesting and valuable matter about China to be derived from any work; for he lived for years in that country, travelled extensively, and learned the language. I am under great obligations to these authors.

The author is under renewed obligations to his readers, young and old, who have been his constant friends during more than forty years, for the favor with which they have received a whole library of his books, and for the kind words they have spoken to him, both verbally and by letter.

WILLIAM T. ADAMS.

DORCHESTER, MASS.

CONTENTS

ix

CHAPTER IX.

CHAPTER X.

CHAPTER XI.

CHAPTER XII.

CHAPTER XIII.

CHAPTER XIV.

CHAPTER XV.

CHAPTER XVI.

CHAPTER XVII.

CHAPTER XVIII.

CHAPTER XIX.

CHAPTER XX.

CHAPTER XXI.

CHAPTER XXII.

CHAPTER XXIII.

CHAPTER XXIV.

CHAPTER XXV.

CHAPTER XXVI.

CHAPTER XXVII.

CHAPTER XXVIII.

CHAPTER XXIX.

CHAPTER XXX.

CHAPTER XXXI

CHAPTER XXXII.

CHAPTER XXXIII.

CHAPTER XXXIV.

CHAPTER XXXV.

CHAPTER XXXVI.

LIST OF ILLUSTRATIONS

FOUR YOUNG EXPLORERS

CHAPTER I

THE BORNEO HUNTERS AND EXPLORERS

THE Guardian-Mother, attended by the Blanche, had conveyed the tourists, in their voyage all over the world, to Sarawak, the capital of a rajahship on the north-western coast of the island of Borneo. The town is situated on both sides of a river of the same name, about eighteen miles from its mouths.

The steamer on which was the pleasant home of the millionaire at eighteen, who was accompanied by his mother and a considerable party, all of whom have been duly presented to the reader in the former volumes of the series, lay in the middle of the river. The black smoke was pouring out of her smokestack, and the hissing steam indicated that the vessel was all ready to go down the river to the China Sea. Her anchor had been hove up, and the pilot was in the pilot-house waiting for the commander to strike the gong in the engine-room to start the screw.

Just astern of the Guardian-Mother was a very

trim and beautiful steam-launch, fifty feet in length. The most prominent persons on board of her were the quartette of American boys, known on board of the steamer in which they had sailed half round the world as the "Big Four." Of this number Louis Belgrave, the young millionaire, was the most important individual in the estimation of his companions, though happily not in his own.

Like a great many other young men of eighteen, which was the age of three of them, while the fourth was hardly sixteen, they were fond of adventure,—of hunting, fishing, and sporting in general. They had gone over a large portion of Europe, visited the countries on the shores of the Mediterranean, crossed India, and called at some of the ports of Burma, the Malay peninsula, Sumatra, Java, Celebes, and had reached Sarawak in their explorations.

They had visited many of the great cities of the world, and seen the temples, monuments, palaces, and notable structures of all kinds they contain; but they had become tired of this description of sight-seeing. When the island of Borneo was marked on the map as one of the localities to be visited, the "Big Four" had a meeting in the boudoir, as one of the apartments of the Guardian-Mother was called, and voted that they had had enough of temples, monuments, and great cities for the present.

They agreed that exploring a part of Borneo, with the incidental hunting, fishing, and study of natural history, would suit them better. Louis Belgrave was appointed a committee of one to petition the commander to allow them three weeks in the island for this purpose. Captain Ringgold suggested to Louis that it was rather selfish to leave the rest of the party on the steamer, stuck in the mud of the Sarawak, while they were on the rivers and in the woods enjoying themselves.

But the representative of the "Big Four" protested that they did not mean anything of the sort. They did not care a straw for the temples and other sights of Siam, Cambodia, and French Cochin-China; and while they were exploring Borneo and shooting orang-outangs, the Guardian-Mother should proceed to Bangkok and Saigon, and the rest of the tourists could enjoy themselves to the full in seeing the wonders of Farther India.

It required a great deal of discussion to induce the commander, and then the mothers of two of the explorers, to assent to this plan; but the objections were finally overcome by the logic and the eloquence of Louis. The Blanche, the consort of the Guardian-Mother, having on board the owner, known as General Noury, his wife and his father-in-law, had nothing to do with this difficult question; but the general had a steam-launch, which he was kind enough to grant for the use of the explorers.

The third engineer of the ship was to go with the quartette, in charge of the engine; five of the youngest of the seamen were selected to make the venture safer than it might otherwise have been. Achang

Bakir, a native Bornean, who had been picked up off the Nicobar Islands, after the wreck of the dhow of which he had been in command, was to be the guide and interpreter.

The youngsters and their assistants had taken their places on board of the "Blanchita," as Louis had christened the craft, and she was to accompany the two large steamers down the river. But the farewells had all been spoken, the hugging and kissing disposed of, and the tears had even been wiped away. The mothers had become in some degree reconciled to the separation of three weeks.

The Guardian-Mother started her screw, and began to move very slowly down the river, amid the cheers and salutations of the officers, soldiers, and citizens of the town. The Blanche followed her, and both steamers fired salutes in honor of the spectators to their departure. The Blanchita secured a position on the starboard of the Guardian-Mother, and for three hours kept up a communication with their friends by signals and shouts.

Off the mouth of the Moritabas, one of the outlets of the stream, the steamers stopped their screws, and the "Big Four" went alongside of the Guardian-Mother; the adieux were repeated, and then the ships laid the course for their destination. Both of the latter kept up an incessant screaming with their steam whistles, and the party on board of them waved their handkerchiefs, to which the "Big Four," assisted by the sailors, responded in like manner, while the engineer gave whistle for whistle in feeble response.

When the whistles ceased, and the signals could no longer be seen, the Blanchita came about, and headed for the Peak of Santubong on the triangular island formed by the two passes of the Sarawak River. The explorers watched the ships till they could no longer be seen, and then headed up the river.

"Faix, the bridges betune oursels and civiloization are all broke down!" exclaimed Felix McGavonty, who sometimes used his Milesian dialect in order, as he put it, not to lose his mother's brogue.

"Not so bad as that, Felix; for there is considerable civilization lying around loose in Borneo," replied Louis Belgrave.

"Not much of it here is found," added Achang Bakir, the Bornean.

"Is found here," interposed Morris Woolridge, who had been giving the native lessons in English, for he mixed with it the German idiom.

"Rajah Brooke has civilized the region which he governs, and the Dutch have done the same in portions of their territory. Professor Giroud gave us the lecture on Borneo, and we shall have occasion to review some of it," added Louis. "But I think we had better give some attention to the organization of our party for the trip up the Sarawak River."

"I move, Mr. Chairman, that we have the same organization we had on board of the Maud," interposed Felix, dropping his brogue. "That means that Mr. Scott shall be captain, and Morris mate, while Louis and myself shall be the deck-hands."

"Mr. Chairman, I move an amendment to the motion, to the effect that Louis shall be captain, while I serve as deck-hand," said Scott.

"I hope the amendment will be voted down, and that the original motion will prevail," Louis objected. "Captain Scott, in command of the Maud, on a voyage of two thousand miles, proved himself to be an able and skilful commander, as well as a prudent and successful leader in several difficult situations. He is the right person for the position. Question! Those in favor of the amendment of Mr. Scott will signify it by raising the right hand."

Scott voted for his own motion, and he was the only one.

"Contrary minded, by the same sign," continued Louis, raising his right hand, Felix and Morris voting the same. "The amendment is lost. The question is now on the original motion of Felix. Those in favor of its adoption will signify it."

Three hands appeared, the motion was carried, and the chairman informed Scott and Morris that they were chosen captain and mate. Scott was outvoted, and he made no further objection. Of the five seamen on board he appointed Pitts cook and steward, in which capacity he had served on board of the Maud. The starboard is the captain's watch; though the second mate, when there is one, takes his place for duty, and the port is the mate's watch.

"I select Clingman for the first of my watch," continued Scott. "Your choice next, Morris."

"Wales," said the mate.

"Lane for the starboard," added Scott.

"Hobson's choice," laughed Morris, as he took the last man. "Clinch for the port; the last, but by no means the least."

"I fancy the watches will have an easy time of it; for I suppose we shall not do much running up and down these rivers, and through dark forests, in the night," suggested Louis.

"If we lie up in the night, I shall divide them both into quarter-watches, and have one man on duty all the time; for we may be boarded by a huge crocodile or a boa-constrictor if we are not on the lookout. But Achang is a pilot for these rivers. Isn't that so, Captain Bakir?"

"I have been up and down all the rivers in this part of the island, though I was not shipped as a pilot then," replied Achang, who had been the captain of a dhow, and on board the ship he had been called by his first name or the other with the title.

"All right; we shall use you for pilot or interpreter as occasion may require; and I suppose you can tell us all we want to know about the country and the people," added the captain.

Clinch, one of the ablest seamen on board, was steering the launch, and Scott kept the run of the courses; but as long as the craft had three feet of water under her, she was all right. The conversation took place in the cabin, as the explorers called the after part of the steamer, though no such apartment had been built there.

A frame constructed of brass rods, properly braced, extended the entire length of the launch. A stanchion at the bow and another at the stern, with five on each side set in the rail, supported a rod the whole distance around the craft. Another extended from the bow to the stern stanchion, directly over the keel, about six inches higher than those at the sides. Ten rods led from the central down to the side rods, like the rafters of a house.

Over the whole, of this structure above was extended a single piece of painted canvas, serving as a roof, and keeping out both sun and rain. It was laced very taut to the rods, and had slope enough to make the water run off. On the sides were curtains, which could be hauled down tight. The launch had been used by the rajah on the Ganges, and when closed in the interior was like "a bug in a rug."

Thus closed in, the standing-room was called the cabin. It was surrounded by wide cushioned seats, which made very good beds at night. Between these divans was a table where the meals of the explorers were to be served. Under the seats were many lockers for all sorts of articles, the bedding, and the arms and ammunition.

Just forward of the cabin were the engine and boiler, with bunkers on each side for the coal. In the middle of the craft was abundant space. The forward part of the boat was provided with cushioned divans, where passengers could sit by day or sleep at night; and this space was appropriated to the sailors. In the centre of it was the wheel. Next to it was the galley, with a stove large enough to cook for a dozen persons, and all needed utensils.

The ship's company had looked the craft over with great interest, and all of them were well pleased with the arrangements. The launch had been put into the water and fitted up for use the day before. The party from both ships had visited her, and almost wished they were to go to the interior of the country in her.

The Blanchita continued on her course up the river. Pitts was at work in the galley; and as soon as the launch was made fast off the "go-down," or business building of the town, dinner was served to the seamen, and later to the denizens of the cabin. The afternoon was spent in examining the place, and in obtaining such supplies as were needed; for the boat was to sail on her voyage up the river early the next morning.

With the assistance of Achang, a small sampan, a kind of skiff, was purchased; for the Bornean declared that it would be needed in the hunting excursions of the party, for much of the country was flooded with water, a foot or two in depth.

CHAPTER II

A VOYAGE UP THE SARAWAK RIVER

THE young hunters slept on board of the Blanchita, and they were delighted with their accommodations. Sarawak, or Kuching, the native name of the town, is only about one hundred and fifty miles north of the equator, and must therefore be a very warm region, though away from the low land near the sea-coast it is fairly healthy. The party slept with the curtains raised, which left them practically in the open air.

Achang had given them a hint on board of the ship that mosquitoes were abundant in some localities in Borneo. The Guardian-Mother was provided with the material, and the ladies had made a dozen mosquito bars for the explorers. They were canopies, terminating in a point at the top, where they were suspended to the cross rods on which the canvas roof was supported. The netting was tucked in under the cushions of the divan, and the sleepers were perfectly protected.

Captain Scott had carried out his plan in regard to the watches. The cook was exempted from all duty in working the little steamer; but each of the other seamen was required to keep a half-watch of two hours during the first night on board. Clinch was on watch at four in the morning. He called the engineer at this hour, and Felipe proceeded at once to get up steam. It was still dark, for the sun rises and sets at six o'clock on the equator.

As soon as there was a movement on board, all hands turned out forward. There were no decks to wash down; and, if there had been, the water was hardly fit, in the judgment of the mate, for this purpose, for it was murky, and looked as though it was muddy; but it was not so bad as it appeared, for the dark color was caused by vegetable matter from the jungles and forest, and not from the mud, which remained at the bottom of the stream.

"The top uv the marnin' to ye's!" shouted Felix, as he leaped from his bed about five o'clock, — for all hands had turned in about eight o'clock in the evening, as the mosquitoes, attracted by the lanterns, began to be very troublesome, — and the Milesian could sleep no longer.

"What's the matter with you, Flix?" demanded the captain.

"Sure, if ye's mane to git under way afore night, it's toime to turn out," replied Felix. "Don't ye's hear the schtaym sizzlin' in the froy'n pan?"

"But it isn't light yet," protested Scott.

"Bekase the lanthern in the cab'n bloinds your two oyes, and makes the darkness shoine broighter nor the loight," said Felix, as he looked at his watch. "Sure, it's tin minutes afther foive in the marnin'. These beds are altogidther too foine, Captain."

"How's that, Flix?" asked Scott, as he opened the netting and leaped out of bed.

"They're too comfor-*ta*-ble, bad 'cess to 'em, and a b'y cud slape till sundown in 'em till the broke o' noight."

"Dry up, Flix, or else speak English," called Louis, as he left his bed. "There is no end of 'paddies' along this river, and I'm sure they cannot understand your lingo."

"Is it paddies in this haythen oisland?" demanded Felix, suspending the operation of dressing himself, and staring at his fellow deck-hand. "I don't belayve a wurrud of ut!"

"Are there no paddies up this river, Achang?" said Louis, appealing to the Bornean.

"Plenty of paddies on all the streams about here," replied the native.

"And they can't oondershtand Kilkenny Greek! They're moighty quare paddies, thin."

"They are; and I am very sure they won't answer you when you speak to them with that brogue," added Louis.

"We will let that discussion rest till we come to the paddies," interposed the captain, as he completed his toilet, and left the cabin.

By this time all the party had left their beds and dressed themselves; for their toilet was not at all elaborate, consisting mainly of a woollen shirt, a pair of trousers, and a pair of heavy shoes, without socks. Felipe had steam enough on to move the boat; and the seamen had wiped the moisture from all the wood and brass work, and had put everything in good order.

"Are you a pilot for this river, Achang?" asked Scott, as the party came together in the waist, the space forward of the engine.

"I am; but there is not much piloting to be done, for all you have to do is to keep in the middle of the stream," replied the Bornean. "I went up and down all the rivers of Sarawak in a sampan with an English gentleman who was crocodiles, monkeys, mias, snakes, and birds picking up."

"Wrong!" exclaimed Morris. "You know better than that, Achang."

The native repeated the reply, putting the verb where it ought to be.

"He was a naturalist," added Louis.

"Yes; that was what they called him in the town."

"I think we all know the animals of which you speak, Achang, except one," said Louis. "I never heard of a mias."

"That is what Borneo people call the orang-outang," replied the native.

"Orang means a man, and outang a jungle, and the whole of it is a jungle man," Louis explained, for the benefit of his companions; for he was better read in natural history than any of them, as he had read all the books on that subject in the library of the ship. "In Professor Hornaday's book, 'Two Years in the Jungle,' which was exceedingly interesting to me, he calls this animal the 'orang-utan,' which is only another way of spelling the second word."

"Excuse me, Louis, but I think we will get under way, and hear your explanations at another time," interposed Captain Scott.

"I have finished all I had to say."

"Take the wheel, Achang," continued the captain.

The sampan was sent ashore to cast off the fasts. The river at the town is over four hundred feet wide, and deep enough in almost any part for the Blanchita. As soon as the lines were hauled in, the captain rang one bell, and Felipe started the engine. The helmsman headed the boat for the middle of the stream, and the captain rang the speed-bell. When hurried, the Blanchita was good for ten knots an hour, but her ordinary speed was eight.

On the side of the river opposite Kuching, or Sarawak, was the kampon of the Malays and other natives; and the term means a division or district of a town. Many of the natives of this village had visited the Blanchita, — some for trade, some for employment, and some from mere curiosity. None of them were allowed to go on board of the launch; for, while the Dyaks are remarkably honest people, the Malays and Chinese will steal without any very heavy temptation.

Achang headed the boat up the river. For five miles the banks were low, with no signs of cultivation, and bordered with mangroves. At this point the captain called Lane to the wheel, with orders to keep in the middle of the river. The " Big Four " had taken possession of the bow divans, the better to see the shores. They were more elevated, which simply means higher above the water.

" When shall we come across the paddies, Achang ? " asked Felix ; " for I am very anxious to meet them, and maybe we shall have a Kilkenny fight with them."

" No, you won't, for you speak English," replied Louis.

" The paddies are here on both sides of the river," added Achang.

" I don't see a man of any sort, not even a Hottentot, and I am sure there is not a Paddy in sight."

" Your education has been neglected, Flix, and you did not read all the books in the ship's library," said Louis. " I only told you the paddies would not answer you if you spoke to them with a brogue. You can try them now if you wish."

" But I don't see a single Paddy to try it on."

" Here is one on your left."

" I don't see anything but a field of rice."

" That's a paddy in this island."

" A field of rice ! "

" Achang will tell you that is what they call them in Borneo."

"Bad luck to such Paddies as they are! But it looks as though there might be some Paddies here, for the houses are very neat and nice, just as you see in old Ireland."

"Certainly they are; but I never saw any such in Ireland," added Louis. "You remember the old woman on the road from Killarney to the lakes who told us she lived in the Irish castle, to which she pointed; and it looked like a pig-sty."

"Of course it didn't have the bananas and the cocoanut-palms around it."

"I admit that we saw many fine places in Ireland, and very likely your mother lived in one of them. But, Achang, is there any game in the woods we see beyond the paddies?"

"Sometimes there is plenty of it; at others there is scarcely any. You can get squirrels here and some birds."

"Any orang-outangs?"

"We found none when we came up the river, for this is not the best place for them. If we run up the Sadong and Samujan Rivers, you will find some," replied the Bornean. "I don't think it will pay to go very far up the Sarawak, if it is game you want; but you can see the country. There is quite a village on the right."

The party were very much interested in examining the houses they saw on the borders of the stream. Like those they had seen in Java and in Sumatra, they were all set up on stilts. A Malay or

Dyak will not build his home on dry land, as they noticed in coming up the lower part of the river, though there was plenty of elevated ground near. The dwellings were all built on the soft mud.

The village ten miles up-stream was constructed on the same plan. The houses were placed just out of the reach of the water when it was higher than usual. The material was something like bamboo, as in India, with roofs of kadjang leaves, which abound in the low lands. In front of every one of them was a flat boat — sampan; and one was seen which was large enough to have a roof of the same material as the house. The boats were made fast to a pole set in the mud.

"There is a bear on the shore!" shouted Morris, with no little excitement in his manner, as he pointed to the woods on the shore opposite the houses, to which the attention of all the rest of the party had been directed.

At the same time he seized his repeating rifle, and all the others followed his example. The animal was fully three feet high, and at a second glance it did not look much like a bear. Whatever it was, it took to its heels when the sound of the steamer's screw reached its ear. But Morris fired before the boat started, and the others did the same.

"That is not a bear, Mr. Morris," interposed Achang, laughing as he spoke.

"What is it, then?" demanded Morris.

"A pig."

"A pig three feet high!" exclaimed the hunters with one voice.

"A wild pig," added the Bornean.

"Is he good for anything?" inquired Scott.

"He is good to eat if you like pork."

"He dropped in the bushes when we fired. Can't we get him?" asked Morris.

Under the direction of the captain the steamer was run up to the shore; and the bank in this place was high enough to enable the party to land without using the sampan. All hands, including the seamen, rushed in the direction of the spot where the pig had been seen. The game was readily found. The animal was something like a Kentucky hog, often called a "racer," because he is so tall and lank. He was a long-legged specimen; and Achang said that was because they hunted through swamps and shallow water in search of food, and much use had made their legs long. He added that they were a nuisance because they rooted up the rice, and farmers had to fence their fields.

He was carried on board by the sailors, and Pitts cut out some of the nicer parts of the pig. They had roast pork for dinner, but it was not so good as civilized hogs produce.

CHAPTER III

SOMETHING ABOUT BORNEO AND ITS PEOPLE

"I don't think we know much of anything about Borneo," said Scott, as the Blanchita continued on her course up the Sarawak, after the dinner of roast pork.

"We all heard the lecture of Professor Giroud on board the ship," replied Louis.

"I should like to hear it over again, now that we are on the ground," added the captain.

"Sure, we're not on the ground, but on the wather," suggested Felix.

As the reader did not hear the lecture, or see it in print, it becomes necessary to repeat it for the benefit of "whom it may concern." The professor, after being duly presented to his audience in Conference Hall, proceeded as follows: —

"Australia is undoubtedly the largest island in the world, and some geographers class it with the continents; but Chambers makes Borneo the third in size, while most authorities rate it as the second, making Papua, or New Guinea, the second in extent. Lippincott says Papua disputes with Borneo the claim to the second place among the great islands of the world; and I do not propose to settle the question. Chambers gives the area of Borneo at 284,000 square miles, the population in the neighborhood of 200,000, and the dimensions as 800 by 700 miles.

"It has a coast-line of about 3,000 miles, nearly the whole of which is low and marshy land. A large portion of the island is mountainous, as you may see by looking at the map before you;" and the professor indicated the several ranges with the pointer. "One chain extends nearly the whole length of the island, dividing in the middle of it into two branches, both of which almost reach the sea on the south. Near the centre of the island are two cross ranges, one extending to the east, and the other to the south-west. It would be useless to mention the Malay names of these ranges, for you could not remember them over night. The general idea I have given you is quite enough to retain.

"The interior of Borneo is but little known; and when Mr. Gaskette makes another map of the island twenty or thirty years hence, it will probably differ considerably from the one before you. In the extreme north is the peak of Kini Balu, the height of which is set down at 13,698 feet, with an interrogation point after it. Other mountains are estimated to be from 4,000 to 8,000 feet high. There are no active volcanoes.

"In the low lands on the coast, it is hot, damp, and unhealthy for those who are not acclimated; but in the high lands among the mountains, the temperature is moderate, from 81° to 91° at noon, and it is sometimes worse than that in New York.   From November to May, which is the rainy season, violent storms of wind with thunder-showers prevail on the west coast.   In hot weather the sea-breezes extend a considerable distance inland.   Vegetation is remarkably luxuriant, as our young hunters will find in their explorations.   The forests produce all the woods of the Indian Archipelago, of which you know the names by this time.   Brunei, on the north-west coast, produces the best camphor in Asia, which is about the same as saying in the world."

"What is camphor, Professor?" asked Mrs. Belgrave.   "I have used it all my life, but I have not the least idea what it is."

"Camphor is an oil found in certain plants, mostly from the camphor laurel.   This oil is separated from the plant, and then undergoes the process of refining. It is mixed with water, and then boiled in a sort of retort.   It makes steam, which is allowed to escape through a small aperture, which is then closed, and the camphor becomes solid in the upper part of the vessel.   This is the article which is sent to market.

"All the spices and fruits of the Torrid Zone are produced in Borneo, with cotton and sugar-cane in certain parts.   The animals of the island are about the same as in other parts of the Archipelago.   The monkey tribe is the most abundant, including the simia, the gibbon, the orang-outang, found in no other island, except very rarely in Sumatra, where our hunters did not find even one; tapirs"—

"What are they ?" asked Uncle Moses.

"They are a sort of cross between an elephant and a hog. They are found all over South American tropical regions and in this part of Asia. The animal is more like a hog than like an elephant, though it has the same kind of a skin as the latter. It is about the size of the average donkey. It has a snout which is prehensile, like the trunk of an elephant, but on a very small scale.

"What does that mean ?" asked Mrs. Blossom.

"Capable of taking hold of anything, as the elephant does with his proboscis. The tapir is one of the gentler animals, and may be easily tamed; though it will fight and bite hard when attacked, or harried by dogs. They take to the water readily, though the American swims, while the Asiatic only walk on the bottom. One book I consulted calls the tapir a kind of tiger, to which he bears hardly any resemblance.

"The other animals are small Malay bears, wild swine, horned cattle, and puny deer. The elephant and rhinoceros are found, few in number, in the north. The birds are the eagle, vulture, argus-pheasant, — a singular and beautiful bird, — peacocks, flamingoes, and swifts."

"What in the world are swifts ?" inquired Mrs. Woolridge.

"They are a kind of swallow, of which you may have seen some as we came down from Rangoon. They make the edible birds'-nests which are so great a delicacy among the Chinese when made into soup.

The rivers, lakes, and swamps swarm with crocodiles, the real man-eaters. Leeches are a nuisance when you bathe in the rivers and ponds, and various kinds of snakes abound. There are plenty of fish in the sea, lakes, and rivers. Diamonds, gold, coal, copper, are mined in the island.

"All of New England and the Middle States, with Maryland, could be set down in Borneo, still leaving a considerable border of swamp and jungle all around them. The United Kingdom of Great Britain and Ireland could be slapped down upon it like a flap-jack, and there would still be more than space for another United Kingdom, without covering up all the mud of Borneo. We do not see how big it is when we look on the map.

"The larger portion of the island is included in the Dutch possessions. Banjermassin, of which something was said as we passed the mouth of the Barito River, on which it is located, contains 30,000 inhabitants, and is the most important in the island. Borneo proper is in the north-west, and is under the government of the Sultan of Brunei. He lost nearly one-half of his territory, taken by the North Borneo Company, and that in the west, which is now Sara-wak, of which I shall have something more to say later. The island of Labuan lies six miles west of the northern portion of Brunei. It was ceded to the English by the sultan, and is principally valu-able as a coaling-station, though it has a considerable trade.

"Sabah is the country of the North Borneo Company. An American obtained the right to this territory in 1865, and transferred it to the present company. It has an area somewhat larger than the State of Maine. No doubt they will develop and improve the country.

"Sarawak has a territory nearly as large as that of the State of Pennsylvania, and larger than the State of Ohio. Its history is involved in the life of Sir James Brooke, who was originally created the rajah, or governor of the country, by the Sultan of Brunei, and retained the title till his death in 1868. He was born in Benares in 1803, and educated at Norwich, England. In 1819 he entered the East Indian army, and was severely wounded in the Burmese war. He returned to England; and his furlough lapsed before he could rejoin his regiment, and with it his appointment. He left the service. He next conceived a plan for putting down piracy in the Indian Archipelago, and of civilizing the savage inhabitants of these islands, a grand and noble scheme to be carried out by a single individual on his own responsibility.

"He bought a small vessel, and made a voyage to China, probably with the intention of improving his finances for the work he had in view. In 1835 he inherited $150,000 at the death of his father. After a cruise in the Mediterranean, he sailed in a schooner-yacht from London for Sarawak, where he arrived in 1839. The uncle of the sultan was engaged in a war with some tribes of rebels, and Brooke rendered him important assistance. He returned to Kuching with the title of rajah, his predecessor, a native, having been compelled to resign.

"The new governor immediately went to work very vigorously to establish a better government, introducing free trade, and framing a new code of laws. At this time the atrocious custom of head-hunting prevailed in the island. Enemies killed in battle were decapitated simply for the sake of the head, and the Dyak who obtained the greatest number of them was esteemed the most valiant warrior.

"A Dyak girl would not accept the addresses of a young man who had not obtained a head, in the earlier time; and murders were often committed for the sole purpose of obtaining the head of the victim, either to conciliate some dusky maiden, or as a trophy for the head-house, of which there is one in every village. The heads were 'cooked,' as they called it, though the operation was merely drying and cleaning the skull. Rajah Brooke made the penalty of this kind of murder death, without regard to the customs and antecedents of the natives; and he soon abolished head-hunting in his dominion.

"The sultan, either directly or by 'winking at it,' encouraged piracy; and the crime was as common as in the vicinity of the Malay states fifty years ago. Sir James Brooke resolutely attacked the pirates,

and with the means at his command soon vanquished
and drove them from the sea and the land. The
Dyaks, in spite of their head-hunting propensities,
were rather a simple people; while the Malays of
the island were cunning, dishonest, treacherous, and
cruel. The simple Dyaks were no match for them,
and were cheated and abused in every possible way.
There was no such thing as justice in the land. The
new rajah corrected all these abuses.

"Having established his government on the basis
of right and justice to all, Brooke went to England
in 1847. He was invited to Windsor by the Queen,
and created a K. C. B. (Knight Commander of the
Bath), a distinguished honor in Great Britain. The
next year he was made governor of Labuan. He
was charged in the House of Commons with receiving head-money for pirates killed; but the charge
was disproved.

"Brooke continued to hold his position as Rajah of
Sarawak while at Labuan; but in 1857 he was superseded at the latter, and returned to his government.
The Chinese, of whom there are a great many in
Borneo, became incensed against him because he prevented the smuggling of opium into his territory. A
large body of them attacked his house in the night,
and destroyed a great amount of his property.

"But the rajah was not a man to submit quietly
to such an outrage. He immediately collected a
force of Dyaks and Malays, and attacked the Celestials. He razed a fort they had constructed, and

thoroughly defeated them in several successive battles. He was very prompt and decided in action, and to see an abuse was to remedy it without unnecessary delay. He established and maintained a model government, and the country prospered greatly under his mild but decisive rule.

"He found a town with 1,000 inhabitants, and left it with 25,000. He died in 1868, and was succeeded by his nephew, Sir C. T. Brooke, who extended his territory, and ten years ago placed it under the protection of the United Kingdom. This is the history of a noble man and a model colony."

"But what are Dyaks, Professor?" inquired Mrs. Belgrave.

"They are natives of Borneo, though all the people are not known by this name. They are divided into Hill Dyaks and Sea Dyaks. At the present time they are a high-toned class of savages; for they do not steal or rob, and they have many social virtues which might be copied by the people of enlightened nations. Head-hunting and piracy are known among them no more. They are the farmers and producers of the island. There is much that is very interesting about them. They build peculiar houses, some of them occupied by a dozen or more families, though they always live in peace, and do not quarrel with their neighbors. The young women select their own husbands, and a head is no longer necessary to open the way to an engagement.

"If any of the party wish to learn more of the

Dyaks, their manners and customs, present and past, you will find a work in two volumes, by the Rev. J. G. Wood, entitled, 'The Uncivilized Races of Men;' and you will find that the author often quotes from Rajah Brooke."

CHAPTER IV

A SPECULATION IN CROCODILES

THE Blanchita continued on her course up the river with Clingman at the wheel. There was no table in the fore cabin; and the dinner of the six men, including the engineer, was served astern after the "Big Four" had taken the meal. Louis attended to the engine while Felipe was at his meals and occasionally at other times. A table is not a necessity for the crew of a ship, and one is not used on board a merchant vessel; but Louis insisted that all hands should fare equally well on board of the little steamer.

The dinner was disposed of, and Wales was at the wheel. The men had nothing to do, and a couple of them had assisted Pitts in washing the dishes and putting the after cabin in order. It was an idle time, and the "Big Four" were anxious to have something more exciting than merely sailing along the river, the novelty of which had worn off; and they had not long to wait for it.

"A crocodile ahead, Captain, on the port bow, sir!" exclaimed Wales, the wheelman, whose duty required him to keep a sharp lookout for any obstructions in the stream.

All of the party had their weapons within reach, including the three seamen who were disengaged; but the latter were not expected to use the rifles till they were ordered to do so by the captain or any one of the hunters. The occupants of the fore cabin, the principal personages on board, had the exclusive use of the forward part of the boat, though the hands were at liberty to use the seats when they were not required by any of the "Big Four." No order to this effect had been given; but the men, under the influence of the discipline on board of the ship, had involuntarily adopted the system.

"Slow her down, Wales," said Scott, after he had observed the situation of the saurian.

The wheelman rang the jingle-bell, and the boat soon came down to half-speed. The five hunters, including Achang, had their rifles ready for use, though they still retained their seats. The reptile was not asleep; and he appeared to have some notions of his own, for he was not disposed to wait for the coming of the boat. He settled down in the dark water so that he could not be seen, but the surface was disturbed by his movements.

"Port the helm, Wales," said the captain quietly. "He is going across the river."

Presently he came to the surface again, and was swimming towards the opposite shore. He kept his head and a small portion of his back next to it above the surface of the water, as the young hunters had seen in Sumatra before.

"Full speed; give her a spurt, Wales," said the captain.

The wheelman rang the speed-bell, and then spoke through the tube to the engineer. The boat suddenly darted ahead under this instruction, and was soon abreast of the reptile, who was not at first disposed to change his tactics. He evidently realized that he was pursued, and it seemed to make him angry.

"The rascal has put his helm to port," said Wales.

"Look out there, in the waist!" shouted Scott to the seamen, a couple of whom were seated on the rail, with their legs dangling over the side of the boat. "Never sit in that way, men, unless you want to be carried to the hospital with a leg bitten off."

"Will they bite, Captain?" asked Clinch.

"Bite? They are regular man-eaters on these rivers."

"I used to go in swimming with the alligators on the Alabama River; but they all kept their distance," added the seaman.

The two men drew in their legs and moved inboard. Alligators, which are generally considered harmless in the rivers of the Southern States, will bite at anything hanging in the water. As Wales had suggested, the crocodile had changed his course, and was now headed directly for the Blanchita. He seemed to have concluded that there was no safety for him in flight, and he had decided to fight.

"Your first shot, Louis," said Scott, who had not even taken up his rifle, as if he thought there would be no chance for him after the millionaire had fired.

Louis waited a minute or more till he could distinctly see the eye of the crocodile, and then he fired. As has so often been said before, he had been thoroughly trained in a shooting-gallery, and was a dead shot, as he had often proved during the voyage. The bullet had evidently gone to his brain, for the reptile floundered about for an instant, and then moved no more. As Felix put it, he was "very dead," though the word hardly admits of an intensifier.

"What are you going to do with him now?" asked the Milesian.

"I don't think we want anything more of him; but, like a poison snake, he is a nuisance that ought to be abated," replied the captain. "I dare say the rajah will be much obliged to us for making the number of them even one less."

"How long is he?" Achang inquired. as he returned his rifle to its resting-place.

"About ten feet," replied Louis.

"More than that," the captain thought. "I should say twelve feet."

"Then he is worth eighteen shillings to you," added the native.

"What is he good for, Achang?" asked Morris.

"He is good for nothing," replied the Bornean. "The crocodile here eats men and women. Some are killed every year, and the government pays one and sixpence apiece for the heads."

"That looks like a war of extermination upon them," said Morris.

"I don't know what that is; but they want to kill them all off," replied Achang, who had improved his language so that his tutor seldom had to correct it.

"That is the same thing. They pay by the foot for crocodiles here."

"The bigger they are, the more dangerous," suggested Louis. "Let us haul him alongside, and see how long he is."

The boat had stopped her screw before Louis fired; and the captain directed Wales to lay her alongside the saurian, which was done in a few minutes. Ropes were passed under his head and tail; and with a couple of purchases made fast to the horizontal rods over the rail, close to the stanchions, the carcass was hoisted partly out of the water. The measure was taken with a line first, to which Lane, who was a carpenter's assistant, applied his rule, which gave twelve feet and two inches as the length of the crocodile.

"That makes him worth eighteen shillings," said Achang.

"About four dollars and a half," added Morris. "We could make something hunting crocodiles. If we could kill ten of them like that fellow it would give us forty-five dollars."

Louis and Scott laughed heartily at this calculation, and thought the idea was derogatory to the character of true sport, though they did not object to turning their victims of this kind into money.

"Must we carry the carcass of this beast down to Kuching in order to get the reward, Achang?" asked Morris.

"The head will be enough; and they can tell how long he is by the size of it."

"How shall we saw the head off? Can you do it, Lane?"

"I can do that," interposed the Bornean, as he went to a bundle of implements he had procured in the town and from the natives.

He drew from it a very heavy sword, from which he took off the covering of dry leaves, and applied his thumb to the edge of the weapon. Then he picked out a straw from some packing, and dropped it off in pieces, as one tries his razor on a hair. It appeared to be as sharp as the shaving-tool, and he was satisfied. All hands watched his movements with deep interest. He secured a position with one foot on the side of the boat, and the other on the back of the crocodile. With two or three blows of his sword, he severed the head from the body, and a seaman secured it with a boathook.

All hands applauded when the deed was done, as the Bornean washed his keen blade. The operation excited the admiration of all the lookers-on, it was so quickly and skilfully done. Louis wished to examine the weapon, and it was handed to him. It was heavy enough to require a strong arm to handle it; and it was sharp enough for a giant's razor, if giants ever shave, for most of them are pictured with full beards.

"I suppose this is a native's sword," said Louis, as he passed it to the captain.

"Dyak *parong latok; parong* same thing, not so . long," Achang explained.

"I suppose that is what the Dyaks used when they went head-hunting," said Felix.

"No head-hunting now; used to use it, the Hill Dyaks. Used in battle too; split head open with it, or cut head off."

"What other weapons did the fighting men use?" asked Louis.

"They carried a shield, and used a spear with the parong latok; no other weapons. Two kinds of Dyaks, the Sea and the Hill."

While the native was talking, the seamen, by order of the captain, had hoisted the head of the saurian into the sampan towing astern, placing it on a piece of tarpaulin. The carcass was cast loose, and probably was soon devoured by others of its own kind.

"We might find some eggs in the crocodile," said Achang, as the body floated past the boat.

"We don't want the eggs," replied the captain, turning up his nose.

"Good to eat, Captain. My naturalist used to eat them. Very nice, like turtles' eggs, which Englishmen always put in the soup."

"None in my soup!" exclaimed Scott, with a wry face, to express his disgust.

"I suppose they would be all right if we only got used to them," suggested Louis.

"As the man's horse did when he fed him on shavings," sneered Scott.

"I did not take very kindly to turtles' eggs when we were in the West Indies; but I got used to them, and then liked them," added Louis. "In Africa the natives eat boa-constrictors, and think they are a choice morsel. Some of our Indians eat clay, and I suppose they like it."

"Something up in the trees yonder, Captain," said Wales, as the boat approached some higher ground, which was not overflown with water, as most of the shore below had been.

"Monkeys," added Achang, not at all excited.

"I don't think I care to shoot monkeys unless it is for the purpose of examining them," said Louis. "They are too small game, and they are harmless creatures."

"Strange monkeys in here," continued Achang. "Not these," he added when he had obtained a sight of one of them. "These no good."

All eyes were directed to the tree; and at least a dozen common monkeys were there, such as they had seen in the museums at home. The steamer continued on her course, and a couple of miles farther on the forest was inundated. Some of the trees appeared to be inhabited.

"Plenty of elephant monkeys in here," said Achang.

"Elephant monkeys!" exclaimed Louis. "I never heard of any such animals. Are they called so because they are so large?"

"No, sir," said Achang; "because they have such long noses."

"There are a dozen monkeys in that tree, and they look very queer," said Louis, as he elevated his double-barrelled fowling-piece, loaded with large shot, and fired.

One of them dropped, and another when he discharged the second barrel. The boat was run in the direction of the tree till it grounded in the mud. The captain proposed to go for them in the sampan, when Clingman volunteered to wade to the tree for the game, and soon returned with the two victims of the millionaire's unerring aim. They were placed in the waist, and all were curious to see them. The rest of the tribe scampered away over the tops of the trees, crying, "honk, honk, kehonk!"

"They are proboscis monkeys, and old males at that; for they have very long noses, which is the reason for the name, and why Achang calls them elephant monkeys," said Louis, as he turned the creatures over. "The noses of these two reach down below the chin. They stand about three feet high, but are rather lank, like the tall pigs."

While the party were examining them, the captain gave the order to back the boat, and then to go ahead. She was moored for the night soon after. The next morning, by the advice of Achang, the Blanchita was headed down the river, for the native declared that they would find no different game on the banks of the Sarawak.

CHAPTER V

A HUNDRED AND EIGHT FEET OF CROCODILE

THE party were stirring as soon as it was daylight; for in the tropics the early hours are the pleasantest, and they had fallen into the habit of early rising in India. The trees were alive with monkeys of several kinds, though the proboscis tribe seemed to be in the majority. Felix came out of the cabin with his gun in his hand, and began to regard the denizens of the tree-tops with interest.

"What are you going to do, Flix?" asked Louis, who was sitting on the rail, busily cutting out a notch in the end of a long piece of board.

"Don't you see there is plenty of game here, my darling?" demanded Felix, pointing up into the trees.

"Game!" exclaimed Louis contemptuously. "Monkeys!"

"Didn't you shoot a couple of them yesterday afternoon, Louis?"

"I did; but I wanted them in order to study the creature. Now every fellow knows what a proboscis monkey is, as he did not before except by name. I got my books out, and read him up with the animal before me. I am glad I did; for the picture of him

I had seen was nothing like him in his nasal appendage, which gives him his name."

"What is the reason of that?"

"The portrait was taken from a young one, before his nose had attained its full growth. But I don't believe in shooting monkeys for the fun of it. Our party are not inclined to eat them."

"I'd as soon eat a cat as a monkey," added Felix.

"Then, don't shoot those long-nosed fellows, for we have all the specimens of them we need," said Louis.

"What are you going to do with them, my darling? You can't keep them much longer, and you will have to throw them overboard, for they won't smell sweet by to-morrow."

"Achang learned something about taxidermy from the naturalist he travelled with, and he has promised to skin and mount one of them for me."

"But what's that you are making, Louis?" asked Felix, who had been trying to take the measure of the implement the young Crœsus was fashioning.

Its use was not at all evident. A triangular piece had been sawed out of the end of a strip of board four inches wide, and the rest of it had been cut down and rounded off, and the thing looked more like a pitch-fork than anything else.

"Is it to pitch hay with?" persisted Felix.

"No, it is not; when you see me use it, you will know what it is for. You must wait till that time before you know," replied Louis, who appeared to

"WHAT HAVE YOU GOT THERE, MR. BELGRAVE?"

have finished the implement just as the other brought his gun to his shoulder."

"That's the handsomest schnake I iver saw since me modther, long life to her, left ould Ireland before I was bahrn."

"Don't shoot him, Flix!" protested Louis vigorously. "Where is he?"

"Jist forninst the bow of the boat. Sure, Oi'm the schnake-killer of the party, and he's moi game."

"I don't want him killed yet," replied Louis, as he moved forward from the waist with the forked stick in his hand. "He is handsome, as you say, Flix."

Creeping very cautiously till he could see over the bow, he discovered the serpent, which was nearly six feet long, working slowly down a dead log towards the water. Springing to his feet on the bow, he struck down with his weapon, directing the fork at the neck of the reptile. The outside of the log was nothing but punk, or the operation would have been a failure. As it was, the two points of the implement sunk into the wood, and the snake was pinned in the opening at the end of the stick.

"What have you got there, Mr. Belgrave?" asked Achang, hurrying to the side of the operator.

"A snake; do you know him?" demanded Louis, as the reptile struggled to escape.

"I saw one like it years ago;" and he gave a long Dyak name to it which the others did not understand. "Wait a minute or two, and I will bring him on board for you."

" I don't know that we want him on board," added Louis.

" He is not poison, and he won't hurt you," said the Bornean, as he made a slip-noose at the end of a piece of cord.

Hanging over the bow, he passed the noose over the head of the snake, and hauled it taut, and then made the end he held fast to the boat. Louis lifted his implement from the neck of the snake, and he squirmed and wriggled as though he " meant business." Achang leaped to the shore, and seiziug the serpent by the tail, tossed him into the boat. He struck on one of the cushions, and the cord prevented him from going any farther.

Scott and Morris had just reached the fore cabin at this moment, and they started back as though they had been bitten by the snake. His head, tail, and belly were bright red, with white stripes upon a dark ground along his back and sides. No one but Achang had ever seen such a serpent, even in a museum. His snakeship was disposed to make himself comfortable on the cushion, and the Bornean loosed the cord around his neck.

" I saw a small snake, not more than two feet long, swimming near the shore of Lake Cobbosseecontee, in Maine, that had nearly all the colors of the rainbow in his skin," said Morris. "I tried to knock him over with my fishing-rod, and catch him; but I failed. I told the people where we boarded about him, but no one had ever seen a snake like him."

"There are plenty of such snakes in South America, some that are not poisonous, which the native women tame and wear as necklaces," added Louis.

"Well, what are you going to do with him?" asked Captain Scott. "I think you had better kill him, and throw him into the river, pretty as he is. He isn't a very desirable fellow to have as a companion on board."

"What is the use of killing him? He would only be food for the crocodiles," protested Louis.

"Do what you like with him, Louis," added the captain.

"I certainly will not have him killed. If Achang never saw but one of the kind, there cannot be a great many of them in this part of the island. Put him ashore, Achang," said the humane young gentleman.

The Bornean complied with this request; and the handsome snake skurried off in the woods, none the worse for his adventure. But the others were not quite satisfied with the policy of the young millionaire. They wanted to shoot whatever they could see in the nature of game, including monkeys, and he was opposed to this destructive action. Of course they could kill whatever they pleased, but the moral influence of the real leader prevailed over them.

"Steam enough!" shouted Felipe from the engine.

"Take the wheel, Clingman, back her out and go ahead," said the captain; and in a few moments they were steaming down the river.

"I suppose you haven't any tenderness for crocodiles, have you, Louis?" inquired Scott, with a smile.

"You seem to believe that I am as chicken-hearted as a girl; but I believe in killing all harmful animals, including poisonous snakes; but I do not like to see these innocent monkeys shot down for the fun of it," replied Louis. "You can kill them if you choose, but I will not."

"The rest of us will not, if you are opposed to it," added Scott.

"Crocodile on the port hand!" exclaimed Clingman. "He is swimming across the river, about three boats' lengths from us."

"Stop her!" said the captain.

"I shot the last one, and I will not fire at this one," added Louis, who was not disposed to monopolize the fun.

"All right; then I will be number two, Morris three, Flix four, and Achang five; and if you are all satisfied, we will fire in this order hereafter," continued Scott, as he took aim at the saurian.

He missed the eye of the reptile, and the bullet from the rifle glanced off and dropped into the water.

"How many shots is a fellow to have before he loses his chance?" asked the captain, as he aimed again.

"I suggest three," said Louis. "Those in favor of three say ay."

They all voted "ay," and Scott fired twice more.

"Your turn, Morris;" and he appeared to be very much chagrined at his ill luck. "I could hardly see the eye of the varmint."

Morris fired his three shots with no better success. Felix took a different position from the others, placing himself on the stem. He fired, and the saurian still kept on his course. He did better the second time; and the reptile floundered for a moment, and then turned over dead. The boat was run up alongside, and Achang was required to bring out his parong latok, with which he decapitated the game at a single blow this time; but the creature was only nine feet long.

Pitts called the cabin party to breakfast at this time. The Blanchita went ahead again, and the repeating rifles were left on the cushions. At Louis's suggestion the captain gave the four men off duty permission to use the arms on crocodiles, but not on monkeys.

Ham and eggs, with hot biscuit and coffee, was the bill of fare; and the young men had sharpened their appetites in the sports of the morning. Before they were half done they heard the crack of a rifle. They listened for the second shot, but none followed it.

"Who fired that shot, Pitts?" asked the captain, as the steward brought in another plate of biscuit.

"Clinch, sir," replied the man. "He knocked the crocodile over at the first shot, sir."

"Then he is a better shot than I am," said Scott, laughing.

"Or any of the rest of us who had their turns," added Felix. "Louis is the only fellow that brings 'em down the first time trying."

"The rest of you would have done better if the sun had not reflected on the water, and shaken your aim," said Louis.

Before the meal was finished, another shot was heard, followed by two more. When the party went forward they found that the little steamer had gone around a bend so that the forest shaded the surface of the water. Wales had fired the last three times at a crocodile still in sight; but he declared that he could not hit the side of a barn twenty feet from him, and did not care to fire again. The men went to breakfast, and the cabin party picked up the rifles. It was Achang's turn; and he missed twice, but killed the game at the third shot.

"I can see four more of them. We seem to have come to a nest of them, and the family are out for a morning airing," said Louis, as he picked up his rifle, while Felix was filling the other chambers with cartridges. "They have all started to go across the river."

"That must be the father of the family at the head of the procession," added the captain. "It is your turn now, Louis."

"Go ahead a little, Pitts," said the next one in turn; for the cook had taken the wheel while Clingman went to his morning meal. "I can't see his eye yet."

"That will do; stop her.   I can see his eye now, and there is no reflection on the water."

As soon as the boat lost her headway, Louis fired. The saurian leaped nearly out of the water, and came down wrong side up.   There were three dead reptiles lying on the water.   It was the captain's next shot, and when he placed the yacht in a position to suit him he fired.   The crocodile lifted his head out of the water, and did not move again.

"Bravo, Captain!" cried Louis.   "You did not have a fair chance last time, and you have redeemed yourself."

"I thought I could shoot better than before, and now I feel better.   But there are two more, and your turn, Morris."

He killed the game with the third shot, and Felix finished the last in sight with the second.   Achang had brought out his formidable weapon, and the six dead reptiles were decapitated.   The last three killed were each nine feet long, while the one Louis had shot was fourteen.   The heads were all put in the sampan, and they made a full load for it.   The Blanchita arrived at Kuching early in the afternoon, and the chief of police measured the heads, and took the figures from Felix.   He made one hundred and eight feet of crocodile, which the official approved as correct, and paid not quite forty dollars for the bounty.

CHAPTER VI

THE VOYAGE UP THE SADONG TO SIMUJAN

THE money received for the heads of the crocodiles was in the hands of Felix, who was the clerk of the captain on board the ship, and it was proper to make him purser of the Blanchita. What to do with it was the next question. Louis's advice was asked for, and he promptly suggested that it should be divided into ten parts, and a share given to all but himself; and this was done. He refused to accept a penny, but all the others received about four dollars apiece.

The money was all in silver, as it is all over India and the Archipelago for general use. The engineer and the seamen shared with the four hunters; for the former had done all the work and some of the shooting. The steamer was made fast at the shore, and all hands except Pitts landed for a walk through the town. Their first visit was to a fruit-store kept by a Chinaman; and most of the shops in the place were in the hands of the Celestials.

Bananas and oranges were the principal, though there were also nearly all the tropical fruits in season. Many of the party purchased useful articles in other places. They had learned in Singapore and

Batavia how to deal with Chinese traders, and they seldom gave even more than one-third or one-half of what was demanded. After diligent search Achang found a certain Dyak tool he wanted, — a sort of axe, which Lane, the carpenter's assistant, ridiculed without mercy.

The young men visited the English Mission, where they were kindly received, and went to the school. The American missionaries are also active in Borneo, and one of them has made a vocabulary of the Dyak language.

It was decided to start down the river the next morning on the way to the Sadong and Simujan Rivers, the latter being a branch of the former. In the early morning, as the hands were casting off the fasts, two Malays came alongside in a sampan, and asked to be towed to the Sadong. Achang had some talk with them, and made the request of the captain for them.   He learned that they were engaged in the business of catching crocodiles for the reward.

"They don't shoot crocodiles, and they have no rifles," added Achang.

"How do they get them then?" asked Louis.

"They fish for them."

"What, with a hook and line?" demanded Captain Scott.

"With a line, but have no fish-hook," replied the Bornean. "You must see them catch one."

"All right," replied the captain; "we will tow them down the river."

After the yacht had been moving about an hour, they came to a colony of saurians apparently, for several of them were in sight at once. Achang directed the reptile-hunters to catch one of them, and they paddled their sampan towards a large one. The Blanchita kept near enough to enable all hands to witness the operation, which the Bornean described to them as the Malays made their preparations, for they had all their fishing-gear in their boat.

The line they used was a rattan about forty feet long. At the "business end," as Scott called it, they attached a float to keep it on the top of the water. The steamer just crawled along on the river in order not to disturb the game, though the reptiles were accustomed to the sight of vessels.

"Now you see that stick the hunter has in his hand," said Achang, though each of them had one. "'Most a foot long, like a new moon."

"Crescent-shaped," added Louis.

"Called an *alir* in Malay. Made of green wood, very tough, pointed at the ends; they fasten the rattan line to the middle of the stick."

Some tough green bark, braided together, was then wound around the stick so that the game could not bite it in two. A big fish for bait was then attached to the alir, and carefully fastened to it so that the reptile could not tear it off.

Thus prepared, the apparatus was thrown overboard, and the sampan paddled away from it to give the game an opportunity to approach it, the Malays each paying out his forty feet of line, one on each side of the boat. The spectators watched the result with great interest. As the sampan receded from the saurians, they approached the bait. Crocodiles and alligators do not nibble at their prey, but bolt it as a snake does a frog.

The bait nearest to the observers on the yacht was soon gobbled up by the hungry crocodile, who appeared not to have been to breakfast that morning; and the Malay at the other end of the line gave a sharp jerk to his gear, the effect of which was to draw the pointed crescent "athwart ships," as the sailors would say, or across his stomach; and the harder it was pulled the more the pointed ends would penetrate the interior of the organ.

The first Malay had hardly hooked his game before the second had another ready to haul in. Both of the saurians struggled and lashed the dark water into a foam; but both of the men in the sampan kept the line as taut as they could with all their strength; and this is the rule in hauling in all gamey fish.

"Tell them we will go ahead, Achang, and all they need to do is to make fast their rattans to the sampan," said Captain Scott, when he had taken in the situation.

In reply to the message the Bornean delivered to them, the Malays nodded their heads vigorously, and smiled their assent.

"Go ahead, down the river, Clinch," added the captain to the helmsman.

"I fancy there will be a lively kick-up on the part of the game," said Louis, as the boat came up to her course.

"Not much," added Scott. "If we put them through the water at the rate of eight knots an hour, the crocs will not feel much like doing any gambolling. We are not making more than four knots now."

"They are as lively now as a parched pea in a hot skillet."

"I will ring the speed-bell now, and see how that will affect them," replied the captain, suiting the action to the word.

The Blanchita darted ahead at her usual speed. Clingman began to overhaul the painter of the sampan, for it did not look strong enough for the present strain. He had scarcely got hold of it before it snapped in the middle, and relieved the strain on the crocodiles. The steamer backed at the order of the captain; and a strong line was thrown into the sampan, which one of the Malays seized and made fast.

When the strain upon them was thus removed, the saurians made violent struggles to escape. The yacht then went ahead again, and the speed-bell was rung immediately. The pressure on the game was renewed, and they ceased to struggle. The apparatus held fast, for the saurian fishers were experienced in their business, and had done their work well.

At eight o'clock the Blanchita reached the mouth of the river. The crocodiles were not dead, but their stomachs must have been in a terrible condition. To Louis it seemed to be cruel to prolong their sufferings; and he wished Achang to request the Malays to kill them, and Scott agreed with him. The Bornean said they could not kill them while they were towing behind, and that, if the lines were slacked, they might get away.

The captain took the matter in hand, and told Achang what he intended to do, which he communicated to the reptile-hunters. On the starboard hand Scott fixed his gaze on a small tongue of land extending out into the river. Taking the wheel himself, he run her close to the land some distance above the point, and worked the sampan and its tow close to the shore. The tow-line of the sampan was then lengthened out to a hundred feet or more, and the yacht went ahead again, rounding the point, so that the peninsula lay between the steamer and her tow.

Then she went ahead again, and the result was that she pulled the sampan upon the point; and as she was flat-bottomed, there was no difficulty in doing so. The Blanchita continued on her course, and the two crocodiles were landed after her. One of the Malays then produced a parong latok; and even more skilfully than Achang had done the job, he cut off the heads of both reptiles. They were out of misery then, and Louis was satisfied.

The yacht was then run up to the point, and Lane was sent on shore to measure the reptiles, while the fishermen proceeded to recover the apparatus from the stomachs of the defunct reptiles. The larger crocodile was twelve feet and four inches long, and the other ten feet and seven inches. The voyage was resumed on the sea to the mouth of the Sadong; and in three hours more she entered the stream, which was a large one, averaging half a mile wide for twenty miles.

"Bujang!" called Achang, as instructed by the captain. "Do you want to go any farther?"

The head man replied in his own language that they wished to go to Simujan, or till they came to plenty of game. The Bornean said Bujang was a great hunter, for he had killed fifty-three crocodiles that year. The yacht, with the sampan still in tow, started up the river, keeping in the middle of it. Just before sunset she reached the junction of the Simujan and Sadong.

On one side of the branch stream there was a considerable Malay village, backed by an abundance of cocoanut palms; and, of course, the houses were built on stilts close to the water. On the other side was the Chinese kampon, or quarter, consisting largely of shops and trading-houses. Louis Belgrave had been presented to the officials at Sarawak as the owner of the Guardian-Mother, and that established him as a person of great distinction.

After the ship departed on her voyage to Siam,

many attentions were bestowed upon him; and when, after the return of the yacht from up the Sarawak, they learned that she was going to the Simujan, one of the officials had given him a letter of introduction to the Chinese half-cast government official, who was the magnate of the place. Figuratively, he took the "Big Four" in his arms, and there was nothing he was not ready to do for them.

He conducted them to the government house, and insisted that they should live there during their stay at Simujan. It had been erected to receive such officials as might have occasion to remain there at any time. It was well built and comfortable, and each chamber had a veranda in front of it. It was set on posts six feet from the ground, like all the other dwellings near it. It was the police station of the region; and the two Malays collected eight or nine dollars for their game, which they did not offer to share with the crew of the yacht — no Malay would do such a thing.

The agent's tender of the rooms to the party was accepted, for the members wished to sleep in a four-posted bedstead once more for a change. The chief Malay of the place called upon them, and treated them very handsomely. The Chinese official gave them much information as they were seated on a veranda of the house.

"You may find the orang-outang up the Simujan; but I don't know that you want such large game," said he.

"We have shot tigers in India, and Mr. McGavonty has shot more cobras than all the rest of us. He has a talent for killing snakes."

"Show me the snakes, and I will finish them," added Felix.

"You will not find many of them in the jungle. There are some water snakes taken occasionally, and people here eat them. They make a very fine curry."

"I should ask to be excused from partaking of that dish," said Scott.

"That is all prejudice," said the agent. "Perhaps you would like to go a-fishing in the Sadong and its branches. We have a peculiar way of taking fish here. We use the tuba plant, which the Malays prepare for use. It is a climbing-plant, the root of which has some of the properties of opium. It is reduced to a pulp, mixed with water. I cannot fully explain the process of preparation, in which the Malays are very skilful. At the right time of tide, the fluid is thrown into the stream. The effect is to stupefy and sometimes kill the fish. With dip-nets the fish are picked up, though some of them are so large that they can be secured only with a kind of barbed spear."

"I don't think I care to fish in that way," said Louis, with some disgust in his expression. "It is very unsportsmanlike, and it looks to me to be a mean way to do it."

"Just what some Englishmen who were here a

while ago said, and perhaps you are right; but it is a Malay art, and not English."

The party slept very comfortably on bedsteads that night, but they were up before the sun the next morning.

CHAPTER VII

A SPIRITED BATTLE WITH ORANG—OUTANGS

THE civilized people of Simujan were not stirring when the party came from their chámbers. Felipe had steam up at half-past five, for the captain intended to begin the ascent of the river; but he did not care to leave without bidding adieu to the kindly agent. But they got under way at his order, and ran up the river for a morning airing. The boat had not gone more than a mile when the young men discovered a sampan containing two Malays paddling with all their might for the shore.

They had no guns, and could not shoot their game, whatever it was; but each of them had a *biliong*. This was the implement Achang had bought in Sarawak. It looked something like a pickaxe with only one arm, the end of which was fashioned like a mortising chisel, and was used as an axe.

The edge of the chisel portion was parallel to the handle; but Achang explained that the Dyaks had another kind of biliong, with the cutting part at right angles with the handle, and this was used as an adze. While Lane, the carpenter, was ridiculing the tool, the Malays on shore moved to a tree in sight of the steamer, which had stopped her screw close to the sampan.

"They are going to cut down a tree with the biliongs," said Achang.   "Sometimes do that to get the game."

"They couldn't cut down a tree a foot through with those things in a week!" exclaimed Lane.

"So quick as you could cut it down," insisted the Bornean stoutly.

"Dry up, now, and let us see the Malays work with the thing," interposed the captain.

"Lane, you shall have a trial with a Dyak or a Malay, and I will give a prize of three dollars to the one that fells the tree first," said Louis.

"I should like to try that with any Dyak or Malay," replied Lane good-naturedly; and he was a stout Down-Easter, who had been a logger in the woods before he was a carpenter or a seaman.

"There are two animals in that tree where they are at work," cried Morris, as he pointed to the scene of operations.   "One of them is a big one, and the other is a little one," he added, when he obtained a better view of the game the Malays were trying to obtain.   "What are they, Achang?"

"Mias! Mias!" exclaimed the native, as a movement of the boat ahead gave him a full view of the creatures.   "One is a big one, and the other is her baby."

"But what are the Malays doing now?" asked Louis.

"Make a stage to stand on," replied Achang.

"What do they want of a stage?" demanded Lane contemptuously.

"You will see if you wait," added the captain.

They were picking up poles where they could find them, and cutting saplings, which they dropped with a single blow of the biliong. In a few minutes they had constructed a rude framework on crotched sticks, driven into the soft ground, with a platform of poles on the top. On this one of the two men mounted with his biliong, with which he began his work with a blow at the tree about four feet above the level of the ground. The other Malay brought from the sampan a couple of spears, a parong latok, and a bundle of ropes and rattans.

"Do they use the sumpitan in Borneo now, Achang?" asked Louis.

"Not Dyaks, Mr. Belgrave; Kyans use it; shoot poison arrows; sure death; very bad."

The sumpitan is a kind of blow-gun, like the "bean-blower" formerly used by American boys, which was a tin pipe, or the "pea-shooter," an English plaything. It was used, it is said, by the Dyaks in former times; but recent travellers do not mention it as used by them. It is about eight feet long, and less than an inch in diameter, made of very hard wood, skilfully and accurately bored, and smoothed inside.

The parong latok, already described, is a heavy sword. It has a head, sometimes carved as an ornament, so that it cannot slip from the hand. At about one-third of its length from this head, it bends at an abrupt angle of about thirty-five degrees, and it makes a very ugly-looking weapon.

"I suppose you all know that a mias is an orang-outang," said Louis. "No doubt the weapons carried up to the tree are to be used in killing the game when the tree comes down. We could easily bring down both; but we won't fire at them, for I think we are all curious to see how the Malays will manage the affair. The chopper has already made a big cut in the tree, and I doubt if Lane could have done the work any quicker."

The carpenter did not say anything, but no doubt he was greatly surprised at the rapid progress the native made with the biliong. He had cut the tree more than half-way through the trunk; and it was evident that he intended it should fall towards the river, for the second Malay was clearing away the ground on that side so that they might have a fair field for the fight that was to ensue. The chopper attacked the other side of the tree, and seemed to deal his blows with even more vigor than before.

The old orang kept up a constant growling. She had a nest just above the limb where she sat, which was quite green, indicating that it had been recently built. It was composed of the branches of the tree small enough to be easily broken off by the "jungle man." They were simply placed in a heap on the limb, with no particular shaping of the resting-place.

"She makes a new nest when the branches of the old one get dry; she like a soft bed," said Achang. "But the tree will come down now; big fight, they kill her."

He had hardly spoken these words before the tree suddenly toppled over, and fell upon the ground with a heavy crash. The orangs seemed to have no idea of what was going on at the foot of the tree, and they were pitched out. The chopper seized one of the spears, and rushed after the old one. The tree prevented the party on board the yacht from seeing the expected battle; and with their rifles in their hands, the "Big Four" sprang ashore, and secured a favorable position. The crew followed them, though the engineer remained at his post.

The first Malay, who had done the chopping, had confronted the orang, and they stood facing each other. Suddenly the animal made a spring towards her enemy, and was received on the point of his spear. The orang was wounded, but this only increased her wrath, and she made a furious onslaught upon the man; but the spear was too much for her, and she was wounded again.

The orang opened her mouth, and showed a terrible double row of teeth flanked by four long tusks. They were enough to intimidate one unaccustomed to the creature's appearance. She made repeated attempts to reach her enemy; but the spear, very adroitly handled, foiled her every time, and gave her a new wound. This sparring, as it were, was kept up for some time, and the Americans wondered that the Malay did not drive his weapon to the heart of the infuriated animal. Doubtless he would have done so if he could ; but the orang had hands as well as feet, and she grasped the spear every time it punctured her skin, and seemed to prevent it from inflicting a fatal wound.

It was a mystery to the observers how the Malay contrived to detach his weapon from the grasp of the orang, though he did so every time. But at last the brute seemed to change her tactics, or she got a better hold of the spear ; for she suddenly snapped the weapon into two pieces as though it had been a pipe-stem. Deprived of his arm, the Malay ran a few rods. The orang is very clumsy on its feet, and she could not catch him. The man only went a few rods to the place where the parong latok had been placed, and with this weapon he returned to the attack.

The skirmishing with this weapon continued for some time longer, and the beast was wounded every time she attempted to get hold of her opponent. In the meantime the other Malay had not been idle. He used no deadly weapons, but substituted for them a long cord he had brought from the sampan. He made a slip-noose in one end of it, and was trying to catch the young one. It might have run away if it had been so disposed, but it seemed to be determined to stay by its mother.

" He wants you, or needs your skill with the lasso,

Captain Scott," said Morris, recalling the feats with the lasso of the commander.

"He is doing very well, and he handles the line well," replied Scott. "Now he has him!" he exclaimed, as the Malay passed the cord over the head of the young orang, and hauled it taut around his neck.

With the line he dragged the orang to a sapling near the fallen tree, and, with other lines he had left there, tied his hands and feet together, and fastened him to the small tree.

He had hardly secured his victim before a yell from the first hunter startled him, and he ran with his lasso and a spear to his assistance. The old one, badly wounded by the sharp weapon of her enemy, had suddenly dropped upon all fours, and crawled to the man; seizing him by his legs, she set her villanous teeth into the calf of one of them. It looked as though the human was to be the victim of the brute.

The Malay, howling with the sharp pain, slashed away with all his might at the hind quarters of the orang; but she did not relax her grip on his leg. His companion arrived at the scene of the conflict. He dropped his lasso then, and began to use his parong latok. After he saw that blows with the weapon accomplished nothing, he plunged the blade into the body of the brute several times in quick succession. These stabs ended the battle. The orang rolled over, and then did not move again.

Both of the human combatants then walked down

to the Blanchita, one of them limping badly. They showed their wounds, and through Achang asked to be "doctored." Pitts had some skill as a leach, and the medicine-chest was in his care. He laid out the patient with the wounded leg, washed the wound, and then applied some sticking-plaster to the lacerated member, after he had restored the parts to their natural position. Then he bandaged the leg quite skilfully, so as to keep all the parts in place. The hands of the other were covered with sticking-plaster and bandaged.

With the assistance of the seamen, the carcass of the old orang was dragged down to the river, and put in the sampan of the Malays. The young one was as ugly as sin itself, and tried to get at the men to bite them. Finally Clingman stuffed a piece of rope into his mouth, and tied it around his head so tight that he could not shut his mouth. He was mad, but he could not bite. He was put into the sampan, and made fast there.

The yacht got under way again, and with the Malay sampan in tow, headed down the river. The tide was running out at a mill-stream pace, for the water in the stream had risen far beyond its usual level. Achang shook his head as he looked at the rapid outward flow of the water; but the steamer went at railroad speed, and the boys enjoyed it hugely.

"What is the matter, Achang?" asked the captain, as he observed the uneasy movements of the

Bornean as the yacht approached the junction with the Sadong.

"Have bore soon; better go no farther," replied the native. "Upset all boats and sampans."

Captain Scott ordered the helmsman to go to the shore, and there the painter of the Malay sampan was cast off, and her men got to the land.

"There it goes up the Sadong!" cried Achang, as he pointed to the broad stream.

A wave, estimated to be about ten feet high, fringing, curling, and lashed into foam, and roaring in its wrath, rolled up the river. It struck two small sampans, upset them, and spilled the men in them into the angry, boiling waters. With less fury it rolled up the Simujan, and Scott rushed to the wheel himself. He "faced the music," and headed the yacht into the wave. She rose some feet in the air at the bow, and passed over it. She was too far from the banks to be thrown ashore, and no harm was done.

These bores are not uncommon on the Sadong; and they were not a new thing to those on board of the Blanchita, for they had seen one in the Hoogly at Calcutta; but even Scott, who was a bold navigator, would not have cared to be in the river when a wave ten feet high swept on his craft.

CHAPTER VIII

A PERFORMANCE OF VERY AGILE GIBBONS

THE cabin party went on shore and breakfasted with their Chinese friend, who had invited them to the meal the evening before. It was a very pleasant occasion, and it occupied half the forenoon. The host gave them useful information, and listened with interest to their account of the battle with the orang-outangs. When they left the house they found the two Malays who had been their companions in the morning waiting for them.

One of them presented a tarsier to Scott. It was a very pretty and curious little creature, belonging to the monkey tribe. It had very large eyes, and was certainly very cunning. It appeared to be play-ful, but his new owner got a nip from its teeth which warned him to be careful. The most curious part of the animal was its legs, the hind ones being much the longer.

Its five slender toes ended in what looked like balls, which proved to be flat, and acted like the foot of a fly, retaining by suction its hold upon the tree where it lived. The spine of its neck was so con-structed that it could describe a circle with its head. Its long hind legs enabled it to leap like a kangaroo.

The other Malay brought with him a flying dragon, a king of lizards, said to be the reptile from which the fables of the original dragons originated. It has a pair of membranes with the semblance of wings, with which it sustains itself in the air in its leaps from one tree or branch to another, as the flying-fish does in its flights over the water.

The party took leave with many thanks of the Chinese agent, and promised to visit him on their return from up the river. Louis stated that they wanted to kill one full-sized orang-outang, for the one killed by the Malays was so cut up and chopped in the fight that she was not in condition to be stuffed and kept as a good specimen.

"You will find them on the Simujan, but hardly anywhere else in the island except in this vicinity, on the Sadong, Batang Lupar, and their branches," replied the agent. "The orangs have been hunted so much, especially by naturalists, that they are becoming scarce; and they are likely to become extinct, for the scientists are looking for the 'missing link,' as they call it."

The speaker laughed as he made the last remark; and it was evident that he was not a Darwinian, or at least that he had not followed out the theory of evolution. Taking their places in the yacht, the captain gave the order to cast off the fasts, the boat stood up the river, and soon passed the scene of the morning's conflict.

"Gibbons!" exclaimed Achang, pointing to a portion of the forest where the trees were sparsely scattered.

There were half a dozen of them, and they seemed to be engaged in a frolic. This ape has been described in a former volume, for it is abundant in Sumatra. Louis wished to observe the movements of the animal, which has very long arms, is wonderfully agile, and a gymnast of the first order. It could travel all over Borneo where forests exist without touching the ground, passing from tree to tree in long leaps. The boat was stopped in the river, in order to permit the party to witness the exhibition which was in process, without the payment of any admission fee.

Every branch was a trapeze, and no troupe of artists could compare with them in the agility of their movements. Their long arms appeared to be the key to their marvellous feats, for their legs were comparatively short, and for the size of their bodies the animals possessed immense strength.

"If some enterprising manager of a theatre devoting himself to athletic exhibitions could secure the services of the half dozen gibbons which are giving us a free show, he would make his fortune in our country," said Louis. "Don't try to see them all at once, but watch that fellow on the right."

The one indicated grasped a horizontal branch with his hands, his arms looking like the ropes of a swing. He was swaying to and fro with great rapidity, apparently trying to see how fast he could go, for he put a tremendous amount of vigor into his efforts. In an exhibition hall he would have "brought down the house," and would certainly have received an "*encore*."

Suddenly, while he was swinging at a dizzy speed, he let go his hold upon the branch, and seemed to be flying through the air; but with his fingered feet he seized another branch, not less than forty feet from the first, and, with his long arms extended to the utmost, continued to swing in this inverted position. The observers were so delighted with this skilful performance that they applauded lustily by clapping their hands. The noise did not disturb the performers, and the actor that had so distinguished himself appeared to put even greater vigor into his movements.

Possibly he was getting up a momentum; for he soon released the hold of his feet on the branch, went flying through the air with his long arms extended ahead of him in the direction of another favorable limb of a tree, and grasped it with his hands. After swinging for a moment, he drew himself up on the branch, and proceeded to walk up to a greater height, using his hands to assist in keeping his equilibrium. This was a fair specimen of the performance of every member of the troupe.

One of the company appeared to see something on the ground that attracted his attention; and he made a flying leap to a lower branch, and then dropped himself upon the soil. Looking about him for a moment, he apparently discovered a bush with some sort of fruit on it, for he immediately began to walk towards it. As a walkist he was far from being a success, and his awkward movements excited the laughter of the interested spectators. In his present *rôle* he would have made an excellent clown in a circus ring.

His short legs seemed to be incapable of fully supporting his body, and he behaved like an inexperienced athlete walking on a tight rope without a balancing-pole. His long arms served as this implement, and with a bend at the elbows and the hands dropped down, he waddled along very slowly.

" It's heavy sea for that fellow, and he looks like a landlubber trying to walk the deck in a rough sea," said Captain Scott. " But I fancy the performance is over, and it is time to shoot some of the actors if that is what you intend to do."

"For one, I don't intend to do anything of the sort," replied Louis, with considerable energy in his tones. " I don't believe in killing for the sake of killing, or for the fun of it. My admiration of the skilful performance we have just witnessed will not allow me to kill the actors or any of them."

" What did we come to Borneo for, Louis ? " asked the captain.

" To see the country, and explore some of its rivers."

" I thought we came here to hunt and fish," added Scott.

" I did not come here to kill harmless creatures

for the fun of it. We want a full-grown orang, and I am ready to hunt for him," replied Louis. "We want him for the purpose of study, and to show to our friends on board of the ship. I don't object to shooting any bird or animal to extend our information."

Louis had his double-barrelled fowling-piece in his hand. Suddenly he brought it to his shoulder and fired. All eyes were directed to the shore, and a large bird was seen to drop upon the ground. The captain started the boat, and ran her up to the bank. Clinch leaped ashore, and soon brought the bird on board. Its plumage was highly colored and very beautiful.

"What do you call that bird, Louis?" asked Morris.

"Chambers calls it simply the argus, but the more common name is the argus-pheasant," replied Louis.

"Faix, he's a magnificent crayter; and what a long tail our cat has got," added Felix, as he spread the bird out on the gunwale.

The last remark referred to the long tail of the bird, which made the entire length from the bill to the end of it about five feet. Only two of the feathers were thus prolonged, adding about three feet to the dimension. The variety of colors were jet black, deep brown, fawn, white, and a number of secondary hues. The bird, deprived of his feathers, is about the size of an ordinary hen.

"But you can't see him at his best now that he is dead," continued Louis, who had read up the animal life he expected to find in Borneo. "Like a peacock, though to a less extent, he can spread out his pretty feathers, but not in the same manner; for they open out in the form of a circle, making a sort of round disk on his back and concealing his head. If you could see the bird alive with his wings spread out you would find every feather had a number of marks that look like eyes, and seventeen have been counted on one of them. Each of these marks consists in part of a jet-black ring, with other different colored rings inside of it, which make the whole figure like an eye.

"You remember a fellow who was called Argus in mythology, who had a hundred eyes, of which only two were ever asleep at the same time. This bird gets his name from him; though the story is that Mercury killed him, and Venus transferred his eyes to the tail of the peacock."

"Thanks for the lecture, Louis," said Scott when he had finished his description. "It was certainly a part of our plan in coming to Borneo to study natural history; and we are doing so instead of shooting all the time."

Just at this moment Felix, who had wandered from the fore cabin to the waist, discharged his fowling-piece. The Milesian was as good a shot as Louis, for both of them had been trained in the same shooting-gallery in New York. All hands rushed to the rail to ascertain what the hunter had brought down. On the bank of the river they discovered a creature about two feet long, lying on its back, and struggling in its death-throes.

Lane leaped ashore, and soon laid the animal on the gunwale of the boat by the side of the argus. It was a queer-looking creature about the head, and no one on board except Achang had ever seen one like it. For the length of the head, the muzzle was very broad, hardly less than three inches. It was covered with a soft and rather long fur on its body, dark brown in color.

"What do you call my game, Mr. Naturalist?" demanded Felix, addressing Louis, who was looking the animal over.

"*Cynogale Bennetti*," replied the young naturalist very gravely.

" Faix, that's jist what I thought he was whin Oi foired at him," added Felix. " Sin O, gal! But what had Ben Netty to do wid it? Or was Netty the name of the gal?"

" I gave you the scientific name because this creature has no plain English name, though the natives here call it the *mampalon*," added Louis.

" That's what we call it; but I forgot the name," said Achang.

" He is one of the otter family; and Mr. Hornaday, whose book I hope you will all read when you return to the ship, thought it might be called the otter-cat. I wish we could have taken him alive, for it would have made a very nice specimen to set up in the cabin of the Guardian-Mother."

"I should like to knock over the big orang-outang you want, Louis, my darling," continued Felix. "There comes a covered sampan up the river," he added, pointing down the stream.

Many such covered boats are used on the rivers. On a frame of bamboo or other wood was a covering of leaves, each of which is six to seven feet long, and two inches wide. They are sewed together with a thread of rattan, overlaying each other, like tiles or shingles, thus shedding the rain. They were in strips or squares, so that they could be readily removed. The sides were sometimes curtained with the same material. The long leaves are taken from the nipa palm, which grows abundantly in the island, and serves a great many useful purposes.

The boat waited to see the covered sampan, and later there appeared to be two of them. As they approached, the familiar voice of the Chinese agent was heard hailing the party. It appeared that this gentleman was bound up the river to a Dyak village, a few miles farther up.

"You had better go with us," said the agent, as his sampan stopped abreast of the steamer. "I spoke to you about a Dyak long-house; and you will have an opportunity to examine one, and to sleep in it if you are disposed to do so. You will be received very kindly, and have a chance to see the people as well as the houses."

"Thank you, Mr. Eng Quee; we will certainly go with you," replied Captain Scott, prompted by Louis. "We will heave you a line, and tow you up."

In a few minutes more the steamer moved up the river with the two sampans in tow.

CHAPTER IX

A VISIT TO A DYAK LONG-HOUSE

As the Blanchita approached her destination many Dyaks appeared on the shores. They were Sea Dyaks in this region; and the name seems to have come down from a former era in the history of the island, for at the present time they have little or no connection with a sea-faring life, and their sampans are mainly if not entirely used on the rivers. But formerly they built large war-boats, or *bankongs*, some of which were seventy feet long.

These craft did not go to sea. The naval battles were fought on rivers and lakes; for the boats were not adapted to heavy weather, and could not have lived even in a moderate gale. They were propelled entirely by oars, single banked, and twenty-four rowers were all that could work. The largest of them had a platform or elevated deck, under which the oarsmen sat, and on which the warriors engaged the enemy.

Some sort of strategy was used; for the small boats were sent ahead sometimes to skirmish with the foe, and lure their canoes to a point where the larger craft were concealed, which then came out and fell upon the enemy. If the craft were used for purposes of piracy, as they were in the northern part of the island, in attacking foreign vessels, it could only be when the strangers were caught within a short distance of the shores.

Mr. Eng came on board of the yacht when his sampans were taken in tow, and was seated with the cabin party on the forward seats. He spoke English perfectly, and explained everything that needed it as the boat proceeded. The explorers had seen Dyaks enough, but had not before taken the trouble to study them; for they seemed not to be in touch with the civilization of Sarawak, and were "hewers of wood and drawers of water," and not proper specimens of the race.

"The men here, Mr. Eng, do not appear to be very powerful physically," said Louis, as they passed several laborers at work in a paddy.

"They are not as strong as Englishmen and Americans," replied the agent, glancing at the seamen in the waist. "The tallest man I have seen among the Sea Dyaks was not more than five and a half feet in height. Five feet three inches is a more common figure, though the average is less than that. They are not men of great strength; but they are active, of great endurance, and in running they exhibit great speed."

"These people are not ruined by their tailors' bills," said Scott.

"They do not need much clothing in this climate; and a piece of bark-cloth a yard wide is full dress here. The *chawat,* as they call this garment, is about five feet long, and is wound around the waist tightly, and drawn between the legs, one end hanging down in front, and the other behind. They wear a sort of turban on the head; and some of them have as many as four rings, large and small, hanging from their ears, through which they pass. Some of them use white cotton instead of bark-cloth, like the Hindoos in India."

The yacht was now approaching the landing-place pointed out by the agent. A crowd of women and children were hurrying to the riverside. They appeared to be lighter in complexion than the men. As a rule they were not handsome, though a few of them were rather pretty. The American visitors were not likely to fall in love with any of the young women on the shore. They were all in " full dress," which means simply a petticoat, reaching from the waist to the knees, made of bark-cloth embroidered with various figures.

A few of the females wore a sort of red jacket and the conical Malay hat; but those are used only on "state occasions." The single garment was secured at the waist by being drawn into a belt of rattans, colored black. Above this was worn a coil of many rings of large brass wire; and all of them seemed to be provided with this appendage. There was some variety in the use of this ornament; for some wore it tightly wound around the body, while others had it quite loose.

In addition to this some of the young girls had a dozen rings of various sizes hanging loosely around their necks, and falling upon the chest, which had no other covering. Their eyes were black, as was also their hair, which was very luxuriant, and generally well cared for, being tied up in a cue behind.

The village did not consist of a great number of small buildings, but from the landing-place could be seen the end of an immense structure with a forest of palms behind it. The rear of it was not perpendicular, but slanted outward, like many of the walls of corn-houses in New England, doubtless to keep the rain from the roof from penetrating. All the party, including the sailors, landed; for Mr. Eng declared that the Dyaks were honest, and even in Sarawak were never known to steal anything, though the Malays and Chinamen were given to pilfering.

The crowd of men, women, and children gathered on the shore had looked the Blanchita over with the closest attention while the Americans were looking them over. The party landed under the escort of the agent, and took up the line of march for the big house. The entire crowd of Dyaks followed them, though they did not intrude upon them; on the contrary, they treated all of the visitors with a respect and deference bordering on homage.

"That 'long-house,' as we call it here, is nearly two hundred feet in length," said Mr. Eng. "It is thirty feet wide. Now you can see more of it; and you notice that it is set upon a multitude of posts, like all Malay and Dyak houses. These posts are firmly set in the ground; and being about six inches in diameter, you can readily see that the house rests on a solid foundation. It is not likely to be blown down in any ordinary gale, though a hurricane might sweep it away. Not a nail, not a wooden pin or peg, is used in the construction of such buildings."

"Then, I should think any ordinary gale would level them to the ground," suggested Louis.

"But the Dyaks have a substitute for nails or pins," replied the guide. "All the poles and sticks and boards are tightly bound together with rattans; and I believe they hold together better than if they were nailed."

"I observed in England and France that the stagings used in the erection of buildings were made partly of round poles, tied together with ropes. I talked with a man who told me they were stronger than if put together with nails," said Morris.

"I think he was right. I can't tell you how the Malays and Dyaks manage the rattan to render it so flexible, but it seems to me they make better work than ropes. On the back of this house, there is not a single window or other opening," continued Mr. Eng, as the party stood at the end of the structure, near the rear corner. "The disagreeable feature of the building, or rather of the habits of the occupants, is that the space under it, ten feet between the ground and the floor, is a catch-all for all refuse matter, and you notice that an unpleasant odor comes from it."

"Is this the only entrance to it?" asked Scott, pointing to a door, which was reached by a log notched like a flight of stairs.

"There is a door at the other end also; and there may be ways of mounting the platform, or veranda, which forms the front of the building, as climbing a post, or dropping from a tree. Some of the posts, of which you see a multitude under the house, are cut off at the first floor, while many of them reach up to the roof, and support it. We will go in now, if you like; and, being sailors, I suppose you can climb the log."

"No doubt of that," replied Scott, who was the first to ascend. "Are all that crowd coming up?"

"Certainly; they are the occupants of the long-house, and they must be at home in order to do the honors of the occasion," laughed the guide.

The villagers followed the party, and immediately manifested their politeness in various ways. The prettiest girl in the crowd spoke to Louis; though he did not understand a word she said, but replied to her in English, when she was as much at sea as he had been.

"What does she say, Achang?" he asked of the Bornean.

"*Tabet, tuan,*" replied the native.

"I heard her say that; but what does it mean?"

"It means, 'Good-day, sir,'" answered the Bornean; and he proceeded to tell her that Louis was the "head man," very rich, and owned a big ship.

She made a very graceful obeisance to him, and then rushed away through a door on the side of the grand hall, as it may well be called. But she returned immediately, bringing a very elaborately worked mat, which she spread on the floor at the feet of the "head man." Then she spread out her hands, and bowed low, saying something which was Greek to him.

"She invites you to take a seat on the mat," Achang explained.

As a matter of politeness Louis seated himself, and looked at the maiden who treated him with so much consideration. By this time the other women were bringing mats for the rest of the party, making no distinction between the seamen and the cabin party. The latter followed the example of the young millionaire, and seated themselves. The foremast hands declined the proffered courtesy; and Achang explained to the ladies that only the four young men who were seated were the magnates of the company, while the others were inferior personages, for the Bornean was not strictly democratic in his ideas.

"We will look at the house now, if you please," said Mr. Eng, after the "Big Four" had been seated a few minutes; and all of them rose to their feet, bowing low to the young ladies who had treated them with so much distinction.

About forty or fifty of the posts extended from the ground, for the visitors had not time to count them; and most of them had suspended upon them various trophies of the hunt, including the antlers of deer, crocodiles' heads, weapons, paddles, and spears. In the middle of the long hall a fire was burning on a foundation of soil, enclosed by a border of wood. In the roof was a sort of scuttle, which was fastened open to admit the air, and to allow some of the smoke to escape, though there was plenty of it remaining in the apartment.

"What is that overhead, Mr. Eng?" asked Louis, pointing to a black mass suspended near the fire, though he had a suspicion of its nature.

"That is a collection of human skulls, relics of the days of head-hunting; for they are generally kept in a building erected for the purpose, though appropriated at the present time partly to other uses. There are about twenty of them, which is not a large number for a village like this. Not one of them is less than twenty years old; for Rajah Brooke put an end to head-hunting long ago, though some of it has been done in spite of his edicts. A lady beckons to you, Mr. Belgrave."

The pretty girl — by comparison — stood by his side, pointing to one of the numerous doors at the closed side of the house. Louis followed her, and she conducted him into a room. A portion of the floor was covered with mats on which the occupants sleep, with an earth section for a fire. There was no furniture of any kind. The roof of the building was covered with square pieces of palm like those used on the sampans, and these could be raised in each room when necessary for air.

"This apartment is occupied by one family, or by a married couple, and unmarried men and boys sleep in the attic overhead," said Mr. Eng. "It has but one door, the one opening into the main hall. This is a house of sixteen doors; and by this enumeration the size of the village is stated, and this number gauges the taxes to be paid."

"Citizens cannot dodge their taxes here, then, as some of them do in the United States," said Scott.

The party walked the entire length of the hall, and then passed out upon the platform, which was not covered, and was used for various purposes, such as drying rice or other articles. The floors were composed of strips of palm, not more than an inch and a half wide, and placed an inch apart. They were lashed to the floor joists, or poles, with rattan.

"Those doors, which indicate the taxable rate of the village, look as though they were cut out of single planks," said Scott.

"And so they are," replied the agent.

"I have seen no saw-mills here, and I suppose they bring the lumber from England or India."

"Not at all, though some may be obtained in that manner. They are made from the buttress of the tapang-tree, which you must have seen."

"I have not noticed any such thing, though perhaps none of us could identify it," replied the captain.

"It is found growing out in triangular form from just above the roots of the tree. In a large one it is twelve or fifteen feet long. It makes a natural plank two inches thick, which may be trimmed into any shape with the biliong."

The party were ready to depart; and they made all sorts of courteous gestures to their hosts, especially the ladies. The women asked them for tobacco, as Achang interpreted the requests. They had none, but some of the seamen supplied them with all they had about them.

CHAPTER X.

THE MANNERS AND CUSTOMS OF THE DYAKS.

AFTER seeing the sleeping accommodations of the Dyaks, consisting of a mat on a rather uneven floor, the Americans concluded to pass the night on board of the yacht. They invited Mr. Eng to supper on board, and he passed the evening with them in the cabin.

"You have seen the Dyaks at home now, young gentlemen; how do you like the looks of them?" asked the guest, after the meal had been disposed of.

"I think they are the pleasantest savages I have ever met," replied Louis.

"I am afraid you did not appreciate the young women who were so attentive to you, Mr. Belgrave," continued the agent.

"Regarding them as uncivilized maidens, they are about the best specimens. The expression on their faces was pleasant, a few of them were pretty, though as a whole they were not handsome, and they seemed to be kind-hearted. I could not admire them, though their eyes were as brilliant as they were black. Their long hair would be the envy of many an English or American belle."

"The women are very vain of their hair. They

bestow a great deal of attention upon it," added Mr. Eng. "The fever of the island sometimes deprives them of their hair, as it may in your country, and that is the greatest calamity that can overtake the younger women."

"I suppose it all right here; but they disfigure and spoil one of the principal attractions of ladies in enlightened nations, the teeth, which they blacken by chewing betel."

"It also makes their lips look as though they had daubed them with blood or red paint; but they do it here, as in India, to make themselves more beautiful. Tastes differ, and the practice makes them ugly to you. The betel-vine grows here, and the leaves are used for chewing. The nut of a certain palm produces the same effect on the teeth."

"I don't admire the brass rings they wear on their waists and around their necks. If I were old enough to get married, I should not look for a wife among the Dyak girls," said Louis, laughing and shaking his head.

"The Dyak women are generally well treated; but they have to work very hard, and much that you would think the men ought to do is done by them. The lords of creation here are inclined to be lazy, while their wives and daughters are engaged in the rice-fields, though their husbands and brothers are driven to labor.

"But the women are not the abject slaves you sometimes find them in the savage state. They have their influence, and exercise a degree of control in household matters. The females are fond of fish, and insist that their husbands shall supply them with this diet. On account of the bores which sweep up the rivers, this is often a dangerous occupation, and the men are unable to procure any fish. Instances are known in which the women bar the door of the house against them if they are unsuccessful."

"I believe the Malays are generally Mohammedans. What is the religion of the Dyaks?" inquired Louis.

"It has been said by some travellers that they have no religion of any kind; but I don't think this is quite true, though it is not far from it," replied Mr. Eng. "Religion is a very indefinite idea among the Dyaks, and they are chary in speaking of what there is of it. Some who have been among them maintain that they believe in a Supreme Being, who has a great many different names among the various tribes. They have almost as many inferior deities as the Hindus.

"They are very superstitious; and there are all sorts of omens, among which there is a particular bird which has obtained the name of the omen bird. His cry on the right of, or behind, a person engaged in any enterprise is an unlucky sign, and he abandons his object; while the cry heard on the left is a favorable omen, and the individual is duly encouraged to go forward.

"I had a story from a Kyan head man which had come down to him as a tradition. A great head-hunting expedition, consisting of a thousand warriors, had set out many years ago. It had not gone far when a little muntjac, which you know is a kind of deer, ran across the path of the warriors. This was a bad omen; and they gave up the enterprise, and returned to their villages.

"I know of a couple just married who separated because they heard a deer-cry within three days after their union, which was a sign that one of them would die within a year. Even little insects intimidate doughty warriors, or assure them that they are far from danger, by their appearance or their cry."

"There is not a little of similar superstition in enlightened nations, though there is vastly less of it than formerly," added Louis.

"I have heard my grandfather say that the ticking of a death-watch used to scare him so that he could not sleep when he was a boy," said Morris.

"What is a death-watch?" asked Scott.

"It is a kind of beetle that conceals itself in the walls of old houses," replied Louis. "The noise it makes is really the call of the bug for his mate, and is the cry of love instead of death, as many ignorant people believe. The breaking of a looking-glass is also a sign of death in the family."

"Mrs. Blossom wouldn't break a looking-glass for a fortune," added Felix. "She says she broke one nine years before her husband died, and therefore it was a sure sign."

"But the death must come within a year to make

the sign hold good," replied Louis. "But if enlightened people have faith in such stuff, it is no
wonder that Dyaks believe in omens. I want to ask,
Mr. Eng, if these Dyaks are regularly married?"

"They are, though with very little ceremony, and
no vows, oaths, nor promises. In fact, the marriage
consists of such rites as the parties please, and often
with no rites at all. Sometimes the betrothed are
married by exchanging bracelets in public, or by eating a meal of rice together. In some communities
the affianced are seated on a couple of bars of iron,
and the head man shakes a couple of live chickens
over their heads, invoking many blessings upon them,
and the birds are afterwards killed and eaten."

"Do these people drink liquor, or have they anything in the shape of intoxicating fluids?" asked
Scott.

"The national drink of Borneo is *tuak*, about the
vilest tipple that ever was invented. I went to a
Dyak feast when I first came to the island, which
proved to be nothing but a series of drunken orgies.
The principal actors at the feast were a number of
pretty girls, such as you saw this afternoon. Their
office was to induce the men present to drink this vile
liquid till they dropped on the floor of the open platform; and they even poured it down the throats of
their victims when no longer able to drink for themselves."

"What sort of rum is it?" inquired Scott.

"It looks like the milk of the cocoanut, and I suppose that it is made from that; but I did not taste it," replied the agent. "It is about my bedtime, and I think I will go to my sampan and retire."

But Captain Scott invited him to sleep on board of the Blanchita; and he accepted after a little pressing, evidently believing that the soft cushions of the yacht made a better bed than the mats of the sampan. Felipe was instructed to have steam on at daylight, and the anchor watch was to call him in season to do so. Fully protected by their nettings from the mosquitoes, which had troubled them to some extent in the evening, all hands slept like tired boys.

When the steam from the gauge-cocks hissed as the engineer examined into the condition of the water in the boiler, the sound waked the captain, and he jumped from his bed. This movement roused all the others; and they went out into the waist, following the example of Scott, who wore nothing but his nightdress.

"I am going to have a swim this fine morning," said he.

"Look out for crocodiles," Morris interposed. "You know they are man-eaters in these rivers."

"I haven't seen any of them around here," replied the captain. "But call all hands, Lane; and tell the men to bring out their rifles."

"I think you are very imprudent to go into the water here," interposed Mr. Eng. "The reptiles are on the watch; and if you must go in, I warn you to keep near the boat."

But the boys all dived from the gunwale into the river, and swam out a few rods. The men placed themselves on the rail, and kept a sharp look out for saurians, though it was still too dark to enable them to see very distinctly. Scott had reasoned that he could not take his bath after it was fully light, for a crowd of Dyak men and women would be on the bank at that time.

The swimmers had not been in the water more than five minutes when the cry of "Crocodiles!" came from Achang, who had stationed himself just forward of the engine. Probably he had a keener vision for the reptiles than the Americans; for the seamen had not yet seen anything that looked like one. He could tell by the appearance of the water that the enemy was approaching, though the disturbance of its surface was near the other side of the stream.

The party in the water turned about, and headed for the boat, swimming with all the vigor they could command. Achang had his rifle in his hand; but even he could not make out the crocodile clearly enough to be sure of his aim. Five minutes more elapsed; for it required that time for the swimmers to reach the yacht. The seamen assisted the party into the boat, and they rushed with all speed into the cabin; for a quartet of Dyak maidens had already reached the bank of the river, and were begging the men for more tobacco.

Achang fired his rifle; but three crocodiles could

now be seen moving towards the yacht. Their approach was not impeded by the shot, for it was impossible to see the eyes of the reptiles in the semi-darkness. But the cabin party were safe, and it was as useless to fire at them as it would have been at a stone wall.

"I advise you not to try that experiment again, young gentlemen," said Mr. Eng as the bathing party came out into the waist.

"I don't think we shall, though we were protected by half a dozen rifles," replied the captain, who had been the leader in the venturesome exploit.

"If you do try it again, do so in the daylight, when your riflemen can see the eyes of the enemy," added the agent. "I must bid you good-by now, for I have business on shore here. I don't think the crocodiles will come any nearer to you, but be prudent. I shall hope to see you at Simujan on your return."

Mr. Eng shook hands with all the cabin party, and went ashore. The captain gave the order to cast off the fasts, and Lane was ordered to take the wheel. The two sampans had before made fast to the shore; and as the Blanchita got under way, one of them put off, and paddled towards the crocodiles. The last that was seen of the craft, it had a saurian hooked after the Malay mode of fishing for them.

After breakfast had been served in the cabin, and the party had gone to their seats forward, the character of the river began to change, becoming much narrower. They came to another Dyak village, where the jungle was cleared off and paddies were near the stream. It looked as though all the inhabitants had gathered on the bank, male and female. A long-house was to be seen on a knoll, and the wheelman was ordered to take the boat within a couple of rods of the shore.

"Are you going to make a landing at this village, Captain Scott?" asked Louis.

"No; we have seen enough of these people, but we will see what we can as we pass along. They are all beckoning us to go ashore; but we won't do so, for any more Dyak maidens would be rather monotonous."

"I quite agree with you, Captain, though there is one with a big stick of bamboo in her hand, who looks more graceful and pretty than any we saw in the village we visited," replied Louis.

"I wonder what that cane is for," added Scott.

"That's to contain some kind of liquid; and she may have four feet of tuak in it," answered the millionaire, laughing at the idea of measuring a fluid by Long Measure. "I think the girl comes nearer to being a beauty than any girl I have seen before."

"She is hooped with brass like all the rest of them," added Scott, as the boat proceeded beyond the group on the shore.

In another half-hour great trees, with an abundant undergrowth of bushes, extended down to the river, and in places some distance into the water.

CHAPTER XI

STEAMBOATING THROUGH A GREAT FOREST

ALTHOUGH there was a wall of green on each side of the boat, and the river was not more than sixty feet wide, the explorers found that everything close to the earth was under water. If the dense jungle had not prevented, they might have sailed inland, they knew not how many miles. As the stream became narrower the current increased in force. The trees were full of monkeys, and hundreds of them appeared to be in sight all the time. They were of the most common kind to be found in Borneo, and the yacht created no excitement among them. They were so tame that any number of them could have been brought down by the hunters.

"The water is not so dirty as it has been everywhere below," said Captain Scott, as the Blanchita stemmed the current without any difficulty, where paddling a sampan must have been a laborious occupation. "It is tolerably clear along here, and we might take our morning bath very comfortably."

"We might if a big crocodile did not break his way through the bushes to pay us a visit," replied Louis.

"After the experience of this morning, I am not disposed to try it again, and I shall take my bath in a wash-bowl with a sponge, though I am very fond of swimming.   But, Louis, don't you think we have had about enough of hunting in Borneo?"

"Enough!   Why, we have not yet been a week on the island," replied Louis, not a little astonished at the captain's question.   "I have enjoyed myself very well so far, and I certainly do not wish to leave till we have killed at least one good-sized orang."

"It is rather stupid hunting here, for about all the country is under water," added Scott.   "There seems to be nothing but monkeys here; and they are very small game, even if we were disposed to shoot them."

"But there are some lakes up the river, Mr. Eng told me; and I think we shall get out of this tangle very soon; and when we come to higher ground we will go on shore, and try our luck on foot."

The captain talked as though he had some scheme in his head which he was not yet prepared to unfold to his companions.   But what could he do? Nothing had been said on board of the ship about coming back to Sarawak for the hunters, and to give up hunting and exploring would be simply to return to Kuching, and idle away the time for the next two weeks. Louis did not like this idea at all; and yet it seemed to be the alternative which Scott must have in his mind.

"Mias!" shouted Achang, when the conversation had proceeded so far.

"Where is your mias?" demanded Louis; for

most of the party had come to calling the orang by his Malay name.

The Bornean pointed into the forest, the trees of which were growing in the water, though there was an undergrowth of screw-pines, which had been abundant all along the river. They were not pines as the explorers understood the word at home. The plant is a bush or small tree with half a dozen or more branches angling upward from the trunk, and twisting a little towards it, from which feature it takes its name. It has long, lanceolated leaves, and therefore is not at all like the American pine.

"Stop her, Lane!" called the captain in a tone that "meant business." "Back her!"

The last order was given because there was an opening through the screw-pines which afforded a full view of the taller trees about twenty rods farther from the stream. The captain then took the wheel from Lane, rang the gong to go ahead; and, putting the helm hard-a-starboard, the boat came about, headed into the opening. Looking forward, there seemed but very few trees or bushes compared with the number along the flowing stream.

"Do you see the mias, Louis?" asked Scott.

"I do; and he is in a very favorable position. He is a big one, and must be a male," replied Louis, who stood at the stem with a repeating-rifle in his hand.

"Do you see him, Flix?"

"I do; and he has a green nest in the same tree with him."

"You are near enough, Captain."

Page 99.

By this time all the party had taken their rifles. The boat moved very slowly. A seaman sounded the depth with a boathook, and reported eight feet. As she approached the orang, the brute showed his teeth, and uttered several successive growls, as though he understood that danger was near; but he did not attempt to escape.

"I wonder can the blackguard swim," said Felix, who had his rifle ready to fire.

"I have read that he is a poor swimmer," replied Louis.

"How does he get about here where the water is eight feet deep?"

"He is not as agile as the gibbon; but he can make his way from one tree to another in the same manner, and his road is through the trees, and not on the ground."

"Here I am, and I can't go any farther," said the captain, as he rang to stop her. "I can't get the boat through this clump of bushes."

"You are near enough, Captain; let her rest where she is," replied Louis, as he aimed his rifle at the orang, which was sitting on a branch holding on with both hands.

Louis fired, and the creature fell with a loud splash into the water at the foot of the tree. But he was not dead, and was struggling to escape. He was evidently wounded very badly, and when the hunter saw his opportunity he fired again. The orang had grasped a screw-pine, and he held on, but he struggled no more. The captain had ordered the sampan to be brought alongside, and two men were at the paddles. Louis and Felix joined them, and they paddled towards the game.

"I think he is dead though he still holds on at the bush," said Louis.

"We shall soon find out," added Clingman, as he threw a slip-noose over his head. "Heave ahead now !" he continued, as Clinch grasped the line with him, and they pulled together.

The orang did not make any movement, and it was certain that he was dead. When they had drawn him within a few feet of the sampan, the line was made fast, and the men paddled to the steamer. A purchase was rigged to the top of one of the stanchions, and the dead animal was hoisted into the sampan.

"Now, Lane, measure him," said the captain.

The body was laid out at full length in the bottom of the boat; and the carpenter took his length on a boathook, which he notched to indicate the height of the animal. He was directed to take several other measurements; in fact, Louis kept him at work for over an hour, with another hand to assist him in spreading out the limbs. The captain became quite impatient; for he was less a scientist than the young millionaire, though he had a taste for natural history.

"Have you finished, Louis ?" asked Scott as the former returned to the yacht.

"All done; but Lane must sum up the results," replied Louis.

"What good will all those measurements do you?" demanded the captain rather contemptuously.

"They will not put any money in my pocket, but I want to know the size of the game I have killed," answered Louis, somewhat nettled by the manner of Scott. "When a man has caught a fish he wants to know what his prize weighs."

"All right; but I want to get a little farther into the woods here, and I can get around the bushes ahead of her," replied the captain, who had been studying up a course by which he could go a considerable distance farther inland.

He backed the boat, and then went ahead very slowly, with Clingman feeling of the bottom with the boathook. It was novel sailing through the forest in a steam-launch, and all hands enjoyed it. The screw-pines were rather scattered, and the forest of large trees was quite open. After the boat had gone about half a mile, as the captain judged, Clingman made a report.

"By the mark, one," said he, as the depth is given with the lead, in fathoms.

"Six feet; we are shoaling," added Captain Scott. "Try it again."

"Five feet," returned the seaman.

The steamer continued on her course, with Scott at the wheel, for some time longer. The dry land could be seen through the trees at no great distance ahead.

The boat continued on her course for a quarter of an hour, when Clingman call out a depth which caused the captain to ring the gong to stop her. The last report was three feet, and the keel was evidently grinding through the soft mud. Then he rang to back her; and when she had increased her depth to four feet, he struck the gong to stop her.

"Dinner is ready, gentlemen," said Pitts.

"We must attend to that before we do anything more," added the captain. "Keep a sharp lookout ahead, Clingman."

The party went into the after cabin, and the novelty of dining on board of a steamer in the woods was sufficiently inspiring to add a big interest to the occasion.

"What have you got for dinner, Pitts?" asked Felix, as he entered the cabin. "Have you got any stewed crocodiles?"

"Not a croc, Mr. McGavonty," replied the cook.

"Any boiled orang-outang?"

"Not an orang. The captain bought six dozens of eggs at the village where we stopped yesterday, and I have ham and eggs for dinner, which I hope will suit you," replied Pitts.

"The best thing in the world for me. Whisper! Are they crocodiles' eggs?"

"Not a bit of it, sir."

The principal dish proved to be very satisfactory to the boys, whose appetites had been sharpened by the exercise of the forenoon. The cuisine had been very good along the rivers, for Pitts had generally been the caterer as well as the cook and steward. Chickens and eggs had been plentiful enough, and at the town he had obtained some fish. There was no fresh beef or mutton. They had a barrel of excellent salt beef from the stores of the ship; and Pitts made a splendid hash, which suited all hands better than almost anything else.

While they were at dinner the steward brought in Lane's report of the measurements of the orang Louis had shot. It was given to the Captain at the head of the table; and he read it off: "'Height, 4 feet, 5¼ inches; arms spread out full length, from end to end of longest fingers, 7 feet, 10 inches; length of arm, 3 feet, 3 inches; length of hand, 10½ inches; length of foot, 12¼ inches; round the waist, 4 feet, 2 inches. Four men estimated on the weight, and the average is 185 pounds.'"

"Big mias," said Achang.

"Do you think you can skin and stuff him, Achang?" asked Louis.

"Know I can; have done it with naturalist."

"Then you may go to work on it as soon as you please, and I will give you five dollars for the job," added Louis. "Take your time, and do it well."

"Where I work? Sampan no good."

"I can make a place in the waist," said the captain; "besides, I want the small boat, for we can see higher land farther in, and I wish to go ashore there; we may find some shooting."

The boxes and barrels were moved farther forward and aft, and a workshop made for the Bornean. The sampan was cleaned out when the hands had finished their dinner, and the " Big Four," embarked in it. They did their own paddling, for there was not room enough for any more in the boat without crowding. Each of them carried a rifle. It was but a short distance, and the party were soon on the dry land.

Louis had hardly put his feet on the shore when he levelled his gun and fired. A moment later Felix followed his example; and each of them had brought down a deer. They rushed forward to secure their game; and then the other two hunters discharged their rifles, and a couple of wild pigs rolled over on the ground. It was plain that they had struck a spot where hunters seldom came. If there was any more game near, the report of the guns had driven it off.

" That was pretty well for a five minutes' hunt," said Louis when he and Felix had dragged the two deer to the water. " I think we had better stay here over night, and hunt on high ground to-morrow."

" That wouldn't do, Louis, and I should not dare to keep the Blanchita here over night," replied Captain Scott.

" Why not ? "

" The water is high and low up here by turns, and I am afraid I should find the yacht on the bottom in the morning," replied Scott. " Then we could not get her out of the woods, and might have to stay here a week or two, waiting for water to float her. No, no; I won't take the risk."

The game was dragged to the shore, and loaded into the sampan; for the appalling picture the captain had made of low water induced them all to hurry on board of the yacht.

CHAPTER XII

A FORMIDABLE OBSTRUCTION REMOVED

THE deer shot by Felix was a little fellow, though he was full grown, Achang said, when it was taken on board the yacht. The one killed by Louis was much larger. The pigs were in better condition than the one shot before. The men were set at work to skin the deer, and the cook cut out the best parts of the two swine. There was plenty of salt pork in the stores, so that the sides were not needed.

Achang kept himself very busy in his workshop. He had a difficult job on his hands; for he had to skin the fingers and toes of the animal, and to keep every part in its original shape. Captain Scott went to the wheel as soon as he came on board, and started the engine. Clingman reported the depth of water the same as when the party went on shore. By backing and going ahead a short distance at a time, he got the boat about, and headed her for the river.

The water was deep enough, and there was no particular difficulty in the navigation, though he was to follow the course he had taken at first. He had carefully observed the shape and location of the trees, and the stream was reached in a short time. Louis declared that it was a great pity they could not remain near the high ground, for he had no doubt that plenty of game would have been found.

"It seems to me that we have got all the game we want," said Scott. "What could we do with a couple more deer and a brace of wild hogs?"

"Perhaps you are right; but the fellows want to hunt, though I think I have had enough of it. I enjoy the sailing up this river, and it will be pleasant to explore the lakes farther up the stream," added Louis. .

"I hope we shall get to some place where we can do some fishing for a change; besides, I am fish hungry," replied Scott.

"Most of the fishing here is done with the tuba plant; and I think it is mean to stupefy the fish, and then pick them up on the top of the water. But the river is clearer up this way, and we will drop our lines when we come to a good place."

"If you want to do any more shooting just now, there is a flock of long-noses" (by which he meant proboscis monkeys), said the captain, as he pointed to them.

"We have one good specimen of that creature, and I don't want any more at present; but I would give something to know why they prefer to be in trees which grow out of the water," added Louis.

"I give it up, for I don't see any reason for it; but I suppose the long-nose understands the matter himself, and he won't tell us. Here we are at the river."

The captain rang the speed-bell as the steamer entered the stream where it was only thirty feet wide. There was a considerable current, and the screw-pines were densely packed together on both sides. The boat continued on her course for half an hour longer, when she seemed to have come to the end of all things, and the gong rang to stop her.

"Here we are!" exclaimed Scott. "And here we are likely to remain, unless we back down stream till we find a place wide enough to turn in."

The obstruction which closed the passage of the river against the Blanchita was a bridge of dead pines which the current had brought down, and they had caught at the sides till they formed the barrier. It was not more than six feet wide, though it might as well have been a hundred so far as blocking up the river was concerned.

"I don't like the idea of stopping here, for I want to see the lakes above; and I hoped we might get some fishing there," said Louis.

"What the matter is?" called Achang from his workshop.

He moved to one side so that he could see the obstruction.

"You can go through that, Captain," he continued, after Morris had corrected his English. "I have come up here before, and we have cut a way through."

"All right; we will see what the bridge is made of," said the captain, as he rang to back the boat.

She backed down the stream about twenty rods,

and then he stopped her. He then ordered Clingman to draw a piece of sailcloth over the stem, to prevent the dead pines from scratching the paint on the bow. As soon as this was done, she went ahead again at full speed, and the captain called to the engineer to give her all the steam he could. She went ahead at a furious rate, and Scott pointed her to what seemed to be the weakest place in the barrier.

"Now hold on, fellows, or she will tip you over!" shouted the captain as the boat approached the obstruction.

She struck the mass of pines, and drove her bow far into it, but stopped without going through it. The barrier was not solid, and was held together by the entanglement of the bushes as they were driven into the nucleus of the mass by the current.

"We can't cut through in that way," said Scott, as he looked at the half-sundered bridge.

"We don't want to take the back track," added Louis.

"There are more ways than one to skin a mosquito, and we haven't half tried yet," replied the captain. "The thing is softer than I supposed, and yielded when the boat hit it. I could go through, but it would take all the paint off the sides. Get out the anchor, Clingman, and we will see what can be done."

"I think we shall stick fast enough without anchoring," said Morris with a laugh.

"Wait a few minutes, my hearty; for I was not thinking of coming to anchor just now," answered

Scott, as he went forward to the stem, and mounted the rail.

The anchor was stowed under the forward seat; and Clingman, after overhauling the cable, passed it up to the captain. It was not very heavy, and with a skilful toss he threw it just over the edge of the barrier on the up-stream side. All wondered what he was going to do, for they saw no way to get through by means of the anchor; but they were willing to believe that the captain knew what he was about, and they said nothing.

"Now pay out about fifty feet of cable," continued Scott, as he rang the gong to back her. "Haul steady on it till you are sure it is fast in the stuff, Clingman."

The seaman humored the cable till he was unable to haul the rope home, and then reported the situation. The boat continued to back till the cable was hauled taut, when he stopped her. Then he spoke through the tube to the engineer, and rang the gong. The craft moved again, but very gently, for Scott was afraid the anchor would not hold; but it did, and speaking through the tube, he gradually increased the speed. The cable swayed and groaned, and it was evident that a heavy strain was upon it. The barrier was shaking and quivering under the pressure, and it was plain that something would yield very soon.

"Hurrah!" shouted Felix, who was looking over the bow at the bridge of pines; and the cry was repeated by the rest of the cabin party, and taken up by the sailors. "Bully for you, Captain Scott! Upon me wurrud, ye's have skinned the muskitty!"

This demonstration was called forth by the rupture of the barrier in two places, so that about one-half of it gave way, and was towed down stream by the steamer. Scott kept the craft moving till he found a place in the green banks of the river to leave the tow, for it was wide enough to obstruct the channel.

"Clingman and Wales, jump on the raft with the boathooks, and crowd the stuff over to the starboard side," said the captain when he had found the place he wanted.

He stopped the boat, and then went ahead, to enable the men to get upon the mass, after they had thrown a couple of boards upon it to stand on. Backing her again, he hugged the starboard side of the stream, and drew the raft abreast of the place, and close to it, where it was to be left. The men on it hooked into the screw-pines, and hauled it into the opening. Pulling vines from the trees, they moored it where it was. As soon as the two men came aboard the boat, the captain went ahead again.

"You did that job handsomely, Captain Scott," said Louis. "I thought the only way we could get through was by cutting a passage for the boat."

"That would have taken too long," replied Scott, as he called Clinch to the wheel. "Mind your eye! for the river is very crooked up here. Look out for the swing as she goes around the bends."

The boat had not gone a great distance when she came to a considerable expanse of territory which had been swept over by fire. The party did not think that the green bushes would burn; but they had burned so that nothing was left of them but the blackened stems, and there was no room for an argument.

"When the fire gets started, it scorches and dries the bushes till they will burn," Louis explained. "But what are we coming to now?" he asked, looking ahead where the country seemed to be level, and covered with a sheet of water, in which the screw-pines were abundant.

"That must be one of your lakes, Louis," added the captain.

"If it is mine, I will sell it to you," replied he.

"I don't want to buy; but I am not so sure that we can get through as shoal a place as that seems to be, for it is only the spreading out of the river. The greater the expanse, the less the depth. How is that, Achang?"

"Plenty water; float the boat," answered the Bornean. "Little Padang Lake. Plenty pandanus."

"What are pandanuses?" asked Scott.

"The plural of the word is pandanaceæ; and they are the same thing as the screw-pines, and sometimes are found thirty feet high. There is one; and you can see roots starting out of the stem, and heading downward. The leaves are very useful to the natives.   We shall get tied in a hard knot if we follow the twists of this stream much farther."

Presently the boat came to the lake.   The captain was considerably exercised about the depth of water; and as they entered the lake, which was not very different from the overflowed region they had visited that day, he ordered the wheelman to stop her.

"There must be some sort of a channel through this pond," said he, looking about him.   "There is a bigger lake than this one farther up.   There are mountains in sight in the distance, and the water from them must find an outlet to the sea."

"I have no doubt you are right; and probably there is a channel through this lake, for its water must get to the sea, unless it dries up on the way," added Louis.

"It will be easier to find this channel near the river than it will when we are half-way across the lake;" and the captain sent two men with Morris in the sampan to search for it.

The water was tolerably clear; and they went to the mouth of the outlet, sounding all the time with the boathooks.   They found the channel at this point, and then followed it up beyond the steamer. Morris shouted that the sampan was in the channel, and the Blanchita moved into it.   The searching-party returned to the steamer.   Morris was the mate; and, with the two men who had gone with him, he was directed to keep the run of the deeper water.

In another half-hour they came to the forest again, though the trees were growing in the shallow lake. Achang was hard at work all the time, taking all the pains with his operation which Louis had required of him; but his occupation did not prevent him from looking about him, and he soon made a discovery.

"Mias! Mias!" he shouted, pointing to a tall tree a few rods from the boat. "Mias fast asleep!"

All the party looked in the direction indicated, and saw the orang. He was lying on his back in the crotch of the tree, holding on with both hands to the branches. He must have been a heavy sleeper or the puffing of the engine would have aroused him. But Louis would not fire at him, as Scott suggested. He had a bigger orang than the one in the tree, and he did not want another. As he would not fire, Felix refused to do so, and the mias was left to finish his nap.

A little later in the day the boat came to Padang Lake; but they were disappointed when they found it was filled with screw-pines, though they could see open water, in one direction quite a large sheet of it. Following the channel, they reached the open space. The boat had hardly passed the limit of the screw-pines before Clingman shouted, "Fish!"

The captain rang the gong, the boat stopped, and fishlines where in demand. The flesh of the orang was used for bait; and in a few minutes Morris hauled up a fish so large that it taxed all his strength and skill to get him into the boat.

CHAPTER XIII

THE CAPTAIN'S ASTOUNDING PROPOSITION

ALL the cabin party had their lines out, but not another fish was caught. The place where they fished seemed to be a hole, and the water was deep and clear. Perhaps Morris's struggle with the big fish had scared the others away, for not another could be seen. The day was done, and it was growing dark. It was decided to anchor where they were, and spend the night there; and they hoped the fish would be in biting condition the next morning.

Achang called the fish the gourami, or something like that; but beyond this nothing was known about him. Louis, who was generally posted, could tell his companions nothing about it. But Pitts had cut it up, and it was fried for supper. The flesh was hard, and the flavor excellent. There was enough of it for all hands, and the supper amounted to a feast. A heavy thunder-shower made the evening very gloomy; but the canvas roof and curtains of the Blanchita fully protected the party from the rain, which fell in sheets for full two hours.

The next morning when the party turned out, the weather was as pleasant as they could desire, and the air was cleared and freshened by the shower.

The first thing they did was to throw over their lines; for they could see the fish through the clear water of the lake. In about as many minutes they had hooked four fish, though not one of them was so large as the one Morris had caught the evening before. But at that point they ceased to bite, and not another nibble was had. Either the fish did not like the looks of the boat, handsome as she was, which would have been very bad taste on their part, or the struggles of those which had been hauled in frightened them away. Very likely the fish could have explained the reason for their sudden disappearance; but they did not, and it remained a mystery.

They had an ice-chest on board, and Mr. Eng had replenished it at Simujan. Pitts dressed the fish, and put them in the refrigerator. For breakfast they had fresh pork, and it was much better than that they had had before. They had learned to drink coffee without milk, for it was not often that it could be procured away from the larger towns.

"I say, fellows, don't you think there can be too much of a good thing?" asked Captain Scott at the head of the table.

"Of course there can be too much of a good thing; for a fellow might eat ice-cream till his throat was frozen," replied Felix.

"Almost anything becomes a bad thing when you have too much of it," added Louis. "But I think we could have stood about four more of those nice fish. What is the moral of all this, Captain?"

"With me the moral is that I have had hunting enough for the present," replied Scott. "I should like a little more variety in our daily life."

"I don't think I should care to go hunting more than one day in a week, or, at most, two," replied Louis. "We have had it right along for a week; and, as you suggest, that's too much of a good thing."

"But it was you, Louis, who went in for three weeks of it," added the captain.

"Simply because I thought it would take the Guardian-Mother and the Blanche about that time to visit Siam and French Cochin-China."

"I suppose if we had made our trip up these rivers in a sampan, we should not have got so far inland in another week," added Morris.

"I don't think we should have come up here at all if the Blanchita had not been available," said Louis. "But we are close to the mountains now, and I am in favor of a tramp on shore."

"All right; and after breakfast we will get under way, for I must attend to the navigation," replied Scott; "and I suppose Felipe has steam enough by this time."

They left the table, and Scott went to the wheel. To save time and trouble, the men took their meals in the after cabin, and the engineer had the head of the table. Both Louis and Felix had run the engine of the Maud a portion of the time on her memorable voyage from Funchal to Gibraltar, and the former was sent to the engine-room. The boat went ahead; and after passing through a section of pandanus, they came to an open lake, which they judged to be five miles long.

The water was shallow, though deep enough for the steamer. The captain opened the binnacle, and headed the Blanchita to the north. It was a very quiet time, and the boat went along at her usual speed. In little less than half an hour she reached the head of the lake; but there was no convenient landing-place for a craft of her draught, and she was anchored at a considerable distance from the shore. Achang and two of the seamen were directed to attend the "Big Four," and they were landed in the sampan.

Each of the cabin party took his fowling-piece, while Achang had a rifle, and each of the sailors carried one, the latter to be used by the young men if they were wanted. They had walked but a short distance before they came to a steep precipice about twenty feet high, at which a notched log had been placed by some former visitors, as they supposed; but as soon as they had mounted it, they came upon a Dyak long-house, which might have been better called a short-house, for it contained but six doors, and therefore the tax upon the village need not have caused any grumbling.

The dwelling was not now a novelty, neither were the Dyak men and maidens; for the latter were not as pretty as several they had seen on the river.

They were very hospitable, and invited the party to enter the house, which they did ; but there was little to interest them there.   Achang talked with them, and the head man said they caught plenty of fish in the lake, and they snared pigs, deer, monkeys, and other game.   He engaged a couple of guides for the mountains.

The game was plentiful, and the hunters shot several deer, a pig, and a Malay bear; but they were not enthusiastic hunters, considering that they had come to Borneo for that purpose.   After a four hours' tramp they all thought they had had enough of it. Felix declared that he preferred to hunt cobras and tigers, for all the game seemed to be very tame to him.   Seating themselves on the ground, they rested for an hour, and then started on their return to the boat.   All the game was given to the Dyak guides, who were very glad to get it.   They swung it on a pole, and trotted along with their load as though it had been no burden at all.

"They do that all day," said Achang.   "Never get tired."

"They have load enough to feed the village for a week," added the captain.   "I should not care for the fun of feeding them another week, for I find hunting here very tame business."

"My sintimints also," added Felix.

After a walk of another hour they reached the Dyak house, and the whole population of the place followed them to the shore.   They were filled with wonder and admiration at the sight of the Blanchita, and went off to her in their sampans. They were permitted to go on board; but when Felipe fed the fire in the furnace, and the steam began to hiss, some of them were frightened, and fled to their boats.

Dinner was all ready when the party went on board; and Achang was instructed to send off the guests, for the boat was to get under way at once. They got into their sampans; but they remained near the Blanchita, evidently desirous to see her sail. They had not to wait long, for the anchor was weighed, and the captain rang the gong. She went off at her usual speed, and the Dyaks expressed their astonishment in various ways.

"Dinner all ready, gentlemen," said Pitts as soon as the steamer was well under way.

"What have you for dinner, Pitts?" asked the captain.

"Baked fish, Captain, in two pieces; for he was too long to go into my oven," replied the cook.

"All right. Take the wheel, Clingman, and make the course due south."

"Due south, sir," repeated the wheelman.

The party hastened to the after cabin; for they were hungry after their long tramp, though they had taken a light lunch with them. The fish, "in two pieces," was placed before the captain; while Pitts stood by his side, ready to pass the plates, and hear any comments the captain might make on the principal viand.

The odor from the steaming fish was emphatically agreeable to the hungry hunters, and so was the soft divan to their tired legs. Scott helped the members of the party to liberal portions of the dainty dish, and without pausing for manners they began to partake. When the captain had tasted the fish, he stopped short, and looked at Pitts. Then he reached out his right hand to him.

"Your hand, Pitts!" and the cook took it, his face wreathed in smiles. "You have cooked a dish here, Pitts, which is fit for any king on the continent of Europe, to say nothing of Asia."

The rest of the party applauded vigorously, and every one of them, following the example of the captain, took the cook by the hand, and bestowed additional praise upon him; and Louis declared that he could not have done better if he had served his time as a *cuisinier* in the Grand Hotel in Paris. But the most telling tribute to the skill of the cook was in the amount consumed; and the captain expressed a fear that the engineer and five seamen would have to "kiss the cook."

"It is only a woman cook that gets served in that way, and then not unless she is good looking," replied Pitts, laughing. "But you need have no fear, Captain, and the second table will have no occasion to kiss the cook, even it were one of the pretty girls we saw at the long-house below; for I have another fish in the oven, and it will be done by the time they are ready for it."

"That's right, Pitts; look out for the men as well as you do for the rest of us," added the captain. "Now, fellows, I am going to the wheel; and I want to see all of you in the fore cabin, for I have something to say, and we may have occasion to vote."

"Vote on what, Captain?" inquired Felix.

"There is no motion before the house, Flix; and when morning comes the sun will rise, not before," replied Captain Scott.

As soon as a plum-pudding had been disposed of, the party hastened to the fore cabin; for their curiosity had been excited by what had been said. The captain took the wheel; and Louis went to the engine, though he could hear what was said while near enough to the levers to act in case of need. Scott had brought from his berth in the after cabin a blue-colored roll, which all understood was a chart, though of what sea they did not know.

"Now, fellows, I have come to the conclusion that we are all tired of paddling about the muddy rivers of Borneo," the captain began, after he had scrutinized the compass in the binnacle. "I have said so before; though I have not enlarged on the subject, or spoken half as strongly as I might. The rest of you may not take my view of the situation; but I do not ask you to do so, and I hope you will all speak out just what you think, as I have done, and shall do stronger than before. We want something that is not quite so tame as shooting pigs and crocodiles at thirty-six cents a foot."

"I am quite of your opinion, Captain," added Morris. "I don't think there is any more fun in shooting orangs, for we are not naturalists nor scientists of any sort. If we had brought a naturalist with us, we should have done better."

"I have had enough of it for the present; but we have two weeks yet before the ship will come to Kuching for us, and what are we to do during that time?" said Louis, walking a little nearer to the wheel.

"That is precisely the conundrum I intend to guess on the present occasion, and for which I have called this meeting without consulting Mr. Belgrave," replied Captain Scott, giving the wheel to Morris, with the course, and unfolding the blue roll. "The Guardian-Mother will go to Saigon before she comes back to Sarawak. That is about a two days' run for her. From Sarawak, or the mouth of the river, the distance is five hundred sea miles. Now, to flash it on you all at once, I propose to sail in the Blanchita to Point Cambodia, where the ship will pick us up as she comes down the Gulf of Siam. Now I am ready to hear you all groan."

"It looks like a risky voyage in such a craft as this steam-launch," said Louis, when there was a prolonged silence.

"I wish you all to look over the chart of the China Sea; this meeting is adjourned to the after cabin at four o'clock, and you may do your groaning there."

The men soon came out of the after cabin, and Pitts was busy removing the dishes and putting everything in order. At the time stated, the party were seated around the table in the after cabin, ready to consider the captain's astounding proposition.

CHAPTER XIV

DOWN THE SIMUJAN AND UP THE SARAWAK

THE proposition of Captain Scott was certainly an astounding one, not unlike the daring of those men who have crossed the Atlantic in a dory or in small sailboats; and so it struck the other members of the cabin party. Scott was not a reckless navigator; and his companions had voyaged with him on stormy seas several times in the Maud, though she was a better sea-going craft than the Blanchita. She was decked over her entire length, so that she could be closed as tight as the inside of a barrel, while the steam-launch was an open boat.

Scott did not regard the venture as an extremely perilous one, though he would not have thought of such a thing as crossing the Atlantic in a craft like the Blanchita, principally because she could not carry coal enough to render the trip a prudent risk. The distance from land to land was about five hundred miles, and the little steamer could easily make this distance inside of three days. But the captain must speak for himself.

"Now, fellows, you can study the chart for yourselves," said he, as he put the point of his pencil on the mouth of the Sarawak River. "If the Blanchita were a sailing-craft instead of a steamer, I should not have a moment's hesitation; for though she is not heavy and clumsy, she is very strongly built. I have looked her over several times, with this trip in my head."

"But she can be rigged as a sailing-craft, and has a short mast and a sail," interposed Morris. "I talked with the rajah about her, and he told me that he had been out to sea in her. He said he had never had occasion to use the sail, but he carried it in case anything should happen to the engine."

"That betters the situation very materially," replied the captain. "If we have anything to depend upon if the engine should break down or the coal should give out we should be all right."

"There must be heavy seas out in the China Sea," added Louis, as he looked over the chart.

"We haven't seen any very heavy seas in any of these waters. The south-west monsoons prevail at this season of the year in these waters. I don't find any decided ocean current laid down on the charts of the southern and western portions of the China Sea. They strike in at the eastward of Java, and flow to the eastward of Borneo, through the Macassar Strait," said Scott, pointing out the direction on the chart.

"That looks favorable; and if there is any current to speak of, it runs in the direction of the monsoons, and therefore will not be likely to cause heavy winds."

"If I thought the trip was a very dangerous one, I certainly should not propose to make it," added the captain.

"Fish!" shouted Clingman at the wheel.

In spite of their interest in the discussion, all the party rushed forward at this cry. The captain ordered the wheelman to stop her, though her headway kept her moving for some minutes after the screw ceased to revolve. The men baited the hooks as soon as fish were indicated. The boat had reached the locality where the catch of the day before had been obtained, and all hands were on the lookout. The lines were thrown over, and the fish bit quickly as soon as the steamer was at rest. In half an hour they had taken seven.

"Keep her moving, Clingman," said Captain Scott, as the party hurried back to the cabin to continue the discussion.

Pitts dressed the fish, and put them in the ice-chest. Achang had completed the skinning of the orang, and the skin was now drying in the sun. The voyage to Siam or Cambodia looked very much like an adventure, and the young men were deeply interested in it.

"I don't think we are likely to encounter any very heavy weather in the western part of the China Sea," said Captain Scott, as he put his pencil on the chart again. "We may be overhauled by a typhoon."

"And what is a typhoon?" asked Felix. "I

know it is some sort of a storm, and that is all I do know."

"There are different names for a storm in different parts of the earth," replied Scott. "What is a hurricane in the West Indies is a cyclone in the northern part of the Indian Ocean, and a typhoon in the China Sea. They are all alike in substance, being revolving storms, in which the wind whirls around in a circle, and at the same time has a forward movement as a whole towards some point of the compass. But there are various signs which indicate the approach of a typhoon or a hurricane; and in these seas the barometer has to be watched constantly."

"I suppose we should be out of sight of land about all the time on the passage," suggested Morris.

"Not at all, my lad; for the first two hundred miles of the course we should not be out of sight of land half of the time, or only for a few hours at a time. Now look at the chart, all of you. Here we are at the mouth of the Sarawak River. About a hundred miles west of that is Cape Datu, the most western point of Borneo. Then for two hundred miles there is a chain of islands extending to the north-west, which is our course. These are the Natuna Islands; the largest one takes the same name, and is forty miles long. There are several other small islands north of this one, and if the weather came on very bad we could make a lee under one of them."

"Channel, sir!" shouted Clingman.

"I think you have got an idea of the whole thing, and we have a couple of days to think of it," said the captain, as he rose from his seat. "I will leave the chart here, and you can all study it."

Scott went forward to the wheel. He had caused a red rag to be tied to the top of a screw-pine while the sampan was looking for a channel through the lake, and Clingman had stopped the boat abreast of it. The captain took the helm himself; and he had carefully observed various marks, and obtained the bearings of the mountain, and other prominent objects which might assist him in taking the steamer through the shallow lake. He started her at once, and rang the speed-bell confidently, as though he had been through the lake a dozen times before.

It was sunset when the boat entered the narrow river, and they were called to supper. Clinch was placed at the wheel. It was a good moon, and the boat continued on her course till she came to the Dyak village where they had visited the long-house. She had been seen or heard as she approached; and the whole village was on the shore, including Mr. Eng.

"We are not going to lie up to-night," said Captain Scott when asked to land. "We are somewhat in a hurry to get back to Kuching, and we shall run down to Simujan this evening."

"I am going in the morning, Captain," added the agent.

"I will tow you down, and you can sleep on board if you wish."

"Thank you; my men will come down with the sampans to-morrow, and I gladly accept your offer," replied Mr. Eng. "But I must first go over to the *pangah*."

"To what? Will it take long?" inquired the captain.

"The pangah, or head-house of the village. I left my portmanteau there, and must get it."

"The head-house! May we go with you? for we did not stop to look at it when we were here before."

"Certainly you may go with me; I will have some torches so that you can see it as well as in the daytime," replied the agent, as he started with the cabin party, attended by four Dyaks who had come to the river with torches. "No head-hunting has been done for many years, as you are aware, and not many heads are on exhibition. In some villages you will find them by the hundred, though the people here were never much given to the barbarous practice. It was not necessary in this part of the island that a young man should get a head before a girl would accept him as her husband. Here it is."

It was a circular building not far from fifty feet in diameter, with a conical roof. In the centre was a place for a fire, which was perhaps required in cleaning the abominable trophies of war or individual murders. All around the apartment was a sort of divan, or bench, while over it were hung up the skulls, all nicely cleaned in the first instance, but now darkened by the smoke.

"This is the public building of the village, and the council when it meets has its place here for deliberation and action," said Mr. Eng, when he had pointed out what was to be seen in the building.

"Rather a sombre place, I should say, for such a purpose," suggested Louis.

"When you got used to the skulls you would not mind them any more than you would any other dry bones," laughed the agent. "I slept here last night, and the young men and boys lodge here. If you were to remain over night, young gentlemen, you would be quartered here; for it is the home of the stranger who visits the village."

"Then, I should be very thankful that we had a cabin in our steamer," replied Louis. "But there is no accounting for tastes."

The agent gave his baggage to a Dyak, and the party returned to the boat. A bed in the cabin was prepared for Mr. Eng, who said he was very tired, for he had walked a great distance that day, and he retired at once. The captain took the first watch, with two of the men. It was plain sailing, and in the middle of the night the Blanchita was anchored in the river in front of the kampon. Scott turned in then, with one of the port watch on duty.

In the morning they could not be induced to accept Mr. Eng's pressing invitation to remain a day or two at Simujan. He promised to take them to the coal and gold mine if they would remain; but all of them were so full of the great project that the invitation was declined. Three of the fish were presented to the agent, who told them something about it, and declared that it was the finest fish on the island.

A quantity of ice was obtained at the town; and Pitts carefully packed the rest of the fish, which were still hard and in nice condition. The captain desired to present a couple of them to Rajah Brooke, and some of the others to officers who had been very kind to them, and had assisted them in many ways. In the early morning they bade a grateful adieu to the agent, and departed on the trip to Kuching.

The tide was going out, and they made a quick passage to the sea. On their arrival there they found a stiff south-west wind blowing, and the bay covered with white-caps. They had not tried the Blanchita in anything like a heavy sea, though the rajah had declared that she was a very able and weatherly sea-boat. Captain Scott was very glad of the opportunity to test her behavior in rough weather. He went to the helm himself as the boat came out of the Sadong. The very first wave that broke on her bow scattered the spray from stem to stern.

Scott ordered the men to batten down the curtains on the weather side. But the boat rose gracefully on the billows, and did not scoop up any water in

THE BOAT ROSE GRACEFULLY ON THE BILLOWS.

Page 132.

doing so.   Boxes, barrels, and other movable articles were secured, and the captain was delighted with the working of the boat.

"I don't want any better sea-boat than the Blanchita," said he with great enthusiasm.   "I doubt if we get it any rougher than this on the voyage to Cambodia Point."

"Unless we run into a typhoon," said Morris, who was observing the conduct of the boat with quite as much interest as his superior officer.

"We won't run into a typhoon," replied the captain.

"How can you help yourself?   As sailors we must take things as they come."

"If navigators have a thousand miles or more of ocean ahead of them, they must face the music. But among these islands, if the weather looks typhoony, we can get under a lee, or make a harbor in some bay.   But don't try to cross the bridge till we get to it, Morris."

"Sail, ho!" shouted Clingman.

It was a steamer about as far off as she could be made out.   The two craft were approaching each other, and the steamer from the west went into the Sarawak ahead of the Blanchita.   She was a small vessel, apparently of not more than three hundred tons.   It soon became evident that she was not a fast sailer, for the Blanchita held her own with her all the way up the river to Kuching.

CHAPTER XV

ON THE VOYAGE TO POINT CAMBODIA

THE Blanchita moored as usual in front of the town, while the steamer anchored in the river. She proved to be the Delhi, from Calcutta; and it was ascertained when the party went on shore later, that she was to sail for Saigon the next day. The first care of the cabin party was to send the fish to Rajah Brooke and two officers whose acquaintance they had made.

Pitts overhauled the ice-chest, and found them in excellent condition; and Achang was appointed to be the bearer of them, with the compliments of the Americans, to the gentlemen who were to receive them. Two native porters were to carry them; and the party knew that the fish were a rarity in the town, and they were in season for the dinner of that day.

The four went on shore together just as a party from the Delhi landed with a boat. The captain of the steamer hailed them in the street in front of the government house, and asked if they belonged to the steam-launch which had just come up the river. He was curious to know something more about the explorers, and Captain Scott told him what they had been doing in the island. He was invited on board of the Blanchita, and was much interested in the young men.

They showed him over the boat; and he was greatly pleased with the craft, and with the excellent accommodations for sleeping, eating, and making the voyagers generally comfortable. They came to the ice-chest, in which two of the choice fish still remained; and Scott presented one of them to their guest.

"We intend to sail for Point Cambodia to-morrow to rejoin our ship," said the captain of the Blanchita, after the fish had been sent on board.

"In this little tub of yours?" asked the commander of the Delhi with a smile of incredulity.

"Is this part of the China Sea subject to violent seas?"

"Not at just this season of the year. With the south-west monsoons smart squalls come up sometimes, but they are not very bad. I don't think you will find it any rougher than we had it outside the river to-day on your passage to the Point," replied Captain Rayburn, who stated then that he had seen the Guardian-Mother when she was at Calcutta.

"You are bound to Saigon, I think you said."

"To Saigon, but a portion of my cargo goes to Kampot. If I found a sailing-vessel here that was going up the Gulf of Siam, I was ordered to reship my freight for Kampot in her; if not, I was to take it there in the Delhi. I find no such vessel here."

"Then you will make your course direct for Point Cambodia, Captain Rayburn?" said Scott.

"Precisely so; and if you can keep up with my steamer, we need not part company on the voyage."

"I think we can keep up with you," replied the captain of the Blanchita with a smile.

The party went on shore again, and arrangements were made for taking in a supply of coal early the next morning. Everything on board of the yacht had been stowed very carefully on the passage from Simujan, in order to make all the room possible for coal; but the boat could carry a supply for four days, and Scott was not at all afraid that he should come short of this needed article. Pitts purchased all the provisions and stores needed for the voyage.

After dinner the four paid their respects to the rajah, and visited the two officers whose acquaintance they had made. They were heartily thanked for the welcome gift of the fish, which the officers declared were a great luxury; and Governor Brooke said that he should make a trip to the lake where they were caught, in the government steam-yacht. These gentlemen thought the young men were rather venturesome to undertake the voyage before them in so small a craft; but the best wishes of all of them went with the party.

At daylight in the morning the coaling was begun; the provisions and stores were all looked over, and all deficiencies were supplied. By nine o'clock everything was in readiness for sailing. Captain Rayburn sent word that the Delhi would sail at ten o'clock, and afterwards went on board of the Blanchita.

"You seem to be well supplied with coal," said he, as he looked about him.

"I think we have a five-days' supply on board," replied Scott. "As I figure it up, we shall make the run to the Point inside of three days."

"The Delhi's time is sixty-three hours," added her commander. "If your coal should come short, I can help you out; but I think you won't need it."

"Thank you, Captain Rayburn; that kind offer removes the only doubt I have in regard to the voyage," replied Captain Scott.

"The Delhi, as you have seen for yourself, is not a fast steamer; but the only fear I have is that you will not be able to keep up with her," added Captain Rayburn. "I am obliged to sail in the interest of my owners, and I must make the best time I can. The south-west monsoons prevail at this season; and by carrying sail I may add half a knot, or perhaps a knot, to her speed. I should be sorry to run away from you, but I must do my duty."

"Certainly; that is understood. If you run away from me, I shall still wish you *bon voyage*. But suppose I should run away from you?" suggested Scott, laughing.

"You will be quite welcome to do so. The Delhi is an old steamer, and not up to modern-built ones; but with a breeze I have made nine knots in her."

"I shall try to keep up with you, for I should be

very sorry to have to part company with so pleasant a captain as you are."

"Thank you, Captain Scott; and if we part company on the voyage, I hope we shall meet again. I am liable to be detained some time in Saigon; for mine is a tramp steamer, and I have to look up a cargo for some port," said Captain Rayburn, as he shook hands with the four, and went into his boat alongside.

The first thing Scott did was to look up the mast and sail of the Blanchita. It had not been covered up with coal, as he had feared; for Clingman had suspended it inboard under the rail. The sail had been stowed away in the bow of the boat, and it was brought out and overhauled. It was nearly new, and needed no repairs. It was a lug-foresail, with a gaff, but no boom. It was stepped just abaft the galley, and the sail could be set in two or three minutes when it was required.

The statement of the captain of the Delhi that he could gain a knot or less in a good breeze had stimulated Scott to be ready for such an emergency. The wind would be on the port quarter during the whole voyage, and the sail would certainly add something to the speed of the yacht. In the crowd that collected at the government storehouse were the rajah and most of the officers of the place. The handshaking was all done over again, and pleasant wishes were extended to the "Big Four" as the Blanchita cast off her fasts.

The Delhi was already under way, and going at full speed down the river. Clingman was at the wheel, and Scott went aft to the engine-room, as it was called, though there was no such room, and the word applied simply to the locality; and the same was true of the galley. The boat had been delayed a little while the party were making and receiving the parting salutations of their friends, and the Delhi had a lead of nearly half a mile.

"Give her a spurt, Felipe," said the captain. "I want to know if that craft has the ability to run away from us."

The engineer threw more coal into the furnace; and in a few minutes he "let her out," as the captain called it. It was very soon perceived that the yacht was gaining on the old steamer, and Scott became correspondingly happy. She was farther down in the water than usual on account of the extra quantity of coal in her bunkers, and all along her sides, to trim her properly.

"I don't believe the Delhi will run away from us, Louis," said the captain as the millionaire joined him, curious to know what he was doing. "She isn't loaded for her best sailing, but she is doing first-rate for her present trim."

"This is smooth water, Captain; what will she do when we get out to sea?" asked Louis.

"We had a chance to try her yesterday in more than half a gale, and she behaved like a lady on a dancing-floor."

"But she was not loaded down with coal then as she is now."

"The extra weight will not disturb her; on the contrary, I think it will make her steadier."

"I talked with the rajah on board, who has used her for over a year, and has made a trip to Rangoon in her. He said she was usually run at eight knots an hour; but on his return voyage, when he was in a hurry, she made nine knots for twelve hours together," Louis explained.

"That is all I want of her; but I shall not drive her up to that unless the Delhi is likely to run away from us; and not then till after I have added the sail to our power of locomotion. We are coming up with her now, and probably Captain Rayburn's fears that his steamer may run away from us are beginning to abate," said the captain, rubbing his hands in his delight at the performance of the Blanchita.

Rather for the occupation it gave him, Scott took the wheel himself, directing Clingman to call the men, and remove the stanchions and connecting-rods on the starboard side of the boat from the galley to the length of the mast aft, so that the sail might not be obstructed when it was set.

Then, while the Blanchita was still making her nine knots, he ran her alongside the Delhi on the port side, keeping at a safe distance from her. Then he called to Felipe to reduce the speed to eight knots. He had gained nearly half a mile in going half-way down the river to the sea; and this fully satisfied him.

"Bully for you, Captain!" shouted Captain Rayburn from the quarter-deck of his steamer.

"I won't run away from you!" returned Scott, as the noise of escaping steam when the engineer reduced the speed must have reached his ears.

"Wait till we get out to sea!" called the captain of the Delhi.

"All right."

The two craft kept abreast of each other till they had passed the mountain at the mouth of the river. The captain laid the course north-west half-west; and this was to be the course for half the distance to Point Cambodia, as he remarked to Louis, who was at his side observing the progress of the yacht.

"How do you spell that word, Captain Scott?" asked Louis.

"Just as I spelled it when I went to school, and it is so put down on my chart; but I noticed in Black's "Atlas" that it was spelled Camboja instead of Cambodia," replied Scott. "I am a sailor, and I stick to the chart."

"I see that Captain Rayburn has laid his course; how does it agree with yours, Captain?" inquired Louis, when they were a mile off the mountain.

"I should say that it was identically the same. I will hail him."

"North-west half-west," was the answer returned by the captain of the Delhi.

"I make it the same," replied Scott.

The cabin party were summoned to dinner at this time, and Clingman was called to the wheel.

"What's the bill of fare to-day?" asked Scott as he took his seat at the table.

"Baked fish and roast venison," replied Pitts, "with plum-duff."

"Very good," returned the captain. "We don't get so much breeze off here as we did yesterday, Louis."

"It does not look at all rough off at sea," added the captain. "But when we get Cape Datu on the beam, we may feel it more."

The Delhi had not yet set her foresail, for she was schooner-rigged, and there was not wind enough to help her much; all the rest of the day the two craft kept abreast of each other, as they had in coming down the river. After supper the watches were arranged for the night. The captain, with Clingman and Lane, had the first, or starboard watch, while Morris, the mate, had the port watch, with Wales and Clinch.

Louis and Felix were appointed second engineers, as the seamen on board relieved them from duty as deck-hands; and the three in that department were to keep four-hour watches, like the officers and seamen. Achang wanted something to do; and he was given the berth of second mate, and as such he served in charge of the captain's watch.

CHAPTER XVI

AN EXCITING RACE IN THE CHINA SEA

EVERYTHING worked as smoothly on board of the
Blanchita as though she had been in commission for
years, for there was not a green hand in the cabin or
forecastle. The experience obtained by the "Four" in
the Maud had made them proficients in the duties of
their present positions. Louis and Felix were not
trained engineers or machinists; though they were
familiar with the machine, which was of very simple
construction. Both of them were competent to run
the engine, and had served their watches in the
Maud. If there was any trouble, the chief engineer
was close at hand.

From eight to twelve it was the captain's watch.
Achang, who had been the master of a vessel, had
been regularly installed as second mate, and was in
charge of this watch; though Scott remained on deck
all the time, for he was anxious to observe the movements of the Delhi. Clingman and Lane had their
two-hour tricks at the wheel, and there was no hard
work for anybody.

The breeze was good, though not heavy from the
south-west; but the Delhi had not yet set a sail. The
Blanchita passed Cape Datu at ten in the evening,

and the second mate made a note of it on the log-slate. Both craft were still making their eight knots, and remained abreast of each other. The wind increased slightly in force, but the conditions were about the same all night. At twelve the watch was changed, and Morris came on duty, with Louis in the engine-room. The captain turned in at this time.

At three in the morning the yacht was off the island of Sirhassen, of which a note was made on the log-slate. Morris had studied the chart enough to enable him to recognize the island, distant as it was, at six bells, or three o'clock in the morning. Of course he could not identify it by its looks, never having seen it before; but the captain had given him the distances between the islands on the course. Sirhassen was forty sea miles from Cape Datu, or five hours as the yacht was running; and when land was reported on the beam, bearing about west, he knew what it was. The chart gave the island as one of considerable size compared with the multitude of small ones in that locality; and this indication afforded him a further clew to the identification.

At eight bells, or four o'clock, the morning watch came on duty, with Achang as its officer. Captain Scott did not turn out when the second mate was called, with Felix to take his place at the engine, and it was six o'clock when he made his appearance. Except when there is only one mate, as in small vessels, the captain keeps no watch; but he is liable to be called at any hour of the night in case of a squall or other peril. His responsibility may induce him to spend the entire night on deck.

When he came out of the cabin, his first care was to observe the signs which indicate the coming weather. Then he went to the wheel, and read the entries made on the log-slate. The sea was about the same as it had been when he left the deck. He had looked at the barometer before he left the cabin. There were no signs of bad weather in any direction.

"What do you think of the weather, Mr. Achang?" he asked of the officer of the deck.

"It will be fine, Captain," replied the second mate. "I have come all the way from Banjermassin to Calcutta with the weather just like this always; but I think we have more wind when the sun come up."

"We can stand more than we have now," added Scott.

"Some of the young gentlemen fear to go to sea in open boat like this yacht; but the dhows and the proas have not much decks," said the Bornean.

"Then you think we shall have weather like this all the way to Point Cambodia?"

"May blow a little more hard some time."

The sun was coming up in the east, and in the course of half an hour Achang's prophecy of more wind was realized. It freshened rapidly for a short time; but it did not come in flaws or squalls, and was a steady breeze. A table had been set up in the fore cabin; and at half-past seven, or seven bells, which is the usual hour for breakfast at sea, the meal was served to the watch below.

"Land on the port bow, sir!" reported Clingman, who was the lookout man, just before eight bells.

"That is Subi," said Achang, looking at the paper Morris had given him when the watch was changed.

"That's right, Mr. Achang," added the captain. "I see the Delhi is setting her foresail, and that means wind enough to add something to her eight knots an hour."

Lane at the wheel struck eight bells a few minutes later; and the officer and engineer of the port watch came promptly on deck from the cabin, as did the seamen from the fore cabin. Breakfast had been served at both ends of the yacht to the watch below, so that they were in readiness to come on duty at the striking of the bell. Breakfast was ready for those who came off watch as soon as they were relieved.

Pitts had his hands more than full in supplying the two tables, but he was assisted by the idlers about the boat. The seamen were served as on board of the Guardian-Mother, where they had a table and a regular meal. On ordinary sea-going vessels the men get their "grub" at the galley in tins, or kids, and eat it seated on the deck, or where they choose.

Captain Scott had graciously ordained, as there was nothing to be done outside of the working of the yacht, that "watch and watch" should be the rule on board; which means that the hands shall have all their time to themselves when not on watch, though they were to respond when all hands were called.

"The Delhi means to run away from us, I suppose, for she has put on all sail," said Louis as he came on deck when he had finished his breakfast.

"But I don't believe she will do it," replied the captain. "We have a sail; but I am waiting to see what she can do under her present conditions, and I have told Felipe to hurry her up a little, just enough to keep up with our consort."

"She is gaining on us a little," added Louis.

"I see she is; but the engineer has thrown another shovelful of coal into the furnace, and I wish to see the effect it will produce. He has opened his valve a little, but he has not steam enough yet."

But it was soon evident to all who understood the matter that the Blanchita was gaining on her consort. It was plain, too, that Captain Rayburn had noticed the fact, for his crew were setting the gaff-topsails on the fore and main masts. Something of the enthusiasm of a race was aroused on board. Felipe had worked up his machine to the nine-knot gauge; and in spite of the added sail on the Delhi, the boat was overhauling her.

"I think that Captain Rayburn must be recalling his talk to us at Sarawak about running away from us," said Louis. "What is he doing now, Captain Scott?"

"He appears to be hoisting a yard on his foremast," replied Scott.

"What is that for?"

"If you watch the steamer for a little while longer, you will see him shake out a fore square-sail, and that will be the sharpest move he has made yet. Morris, have the mast stepped, and set the sail," continued the captain.

Clinch was at the wheel; and Clingman was called upon to do the work, with the assistance of the other two hands. The great squaresail of the Delhi had been shaken out, and it was drawing for all it was worth. The effect was simply to prevent the Blanchita from passing her, as she would have done in a few minutes more. The enthusiasm of a race was fully developed on board the yacht, among the seamen as well as the cabin party. Clingman and the others had worked very lively, and in a few minutes the sail was set. The captain gave the orders for trimming it; and as soon as the sheet was made fast the yacht heeled over till her rail was nearly down to the water.

"Our sail is a big one," said Scott, who saw it spread out for the first time; "and if we desire to run away from the Delhi, I am satisfied that we could do it."

The boat dashed the spray at her bow, and proved to be very wet in the fore cabin. The captain ordered the curtains to be hauled down to keep the water out, and the forward part of the craft was then as dry as it had been on the river.

Scott was not quite satisfied with the steering under the altered conditions, and he went to the wheel himself. He was a very skilful boatman in a sailing-craft, as had been fully proved by his bringing his yacht, the Seahound, from New York through the Bahama Islands. The seaman was inclined to follow the compass too closely, while Scott regarded the effect of the sail.

"We are gaining on the Delhi," said Louis, as he seated himself near the captain.

"Of course we are; I knew she would do it with the sail in this wind," replied Scott. "The Blanchita is a light craft, and skims over the water like a racer."

"But it is a little too much sail for her," suggested Louis. "She is taking in a bucket of water over her lee rail once in a while."

"Try the pump, Lane," added the captain. "I don't believe she has shipped more than a teaspoonful or two."

"We are pretty well down in the water," added Louis.

"Clingman, let off about six inches of the sheet," continued Scott; and the order was promptly obeyed. "I think you are getting a little nervous, my dear fellow," he added to Louis.

"Perhaps I am; I should not like to see the yacht

heel over and take in a couple of hogsheads of water, for she is loaded so heavily with coal that she would go to the bottom."

"But I should not let her ship such a sea as that. The wind is quite steady, with no heavy flaws, and the boat is under perfect control. I should like it better to sail the Blanchita with less cargo in her, but she is doing splendidly."

"But a flaw might come, even if we have had none to-day; what could you do in that case?" asked Louis.

"Clingman, stand by the sheet!" called the captain.

The seaman was seated on a box not more than three feet from the cleat at which the sheet was made fast. He took his place within reach of it.

"Now she heels over again!" exclaimed Louis, as the water came quite up to the rail, though she took none in.

"Cast off the sheet, Clingman!" called the captain; and the order was obeyed in an instant.

The boat flew up to an even keel almost as though she had been hoisted up by some giant power.

"That is how I should keep her from shipping a big sea," said Scott, as he looked at his companion with a smile on his brown face.

"I give it up, Captain Scott. Of course you know what you are about every time, and I won't say a word again about the boat. But suppose you were not looking when the flaw came?"

"It is not necessary to be looking; for a skipper steers more by the feeling of the boat than by sight. Make fast the sheet, Clingman."

The Blanchita went ahead again; and by this time she was abreast of the Delhi, and gaining upon her. Captain Rayburn was on his quarter-deck.

"Don't run away from me, and I won't run away from you!" he shouted.

But he had hardly spoken before a noise like the distant report of a cannon was heard on board of the yacht.

"He has split his fore squaresail; and if his game was not up before, it is now," said Captain Scott. "The sail was old and rotten, and I don't believe he would have attempted to carry it except on an occasion like the present."

"He was a little too pronounced when he expressed his fears that the Blanchita would not be able to keep up with him, and I fancy he is sorry he said anything about it by this time," added Louis.

The split sail could not be repaired at once; and if it could it was not strong enough to be of any use in the fresh breeze. The crew took it in at once, the yard being lowered to enable them to do so. The captain of the yacht ordered the engineer to reduce his speed to the ordinary rate, though the sail was not furled. Between the steam and the wind the Blanchita ran ahead of the Delhi. The sheet was slacked off as far as it could be without permitting the sail to shake, and the two craft kept well together the rest of the day, passing Great Natuna Island at four in the afternoon.

The captain took the sun at noon, and worked up the position of the boat. The run from the mouth of the Sarawak at that time was two hundred and four sea miles.

CHAPTER XVII

THE END OF THE VOYAGE TO BANGKOK

THE routine of daily duty on board of the Blanchita has been given; and after the race in the China Sea had proved that she could run away from the Delhi, there was no further excitement on the voyage. On the contrary, it was rather monotonous, and there were no incidents worthy of record. After passing Great Natuna on the afternoon of the second day from the mouth of the Sarawak, no land was seen again till the island of Pulo Obi, about twenty miles south-west of Point Cambodia, was seen on the third day; and the Point on the mainland was passed a little later.

At noon on this day the two vessels were forty-four miles up the Gulf of Siam. The prophecies of Captain Rayburn and Achang in regard to the weather proved to be correct. The monsoon blew steadily all the way, and the yacht carried her sail. Not even a squall disturbed the serenity of the voyage, and everything went on as during the first and second days. The "Four" would have been glad to explore the Great Natuna Island, and determine whether or not it was inhabited; for they could obtain no information in regard to it from any of the books they had brought from the ship, and they forgot to inquire about it at Kuching.

At noon on the third day, in the Gulf, the captain of the Delhi hailed the yacht, and came on board of her.

"I shall have to bear more to the eastward now, Captain Scott, and we shall soon part company," said the commander of the Delhi. "We had quite a lively race on our second day out, and you beat me handsomely. I had no idea that your yacht could sail so fast. I was afraid you could not keep up with me; but I found that you could run away from me, as you suggested before we sailed."

"I did not know myself what speed the Blanchita could make, though I was informed that she had gone nine knots for twelve hours together," replied Scott.

"I am very glad that I met you, and I hope I shall see you again. You have a very agreeable party, and I should think you might enjoy yourselves."

"I think we are likely to meet again at Saigon. The Guardian-Mother will be there, and I hope you will come on board of her," replied Captain Scott, as they shook hands at parting, and the visitor returned to the Delhi.

The Blanchita started her screw again; and the captain gave out north-west as the course for the mouth of the Menan River, on which Bangkok is situated.

"Where do you expect to find the Guardian-Mother, Captain Scott?" asked Louis.

"At Bangkok," replied the captain, as he took his memorandum-book from his pocket. "Captain Ringgold gave me his time for leaving there, and also of sailing from Saigon."

"When was he to leave the capital of Siam?"

"On the first tide Monday morning. This is Saturday, a little after noon," replied Scott. "We have three hundred and twenty-five miles to make. The monsoon is about as fresh here as it has been all the voyage; and we have used up about half of our coal, so that we are considerably lighter than when we left Kuching, and with the sail we can easily log nine knots an hour. We shall go into the Menan River before sundown to-morrow, and it will take two or three hours to go up to the city. We shall be alongside the ship some time in the evening; and that is just the time I should like to be there."

"We shall give our friends a tremendous surprise," added Louis.

"That is so; for while your anxious mamma is worrying for fear you have been chewed up by an orang-outang, and Flix's grandma is dreaming that he has been swallowed whole by a big boa-constrictor, we shall drop in on them while they are singing gospel hymns in the music-room."

"I shall be sorry to disappoint grandma; but if she insists upon dreaming such nonsense, it is not my fault," added Felix. "She ought to know by this time that snakes don't swallow me till they get a bullet through their heads."

"I don't think my mother has been greatly worried about me, for she has learned that I am able to take care of myself," said Louis.

"But the mothers will hug their boys as soon as they get hold of them."

"I wish the hugging might be confined to the mothers, for it is perfectly proper for them to do that thing; but when it comes to a grandma who hasn't a drop of Irish blood in her veins, I beg to be excused, and, what is more, I won't stand it," protested Felix, making a very comical face.

"But you can't help yourself, Flix," laughed the captain.

"You see if I don't!" replied the Milesian, shaking his head as though his plan to avoid the endearing reception had already been formed.

"We shall see what we shall see," added the captain. "It seems to me that the breeze is stronger here than it was out at sea."

"There is a hot country to the east of us, and perhaps the wind is hurrying up to fill a partial vacuum there," suggested Louis.

"You are a philosopher, my darling Louis, and that must be the reason," added Felix.

The Blanchita seemed to be flying through the water, for her speed had sensibly increased since she came into the Gulf. There were several large islands along the coast of Cambodia; but the course was fifty miles outside of the mainland, which could not be seen.

"Why do you keep so far from the shore, Captain Scott?" asked Louis; for all the party would have been glad to observe the shore.

"Because we all wish to get to Bangkok to-morrow evening. What is the shortest way between two points, Louis?"

"A straight line, of course."

"That's the reason we keep her so far from the land. A north-west course from a point outside of Obi Island to Cape Liant takes the yacht on the course we are running now."

"That explains it all," replied Louis.

The watches were regularly kept, and the captain was satisfied that the Blanchita was making over nine knots an hour. There was no excitement of any kind on board, and the rest of the day was without anything worthy of note. The Delhi had gone in behind an island, and in a few hours she was no longer to be seen. And so it was all day Sunday. Cape Liant was passed about one o'clock. A river pilot was taken about five o'clock. He could not speak English, but Achang spoke to him in Malay.

"Ask him if the Guardian-Mother is in the river, Achang," said the captain.

The pilot could not make out the name, and the interpreter described the ship so that he understood him at last. The face of the Siamese lighted up when he got the idea, and it was seen by the four that the ship was there. Achang informed them that the Guardian-Mother was anchored in the river.

The river was full of boats, and on many of them houses were built. The people were new to the Americans, though they were not very different to the ordinary observer from the Burmese and other natives they had seen. Before the yacht was half-way up to the city, it was too dark to see anything distinctly, and the party were more interested in the expected surprise of their friends on board the ship than anything else.

When the yacht was within a short distance of the ship, the pilot pointed her out. The singing in the music-room could be distinctly heard, and everything was working precisely as Scott had said it would. At the gangway the barge of the Blanche was made fast; and it was evident that General Noury and his wife were on board, and perhaps Captain Sharp and his lady. The boat was worked very carefully and noiselessly up to the platform of the gangway, where several sailors were seated.

"The Blanchita!" exclaimed Quartermaster Bangs, as he recognized the craft. "Captain Scott! I will inform the captain that you are alongside."

"Don't do anything of the kind, Bangs!" replied Scott. "Don't say a word, and don't make any noise, any of you. We want to drop in on the party without any notice."

The quartermaster was a very intelligent fellow,

and he took in the situation at a glance. The "Big Four" stepped lightly on the platform, and Felix had taken pains to be the last one to mount the gangway. Scott led the way, and halted at the door of the music-room. He waited there till the hymn they were singing was finished, and then threw open the door, and marched in. He took off his cap, and bowed as gracefully as a dancing-master to the assembly.

Louis and Morris followed him, and imitated the example he had given them; but Felix had disappeared, and they did not know what had become of him. The musical party seemed to be so utterly confounded at the sudden and unexpected appearance of the hunters from Borneo that they seemed to be struck dumb with amazement.

"Louis, my son!" Mrs. Belgrave screamed as she rushed upon her boy, and folded him in her arms, kissing him as though he had come back to her from a tomb or a grave beneath the ocean.

"Morris!" cried Mrs. Woolridge, as she imitated the example of Mrs. Belgrave.

"My brother!" exclaimed Miss Blanche, as she divided the neck and arms of the returned hunter with her mother.

"This is somewhat unexpected, Captain Scott," said Captain Ringgold, as he came forward, and took the hand of the captain of the Blanchita, who alone of the trio was not in the arms of a mother.

"I should say that it might be, Captain," replied

Scott as coolly as though the meeting was nothing unusual.

"But how under the sun did you get here, Scott?" demanded the commander, scrutinizing the expression of the third officer, — which was his rank on board of the ship, — to ascertain if there were any signs of a calamity there.

"We came by water, Captain," answered the young officer, with a cheerful smile, which indicated anything but a disaster.

"Of course you did, inasmuch as there is no other way to get here. In what steamer did you come? for I believe there is no regular line from Sarawak to Bangkok," added Captain Ringgold.

"We came by the steamer Blanchita."

"I don't understand it at all," said the commander with a perplexed look on his face. "Do you mean that you made the voyage in the steam-yacht, Mr. Scott?" and there was a decided expression of incredulity on his face.

"That is exactly what I mean to assert; and if you have any doubts about the truth of what I say, I appeal to Louis and Morris to substantiate my assertion.

"If you really say so, I do not doubt the truth of what you declare. It looks like a foolhardy risk, but boys will be boys. I will not detain you now; for others wish to welcome you back, and I know they are all glad to see you, unexpected as your return is."

"BUT WHERE IS FELIX?" DEMANDED MRS. BLOSSOM.

Page 161.

As soon as his mother released him from the bondage of her loving arms, Louis hastened to Miss Blanche, and she grasped his hand as he approached. No loving expressions passed between them, but what they might have said that could be classed under this head was seen on their telltale faces.

"But where is Felix?" demanded Mrs. Blossom, who had been looking for him since Scott came into the room. "Where is he, Mr. Scott?"

"I am sorry to say that he was swallowed by a big boa-constrictor one hundred and sixty feet long, and twelve feet in circumference," replied the captain of the Blanchita, as seriously as though there had been such a monster snake in existence.

The poor lady was impervious to a joke; she screamed once, and then dropped in a sitting posture on a divan. Nearly all the rest of the party laughed heartily. At this point the head of Felix dropped down a foot through the skylight over the centre of the room. He had made his way to the upper deck, and stationed himself where he could see and hear all that passed in the apartment.

"Good-mahrnin' to ye's all this foine avenin'!" he shouted. "Don't ye's make a row, Aunty. The schnake was a bit troubled wid indigestion of the brain, and, faix! I was too much for him! Loike the sodjers surrounded by the inimy, Oi cut me way out, and here Oi am."

"I don't believe you were swallowed by a snake," protested Mrs. Blossom.

"Don't you believe that Jonah swallowed the whale, Aunty?" demanded Felix.

"Of course I believe that because it is in the Bible. If you had told me that you had swallowed the snake, I might have believed that," added the good lady.

At this point General Noury came forward, and grasped the hand of Scott, passing from him to Louis and Morris, and then doing the same with Felix, who had dropped down from his perch at the skylight. As soon as Mrs. Blossom saw him on the floor, she rushed towards him with outspread arms; but the Milesian warded off the assault, and took her right hand.

"Don't hug me, Aunty, for the snake swallowed me clothes and all, and you may get some of the poison on you," said he.

For some time longer there was a general hand-shaking, and Louis was kissed by the Princess Zuleima.

CHAPTER XVIII

LOUIS'S DOUBLE-DINNER ARGUMENT

AFTER the welcome of the Bornean hunters had spent itself in kissing and handshaking, the question came up as to why the "Big Four" had abandoned their explorations after one week in the island instead of three, the time arranged for them to remain there; and they had fixed the time themselves.

"I thought three weeks was a rather long time for you to be in the island," said Captain Ringgold after the question had been opened for discussion.

"We fixed the time before we knew anything about the island," replied Louis. "But I want to say, in order to counteract the impression which appears to prevail in this company, that our trip was not a failure; for we had a fine time, and enjoyed our trips on the rivers."

"If you had a good time, why did you cut it short by two-thirds of the period allotted to the excursions?" asked Uncle Moses.

"We went up the Sarawak, the Sadong, and the Simujan, up the last to the mountains, passing through Lake Padang, and we have shot an orang-outang, and might have killed more of them, to say nothing of other game," replied Louis, whom Scott had requested to do the talking. "We visited three Dyak villages, sailed the Blanchita through a forest, and killed a good many crocodiles."

"You seem to have had sport enough," added Uncle Moses. "Why did you give it up in the cream of the thing?"

"I believe you like a good dinner, Uncle Moses; such a dinner as you always have on board of the Guardian-Mother," continued Louis, who was evidently pluming himself to make a point.

"I do like a good dinner, and enjoy one very much," replied the worthy trustee of the young millionaire. "But I doubt if I am any more devoted to such a banquet as we get every day than my beloved friend, Brother Adipose Tissue, and all the rest of the voyagers all over the world."

"I plead guilty to the charge of Brother Avoirdupois; and I acknowledge myself to be a worshipper at the shrine of Mr. Melancthon Sage, and I invoke a blessing upon the head of Monsieur Odervie, the chief cook. Our life on the ocean wave is a constant promotive of the appetite. If the proof of the pudding is not in the eating of the bag, it is in the eating of the dinners; and I think we pay an abundant tribute to the talent of Mr. Sage, the prince of stewards, in the quantity of the well-cooked food he causes to be placed before us."

"We get through dinner about seven o'clock. I see that the accomplished chief steward is standing at the door," continued Louis. "Now, Mr. Sage, would it be possible and convenient for you to have another dinner on the table, say at eight o'clock, an hour after the first feast had been finished?"

"Quite possible, and even convenient; the only persons to complain of such an arrangement would be the cooks and stewards," replied Mr. Sage.

"Captain Ringgold, might I so far presume upon any influence I may have with you as the owner of the Guardian-Mother to request you to order a second dinner to be served at eight in the evening, beginning, say, with to-morrow evening?" asked the young millionaire, looking as serious as though he was about to preach a sermon, though the party were generally laughing.

"As I have always told you, I take my orders from the owner; and if you desire such a dinner, I shall certainly give Mr. Sage an order to that effect," replied the commander.

"But who is to eat the dinner after it is provided, an hour after the passengers have gorged themselves at the table?" demanded Dr. Hawkes. "Is this a conspiracy to make more work for the surgeon?"

"Not at all," protested Louis. "It is to give the gentlemen who question so closely an opportunity to have an abundance of a good thing."

"But we could not eat the dinner," said Uncle Moses. "We are not hogs."

"Oh, you are not!" chuckled the owner

"But what has all this to do with hunting and exploring in Borneo?" inquired Mr. Woolridge.

"Well, sir, after we had taken a full dinner in Borneo, Uncle Moses and the commander ask us why we did not eat another dinner immediately on the top of it, as I observe that they are not disposed to do on board of the ship," returned Louis.

Some of the party had penetrated to the conclusion of Louis's argument, but most of them did not see the point of his illustration till he made his last remark; then Mr. Woolridge began to clap his hands, and the whole company applauded vigorously.

"I suppose the interpretation of the whole matter is, that the hunters in Borneo were gorged with hunting," said Captain Ringgold; "and that when they stipulated for three weeks of the sport, they overdid the matter."

"That was precisely the situation, Mr. Commander; and if you had been with us on the waters of Padang Lake, you could not have defined it better," replied Louis.

"But it is almost incredible that a quartet of such Nimrods should have become disgusted with their favorite sport in a single week," added Captain Ringgold.

"We are not hogs, as Uncle Moses gently suggested, and we could not eat a second dinner on top of the first so soon. If we had gone to Borneo a second time, after a reasonable interval, I am confident we should have enjoyed a second week of hunting, even along the muddy rivers and inundated jungles," Louis explained.

"In other words, you bit off a bigger mouthful than you could swallow," said the commander with a hearty laugh; for he had predicted that three weeks of hunting at one time was too much. "But we understand the situation now up to the time of the departure of the Nimrods from their happy hunting-ground. It was a rather daring enterprise to make a voyage of nine hundred miles in an open boat; and I should like to ask who was the originator of the idea."

"If there is any blame for this trip, we were all in the same boat, and we share the responsibility," answered Louis. "Captain Achang Bakir was with us; and he has sailed in all the seas of the Archipelago in an open boat, and we had his advice. Then we sailed all the way to the entrance of the Gulf of Siam in company with the steamer Delhi, whose captain agreed to stand by us, and to supply us with coal if we came short."

"That puts a new face on the matter."

"It was in the head waters of the Simujan that the plan was discussed, and Captain Scott was the originator of the idea," continued Louis. "I was in favor of it first because it would save the Guardian-Mother the voyage from Saigon back to Kuching, about a thousand miles."

"Where is Kuching?" asked Dr. Hawkes.

"It is the native name for Sarawak."

"I am heartily glad you have come to us, Louis, for the reason you have given," added the commander.

"How did the steam-yacht work, Mr. Belgrave?" asked the rajah.

"Exceedingly well, sir; nothing could have done any better; but Mr. Scott can answer you better than I can, sir."

The third officer of the ship, late captain of the Blanchita, described the working of the yacht, and gave her liberal praise. He related in what manner she had beaten the Delhi in the race, and that he had carried sail all the way nearly from the start. He gave the party the routine of the boat, — how they had taken their meals, and how they had slept on board.

"But I think it is time for us to return to the Blanche," interposed Captain Sharp, as the clock struck eleven.

"I must make an announcement before you go," said Captain Ringgold. "We shall not be able to sail for Saigon to-morrow morning, as arranged before. We have to clean the Blanchita in the morning, and she has to be put on the upper deck of the Blanche. As the Nimrods have come to Bangkok, I wish to give them a day on shore to see the temples, and call on the king if they are so disposed. We will sail on Tuesday morning on the early tide."

"But we have not had any account of the adventures of the Nimrods in Borneo," suggested Uncle Moses.

"We shall do so at eight o'clock in the morning; and you will all assemble for the purpose at that time. The lecture on Siam and Cambodia has been postponed till all hands could hear it; and if General Noury is ready, that shall follow the adventures," replied the captain.

"I will be here at the time stated, for we all desire to know what the Nimrods have been doing," replied the general, as the party from the Blanche retired from the music-room.

The rest of the company went to their staterooms, while the commander gave his orders for the work of the morning. All hands were called at daylight; and the young adventurers shook hands with the officers they found on deck, and spoke a pleasant word to the seamen on duty. The latter were hoisting the coal, provisions, and stores of the Blanchita on board of the ship; and by breakfast-time the yacht was as clean as a Dutch chamber.

At the appointed time the company, including the party from the Blanche, were seated in the arm-chairs of Conference Hall; and Louis went through his narrative of the adventures of the Nimrods in Borneo. During the morning, Achang had placed the stuffed orang-outang on a shelf the carpenter had erected at the head of the platform, with the proboscis monkey on one side, and the argus-pheasant on the other. The Bornean had had some experience as a taxidermist, and Dr. Hawkes declared that he had done his work well.

Louis explained these specimens, and gave the measurements of the orang. The proboscis monkey and the bird were also described. When he said he had not been disposed to shoot monkeys and other harmless animals for the fun of it, the audience applauded. He had killed a specimen of several animals, and several pigs, deer, and one bear, most of the latter for food. The cook had packed the last of the fish in the ice, so that it had kept well, and it had been served for breakfast that morning. Everybody had praised it. The surgeon called it the gourami, and said that some successful attempts had been made to introduce the fish in American waters.

The audience laughed heartily when Louis related in what manner they had killed and sold one hundred and eight feet of crocodile for about forty dollars. He told what he had learned about the Dyaks, and described the long-house they had visited, and the headhouse, and gave the story in full of Rajah Brooke, and their visits to his nephew and successor, the present rajah. He might have gone on with his narrative till lunch-time if he had not known that General Noury was waiting for him to finish his account.

"Did you see the Dyak women, Louis?" asked his mother.

"Plenty of them. The older ones reminded me of the French women; for when they begin to grow old, they wrinkle and dry up. The morality of the Dyaks is much higher in tone, even among the laboring-classes, men and women, than in civilized countries. They are all honest; and they steal nothing, even in Kuching, though the Malays and Chinamen do it for them."

"Were the young women pretty, Mr. Belgrave?" inquired Mrs. Woolridge.

"To a Dyak gentleman I suppose they are; but I was not fascinated with them, though I saw some on the Simujan who were not bad looking. The prettiest one I saw was at a village near the mountains. But the general is waiting for me to finish, and I must answer no more questions at present," replied the speaker, as he bowed, and hastened from the rostrum.

Then it was found that Mr. Gaskette had not hung up the map of Cochin China, for Achang and the carpenter had taken up the space before appropriated to it. Mr. Stevens, the carpenter, suggested a way to get over the difficulty; but it would take him half an hour to put up a frame in front of the orang.

"I shall not be able to get half through Cochin China before lunch-time," said General Noury, consulting his watch.

"I am afraid your audience will be scatterbrained, General, there is so much going on about the decks. Perhaps we had better postpone the lecture till after we have sailed to-morrow morning, especially as the Nimrods will be on shore this afternoon," suggested the commander.

"I approve the suggestion; let it be adopted."

The Blanche party lunched on board, and spent the afternoon there.

CHAPTER XIX

A HASTY GLANCE AT BANGKOK

WHILE the carpenter and the second officer were busy making a place for the large map of Cochin China, the returned hunters from Borneo were invited to the cabin of the commander.   They were pleased with the change of scene from the mud and water of their week in Borneo; though they felt that they would like to go there for another week — not more than that — at another time.

"After lunch you will visit the city of Bangkok, and spend the afternoon there; for you ought to see the place, as you are here," said Captain Ringgold. "It is a large city."

"How large is it, Captain?" asked Louis.

"That is more than anybody in Siam, or anywhere else, can tell you.   In these Oriental countries, when they count the people, they do not include the females in the enumeration, so that we get but half an idea of the whole number.   Chambers puts it at 300,000; the 'Year Book' does not give it at all; Bradshaw puts it down at 500,000; Lippincott the same. Probably the larger number is the nearer correct, and the authorities quoted are issued the present year."

"I see no end of Chinamen flitting about the river," said Scott.

"They compose about one-half of the population of the city; and most of the trade of the place is in their hands, as you have found it to be, though to a less degree, in other cities you have visited in the East. The Celestials are taxed three dollars when they come into Siam, and pay the same amount every three years. But there is the lunch-bell. If you have no objection, Professor Giroud will go on shore with you."

"I should be delighted to have his company," replied Louis; and the others said the same thing.

The conversation at the table related more to Borneo than to anything else, and the Nimrods had all the questions they could answer put to them; and some of the ladies wished they had remained there a few days.

"If I had supposed the Nimrods would stay there only a week, I should have been quite willing to remain at Sarawak that time," added the commander.

"We fixed the time at three weeks because we thought it would take you all of that time to see Siam and Cambodia, and get back to Sarawak," replied Scott.

"I think it would have been delightful to sail on those rivers, and see the uncivilized people of the island," added Mrs. Belgrave. "But I suppose we should have been in the way of the hunters."

"Not at all, madam," answered Scott. "We had

a sampan, in which we could have done our hunting, while you were examining the long-houses and the head-houses.   I don't know but that we should have wished to remain the whole three weeks if the ladies had been with us."

"Gallant Captain Scott!" exclaimed the lady.

"We did not go up the Rajang River as we intended, and we should have done that if you had been with us.   I am very sure the Dyak ladies would have been delighted to see you, more than you would have been to see them," replied Scott.

"The steam-yacht must have been very delightful on the rivers and lakes; but the crocodiles, the snakes, and the savage orang-outangs would not have been pleasant to us."

"But with eleven Winchester repeating-rifles ready for use, you would have had nothing to fear."

Captain Ringgold rose from the table; and this terminated the conversation, and the party went on deck.

"Captain Ringgold said you had offered to go on shore with us, Professor Giroud," said Louis, as he joined the instructor.   "We shall be delighted with your company."

"Thank you, Mr. Belgrave.   I have been on shore every day, with or without the party, and have learned something about Bangkok.   I may be of service to you," replied the professor.

"I am sure you will," said Scott.

The first cutter was in the water when they

reached the gangway, with the crew in their places. They went on board, and the bowman shoved off. Stoody, the coxswain, gave the orders, and the boat was immediately under way. She was steered towards the shore till she came abreast of the various craft moored there, and then headed up the river.

"Where are you going, Stoody?" asked Scott.

"Captain Ringgold told me to take the party up the river, to show them the boats and houses," replied the coxswain.

"That is a good idea, Mr. Scott," added the professor.

"The houses here are all afloat," said Morris. "They are three or four deep."

"Everybody is not allowed to build his house on shore; for that is a royal privilege, doled out to a few of the highest nobility," said the professor. "I suppose there is not room enough in the city for much besides the palaces and the temples, but beyond its limits we shall find plenty of land-houses."

"But I should think these floating houses would be smashed to pieces in a heavy blow; and I see there are plenty of steamers and tugboats in the river, which might bump against them," Morris objected.

"You see that the middle of the river is kept open, though it is very crooked; and these things regulate themselves."

"These houses are no better than card-boxes.

They seem to be built of bamboos, with wicker-work and plants. Each of them has a veranda in front, which is a nice place to sit and read, with a kind of ell at each end. I think I should like to live in one of them for a week or two," continued Morris.

"You would not like it," said Achang, who had come with them to act as interpreter.

"This is a walled town, with six miles of fortifications around it."

"A little less than two miles across it; and we shall not have to take any very long walks, for I have read that carriages are seldom seen except among the palaces, and probably belong to the nobility," said Louis; "but we are good for six miles this afternoon."

"The river is the great thoroughfare for business and for pleasure. It is covered with boats of all sorts and kinds. The walls of the city are from fifteen to thirty feet high, and twelve feet thick; but I suppose the heavy guns of modern times could knock them down in a very short time," added the professor.

"What is that opening into the river?" asked Felix, who had kept his tongue very quiet so far.

"That is a canal," replied Achang, as the professor did not reply. "I have been here three times, and once I went up that canal. There are only a few good streets in the city, and inside business is carried on by the canals."

"As Paris is to France, and Paris is France, so Bangkok is Siam; and that is the reason why the commander goes no farther. Now we have come to the wall, and you can see the outside town."

"The houses here are all on stilts, as in Sumatra and Borneo," observed Scott. "Some of them are built over the water."

"It is said here that the city suffered terribly from the ravages of cholera; and when the king found out that the disease was caused by the bad drainage of the houses, he ordered his people to build on the river, where the drainage would dispose of itself," said Professor Giroud. "This story was told me by a Frenchman here, but I cannot vouch for the truth of the statement."

"Can you tell me, Achang, why they build their houses on piles in this country?" asked Morris.

"Because they have waterations here."

"Have what?" demanded the questioner, while all the party laughed except the Bornean. "I never heard of waterations before."

"When the water rise up high," Achang explained.

"Inundations, you mean."

"Yes; thunderations," added Achang.

"Inundations!" roared the Bornean's preceptor.

"That's what I say; and that's the first reason. The second is that there are many snakes" —

"Then, it's the place for me!" exclaimed Felix.

"Many snakes and wild beasts; the stilts help to keep them out of the house."

"But most snakes can climb trees," Scott objected.

"Fixed so that snake can't get off the post into house," the Bornean explained.

"The little corn-houses in New England and other places are protected in the same way from rats. Four posts are set up for it to rest on, with a flat stone, or sometimes a large tin pan turned upside down, placed on the post. When the building is erected with the corners on the large, flat stone or the pans, rats or other rodents cannot get over these obstructions, and the corn is safe from them," continued Louis, illustrating his subject with a pencil for the post, and his hand for the stone or the pan.

Scott, who was an officer of the ship, ordered Stoody to take the party to the landing nearest to the Temple of Wat Chang, as the professor requested.

"The religion of Siam, like that of Burma, is Buddhist, in whose honor most of the temples whose spires you can see are erected," said the professor, as he pointed to several of them.

"We don't care to see them in detail, even if we had the time," suggested Louis. "I know they are magnificent pieces of architecture, and wonderful to behold; but we have had about enough of that sort of thing."

The party landed, and walked to the temple. It looked like an exaggerated bell, the spire being the handle, and the lower portion looking like an enormous flight of circular stairs for the roof. It was over two hundred feet high. Attached to it in the rear was a structure with a pitched roof. They bought photographs of it at the stand of a native who spoke a little French. At this point Achang procured a guide who spoke French, and he conducted them to the Temple of the Sleeping Idol.

"It is not much of a temple compared with the one we have just visited," said the professor. "We must go into it."

They entered, conducted by the guide. The building looked like three pitched-roof structures set together, the middle one into the largest at the bottom, and the smallest into the middle one. It contains an enormous figure of Buddha, one hundred and sixty feet long, which about fills the interior of the temple. It is constructed of brick, plastered and then gilded, so that it looks like a golden statue in a reclining posture. The feet are sixteen feet long, and the arms six feet in diameter.

The party looked in at another temple, which contains a brass statue of Buddha fifty feet high, with other smaller statues, and a variety of objects that were unintelligible to the visitors. Various other temples were examined hastily on the way to the royal palace, but they were only a repetition of what they had often seen before.

The palace was a magnificent building, or series of buildings, for a half-civilized country. The tourists were permitted to enter at the gate, though the guide was excluded. They saw a squad of the royal guards who were drilling on the pavement, and they regarded them with great interest. They wore a Zouave uniform, though with a short frock-coat buttoned to the chin, with round caps in cylindrical form, and visors. They were armed with muskets, and commanded by native officers.

"This palace is a big thing," said the professor, "and is a mile in circumference, surrounded by walls."

It contained, besides the palace of the king, the public offices, temples, a theatre, barracks for several thousand soldiers, and apartments for three thousand women, six hundred of whom are the wives of the king. But what interested them more than most of the sights was the famous white elephant. He is said to be of equal rank with the king, and is treated with all possible deference and respect. He has a palatial stable; and being a king, he lives like one. His servants and attendants are all priests. But he is not a pleasant sprig of royalty, and the visitors were warned not to go too near him.

But it was time to return to the ship, and they found the boat in the canal which Achang had indicated. At dinner the conversation was concerning the city, and the party mentioned many things the Nimrods had not seen. On Tuesday morning the ship sailed on her voyage to Saigon.

CHAPTER XX

A VIEW OF COCHIN CHINA AND SIAM

THE ship sailed at six o'clock in the morning, but nearly all the passengers were on deck as soon as the screw began to turn. They were still in the Torrid Zone; and they saw the sun rise, though the days had become a trifle longer. The Menam River is the great thoroughfare of Bangkok, and the floating houses lined the river three or four deep for a considerable distance below the city. The party found plenty of objects to engage their attention as the steamer slowly made her way towards the Gulf. Breakfast was served at the usual hour; and as soon as the pilot was discharged, the company gathered at Conference Hall for the lecture.

The siamangs and the baby were still great favorites with all on board; and Mr. Mingo, Mrs. Mingo, and Miss Mingo, as they had been named, had made great progress in civilization. All of them were regular attendants at the meetings in Conference Hall, and always behaved themselves with the greatest propriety. The mother usually occupied one of the arm-chairs, while the baby was held in the lap of one of the ladies. They looked at the speaker just as though they understood what he was saying.

They joined in the applause when the lecturer presented himself before his audience with their "Ra, ra, ra!" finishing with the squeak which was a part of their language.

General Noury took his place on the platform after he had shaken hands with Mrs. Mingo, who gave him an encouraging smile as he mounted the rostrum. The Sumatra lady looked at him very earnestly, and Miss Blanche declared that she understood everything that was going on. Mrs. Noury, the Princess Zuleima, had the baby; and the little siamang seemed to take as much interest in the proceedings as her mother. Mr. Mingo was not literary, and perched in the fore-rigging.

The great map seemed to have been drawn and colored with even unusual care, perhaps because Mr. Gaskette had had more time to attend to it. It was displayed on the new frame which the carpenter had built for it, and included the entire peninsula east of the Burmese possessions, and south of China and the Shan States. When the applause which greeted the general had subsided, he directed the pointer at the map.

"Perhaps some of you will be considerably confused by the various names of the territory we are engaged in visiting at the present time," he began; and Mrs. Mingo gave a louder squeak than usual as a special greeting to the distinguished gentleman. "Cochin China, I think, is the most common name, though Indo-China is very generally used. It is also called

Farther India and Annam. Its various divisions are the Shan States, tributary to Siam, taking their name from a race of people who are of the same descent as the natives of China. You observe that there are more of these states in the territory of Burma, to which they are subject. These states tributary to Siam contain a population of about two millions.

"Next south comes Siam proper. Lying east of the Shan States and Siam is a territory called the Little Lao States, which are subject to the several countries around them. On the east, bordering on the China Sea, is Annam, a part of which is sometimes labelled Cochin China. A part of Annam is Tonquin, in the north, next to China. What is called Cambodia, next south of Siam, and appearing to be a part of it, is an indefinite factor of Cochin China, and may properly enough be counted in with Siam. What is called Independent Cambodia, if it is independent, is a triangular country south-east of Siam. French Cochin China occupies the most southern portion of the peninsula.

"Nearly the whole of the territory of Cochin China is under the protection of France; and in my judgment, which you can accept for what it is worth, the whole peninsula will eventually become French, under whatever form it may be accomplished. Very recently the relations between France and Siam were very much strained over a disputed boundary question. France had ships of war at the mouth of the Menam, and sent some of the smaller craft up the river. It looked very much like war; but before the ships bombarded Bangkok, Siam yielded, and gave up the portion of territory claimed; and no doubt it will be the same story told over again from time to time, until Siam exists only as a dependency of France.

"Though you see mountains laid down on Mr. Gaskette's map, the elevations hardly deserve that name; for nearly the whole of Cochin China is low ground, almost flat. The Mekhong River is the largest in the peninsula, being 2,800 miles long. It rises in Thibet, and is navigable only in its lower waters. On account of the low level of the country there are many canals, or bayous as you call them in Louisiana, which connect many of the rivers. Let us now return to Siam. By the way, I find the latest map I have seen of this region in Chambers's, published last year; and it is quite different from the one before you."

"But not from the one that will be before you in half a minute more," interposed Mr. Gaskette, as he unrolled and hung up a smaller one which he had just completed. "I made this one this morning, after the commander had shown me the one to which you allude; and you can see that it is a very crude one."

"I thank you, Mr. Gaskette, for the new map; and though you took it from a book not more than a year old, I am afraid that it is not entirely correct for to-day. You observe, my friends, that Siam occupies nearly the whole of the peninsula east of Burma. Annam is cut down to a very thin slice on the China Sea; and Tonquin, where France has kept many soldiers employed for several years, is swelled into a considerable territory. I doubt if the last change in the boundary of Siam is shown before you. The limits of Cambodia are closely defined.

"Nearly the whole of the peninsula was included in the ancient kingdom of Cambodia, existing at the Christian era; and Buddhism is believed to have been introduced into it in the fourth century. Some remarkable ruins, with interesting sculptures, have been found as testimonials to the greatness of this ancient country. The Temple of Angkor had 1,532 columns, and the stone for the structure was brought from a quarry thirty-two miles distant. Massive bridges, so solidly built that they have resisted the ravages of time and the inundations of more than a thousand years, are still to be seen. One of them is four hundred and seventy feet long, and has thirty-four arches. An account of these wonders was given by a Chinese traveller of the thirteenth century, and they seem to bear some comparison with the works of the ancient Egyptians.

"The native name of Siam is *Muang Thái*, which you will please to remember; and I mention it only to tell you that it means 'The Land of the Free,' and it must be a first cousin of your country, Mr. Commander; but I suppose you will not accept the relationship because 'The Home of the Brave' is not included. Siam has an area of about 250,000 square miles, as estimated by geographers; and one authority gives it a population of 6,000,000, and another 8,000,000, but they agree in giving it 2,000-000 Siamese, and 1,000,000 Chinese. The rest of the number is made up with Malays, Laosians, and other tribes.

"The Menam River is six hundred miles long, and it has several branches. On the banks of these streams very nearly all the people live, for the regions away from them are a wild jungle which is not cultivated. The country is healthy enough for a tropical region, though malarial fevers are very trying to European residents and visitors. The wet season is from May to November, when it rains about every day; and the rest of the year it does not rain at all. The average rainfall is fifty-four inches a year, and the average temperature 81°, though the glass goes up to 94° in April; but New York beats that in summer.

"Agriculture stands at a low ebb; but the abundant rains and the rich soil produce very large harvests of rice, the principal crop, and all the productions of the Torrid Zone thrive. The labor of Siam is done by Chinese coolies; for the native workers are hampered by a law which requires them to give one-fourth of their labor to the state. Domestic elephants are used in hauling timber, — for teak is one of the products of the forests, — and also for travel and as bearers of burdens. Wild elephants are hunted and trapped in Siam; and tigers, bears, deer, monkeys, and wild pigs abound in the jungles. Crocodiles live at the mouths of the rivers; and the cobra, python, and other reptiles are plentiful enough.

"The Siamese are peaceable people, lazy, and without what you call 'snap.' They are fond of jewelry and high colors. They are rather small in stature, and very like the natives of the several islands you have visited. They live for the most part on rice, used largely in various curries, dried fish in small quantities, though the rivers and sea swarm with fish. Tea is the favorite beverage, taken without sugar or milk. Though they distil an intoxicating liquor from rice, a tipsy person is rarely seen. They chew betel-nut, males and females; and their teeth are always black, which is their ideal of beauty, and they use other materials to make them black and shining.

"The worst vice of the Siamese is gambling; but it can be practised only in houses licensed by the government, though on certain holidays, New Year's in April especially, the people are privileged to gamble at home, or even in the streets. Marriages are arranged by women of mature age. The birthdays of the contracting parties must be agreeable; for the people are superstitious, and consult the stars for their horoscopes. The old ladies agree upon the amount of money the parents of the bride and groom must pay to set up the young couple in life. The ceremonies last three days or more; and the principal observance is the chewing of betel, winding up with a feast to all the friends. Priests are sometimes called in to say prayers, and sprinkle the couple with consecrated water.

"The Siamese believe that the arteries of the body are filled with air, and that disease is caused by some disturbance in these internal breezes. A wind blows on the heart, and bursts it, causing death by 'heart failure.' Almost everything is pressed into the *materia medica* for service, including such things as cats' eyes, the bile of snakes, sea-shells, horns, and probably dogs' tails, kittens' teeth, and monkeys' tongues. Doctors are paid by the job, and not by the number of visits. The price of a cure is agreed upon; and if the patient dies, or fails to get better, the physician gets nothing.

"After poor people, dying, have been kept a few days, they are cremated, as in India; but they keep a high noble nearly a year before they commit his remains to the fire. When called upon, a Siamese farmer or other person is compelled by law to furnish transportation and board to travelling officials. The law of debit and credit is curious, and amounts to actual slavery. A man may borrow money, and give his person for security. If he fails to pay as agreed, the creditor can put him in irons, if need be, and compel him to work for him till the debt is discharged, — the principal only, for his labor is the equivalent of the interest.

"Missionaries are sent here from America, includ-

ing many female physicians; and they have a great
deal of influence among the natives.

"The present king of Siam is Chulalongkorn I.
The former system of having the country ruled by
two kings has been abolished, and the present monarch is the only king; and I never could find out
what the second king was for.   The throne is now
hereditary, but the king formerly had the privilege of
naming his own successor.   Chulalongkorn is an ami-
able and dignified ruler, well educated, and speaks
English fluently.   The laws are made by the king
in connection with a council of ministers.   The forty-
one provinces of the kingdom are in charge of com-
missioners appointed by the king.   Such a thing as
justice is hardly known, and what there is of it is
very badly managed.   Thieving and plundering are
carried on almost without check in Bangkok, which
includes about all there is of Siam except a great
deal of spare territory, and property is very unsafe
there.   I think I have wearied you, Mr. Commander,
and ladies and gentlemen."

"Not at all!" shouted several.

"Did you ever see the Siamese twins, General
Noury?" inquired Uncle Moses.

"I never did; but I have read about them, and
looked them up this morning," replied the lecturer.
"They were born in Siam in 1811, but their parents
were Chinese.   I don't quite understand in what
manner they were united."

"There was a ligament, which looked something

like a small wrist, reaching from one to the other at the breast-bones. Their garments were open enough to enable the spectators to see this connection. There was a great deal of speculation among the doctors about them, I remember, and it was even proposed to separate them with the knife; but that was never done, for it would have spoiled the exhibition business," the trustee explained.

"They were purchased of their mother at Meklong by an American in 1829, and taken to the United States, where they were exhibited all over the country, and then taken to England. It was a good speculation to Mr. Hunter and to Chang and Eng, the twins; for they all made their fortunes. They were married to two sisters, and settled in North Carolina, where they had children. They lost their property in the Civil War, and again exhibited themselves in England in 1869. They died in 1874, one living two hours and a half after the death of the other."

The general retired from the rostrum; and the party separated, Mrs. Mingo ascending the fore-rigging, while the others went to various parts of the ship to see the shores, which were still in sight.

CHAPTER XXI

ON THE VOYAGE TO SAIGON

THE steamer was obliged to descend the Menam at less than half speed, to avoid running down any of the multitude of boats and vessels that thronged the river, and because the stream was so crooked.

"How far do you think Bangkok is from the Gulf, Captain Ringgold?" asked the general, at the close of the session.

"About twenty miles," replied the commander.

"One description of the city that I have read makes it forty miles, another twenty-six, and three others make it twenty miles," added the pacha; "and I suppose the last is the right distance."

"I have come to that conclusion after consulting all the books we have on the subject. You have said the second king of Burma had been abolished, General; are you confident that such is the case? We certainly did not see him, and I did not hear anything about him," added the captain.

"In the first place, I consider Chambers excellent authority, and you have the latest edition in the library, and the date is last year; and it says in so many words that the second has been done away with. The king who was the father of Chulalongkorn died in 1868. His prime minister was a progressive man, who introduced many reforms in Siam; and I am sure that he could not have helped seeing the absurdity of the second king. The present king is well educated, and also a progressive man, as his father was not. I am sorry we did not look the matter up, which we might easily have done with the assistance of the missionaries. But I am satisfied that I was correct in regard to the statement."

In the course of another hour the ship came to the mouth of the river. Crocodiles appear to prefer the mouth of a stream, and a considerable number were seen at the entrance to a canal or cut-off. The pilot stopped the screw, and backed it, in order to avoid a collision with a couple of vessels in the channel. As the two vessels were under sail, it looked as though it would be some time before the channel was clear; and the "Big Four" hastened to their staterooms for their repeating-rifles.

Their appearance thus armed created a sensation on the upper deck, and all the party secured positions where they could see the sport. Mrs. Belgrave manifested some anxiety when she saw the arms, for she was somewhat afraid of such weapons.

"What are you going to do, Louis?" she asked as her son passed her.

"Don't you see that there are a dozen crocodiles at the mouth of that cut-off, mother?" replied Louis. "We are going to shoot some of them."

"But you can't get them if you do kill them."

"We don't want to get them. They are not good for anything to us."

"Then, why do you want to kill them? They do you no harm," protested the lady.

"But they would if they got the chance. Suppose by any accident some one should fall overboard; those brutes would snap the person up as a fish snaps the bait," answered Louis. "In Borneo they are regular man-eaters, more dangerous than sharks; and I have no doubt they are the same here. As I told you, they pay so much a foot for killing them in that island. Ask the pilot how it is here, mother."

Achang was called, and was asked to inquire of the Siamese if the crocodiles were dangerous. He promptly replied that they were not only dangerous, but a nuisance; for they went ashore and swallowed all small animals, and even attacked a cow. The lady offered no further objection. She only hoped the Nimrods would not shoot each other; and they descended to the platform of the gangway, which had not yet been hoisted up, and the crack of their rifles was soon heard.

Each of the rifles could send out nine bullets, fixed ammunition, contained in cartridges, nine of which was the capacity of the magazine. Those on deck watched the group of saurians; but Louis fired the first shot, and immediately there was a sensation among the reptiles. One of them made a spring, and came over on his back.

"Mr. Belgrave fired that shot," said Achang to

the hunter's mother. "He is dead shot, and he never miss his aim."

"There is another turning over on his back," added the lady.

"I think Mr. McGavonty fired that one; for he is a dead shot too, but not quite so sure as Mr. Belgrave," said Achang; and he was correct in his supposition. Both of them hit the crocodile in the eye.

The next report that reached the ears of the party was followed by five more in quick succession; and the Bornean explained that the hunter had missed his aim five times out of six, but his victim turned over after the last one.

"Mr. Scott is better with lasso than with rifle," criticised Achang, with a smile.

The next shot caused the fourth of the reptiles to upset himself on the water, and then the screw of the ship began to turn again. The crocodile's reasoning powers did not seem to be well developed, as Mrs. Belgrave suggested when she saw one of their number killed; for they might have known there was mischief in the air. The Nimrods came on deck, and then carried their rifles to their staterooms, where the commander required them to lock up the weapons in their closets.

The third officer was ordered to have the gangway hoisted up when he returned to the deck, and the ship proceeded to sea. The weather was pleasant, and not very warm for the tropics; in fact, they had suffered more from the heat in New York and in Von Blonk Park than in Bangkok, though it is sometimes extremely hot there. The south-west monsoon cooled the air where they were, though the sun poured down its blistering rays.

There was an awning over the platform where the conferences were held, and another over the after part of the promenade deck. But the former, with its arm-chairs, was the most desirable location to be had; and in a short time the company had seated themselves there without any call to attend a lecture. As soon as deep water was indicated by the soundings, the pilot was discharged, and the captain then gave out the course south by east. Everything was in working order on board; and the commander joined the party on the promenade, as it had always been called before Conference Hall was located there. It commanded the best view on both sides, though not forward, where it was obstructed by the pilot-house.

"What have you seen in Bangkok, Miss Blanche, that the absentees have not seen?" asked Louis, who had seated himself at her side, after patting Miss Mingo, whom she was holding in her lap.

"A great many things," she replied. "One was the royal barge, which they said was rowed or paddled by one hundred and fifty men; but a good many of us did not believe it contained so many."

"I have read about it, though I did not see it. It is said to be one hundred and fifty feet long, and the book I read said it was paddled by one hundred and twenty men," added Louis. "But it does not make much difference, and the books do not agree in regard to a great many things in this part of the world. What did you think of the people you saw, Miss Blanche?"

"A lady and gentleman were pointed out to us by one of the kind missionaries who guided us, and I could hardly tell which was the lady and which the gentleman till I had studied them a while," returned the fair maiden. "Both of them wore what appeared to be trousers; but it proved to be a cloth as big as a sheet wound around the waist, and so disposed about the legs as to look like trousers; but the garment was the same on both of them. The lady had something like a shawl, which was passed over the left shoulder, and under the right arm, with some kind of a jacket under it. The gentleman wore a sort of tunic, which was regularly buttoned up in front like a coat. The hair of each was shaved off close to the head, except a tuft on the crown, which was bunched up. They wore no ornaments of any kind, perhaps because it was not a dress occasion. I saw one woman who had a kind of necklace on the top of the shawl."

"I saw a woman's band of five pieces, and the music they made was not bad," added Louis.

"I heard a band like that; but I could not tell whether they played a tune or improvised their music. The missionaries took us into the garden of a nobleman, where we saw what was called a theatrical exhibition; but it was no more like a theatre than it was like a cattle-show. We saw the king too, and he was a nice-looking man forty years old. He had what looked like a tunnel on his head. He was sitting in a kind of big arm-chair on poles, and eight men were bearing him to a temple. All the natives in the street dropped on their knees as he passed, and some lay flat on their stomachs. That is the way they always do before him. But he chews betel; and his mouth was as black as though he had just eaten a piece of huckleberry-pie, and it looked horrid. That is all the fault I have to find with him."

"It is a bad habit the people here have; but it is not so bad as drinking whiskey, and we must be charitable while our country has its faults; and theirs only spoils their looks, though I have been told there is a 'kick,' or exhilaration, in the use of betel. I don't think I should ever fall in love with a girl who chewed-betel-nut. Some Dyak maidens would have been passably good-looking if their teeth and lips had not been blackened with this drug."

"The missionaries took some of us into the private chapel of a nobleman. There were about a hundred priests, all clothed in yellow robes, with their heads shaven; the service consisted of the constant repetition of a sentence, which a missionary told me meant 'So be it.' It reminded me of the howling dervishes we visited at their monastery, whose service was a monotonous repetition of ' Allah il Allah.' You went to some of the temples, Mr. Belgrave, and they seem to me to be all alike. Now can you tell me how far it is to the place where we are going next ? "

"It is about six hundred miles to Saigon, the chief town of French Cochin China, and we shall get there to-morrow," replied Louis. "You must brush up your French, Miss Blanche, for we have not used it lately."

"We are off Cape Liant now, and I must give out a new course," said the commander, rising from his chair by the side of Mrs. Belgrave.

"South-east half-south ! " called the captain at the side window of the pilot-house.

"South-east half-south," repeated the quartermaster at the wheel.

"We are going to Saigon, you said, Mr. Belgrave; but I cannot pronounce the name," added the young lady.

"As to that, you pays your money, and takes your choice," laughed Louis. "The French call it Sah-gong, shutting out the full sound of the last g," added the speaker, pronouncing it several times with the proper accent. "The English call it Sy-goń, I believe; but I have heard it called variously at Sarawak."

"But we want to know something about it before we go there," said the young lady. "We had to ask no end of questions about Siam because the lecture was postponed for the absentees."

" After lunch to-day a short talk will be given in relation to Saigon," replied Louis, as the bell rang for that meal.

When the company gathered in Conference Hall, Louis was introduced as the speaker for the occasion, and promptly presented himself before his audience.

"I have very little to say, Mr. Commander, for General Noury has covered the whole subject under the head of Cochin China," he began. "What is more particularly known as French Cochin China contains 23,000 square miles, and a population of 1,800,000. The part in the north is called French Indo-China. The country is precisely that described so carefully by the general, and I need not repeat it. The Cambodia, or Mekhong River, flows through it with many bayous or cut-offs. On one of these, which is called the Saigon River, is the city of Saigon, the capital of the French possessions in the East, Lippincott says thirty-five miles, and Chambers sixty miles, from the China Sea; and of course both of them cannot be right, and you are all at liberty to take your choice. The town has grown up within the last thirty-two years; and, after the style of French cities, it is handsomely laid out, with fine streets, squares and boulevards. It contains numerous canals, with stone or brick quays; and perhaps it will remind you of Paris along the Seine. It is said to be one of the handsomest cities of the East. It has a navy-yard and citadel, and is the most important port between Hong-Kong and Singapore. The people are French, Annamese, and Chinese. It has a large trade, and contains two colleges, an orphan asylum, a splendid botanical garden, to say nothing of convents and other institutions. The population is put by one at ninety thousand, and by another at about half that number. I have nothing more to say."

Louis retired, and the next day the ship arrived at Saigon.

CHAPTER XXII

IN THE DOMINIONS OF THE FRENCH

It was not a long voyage from Bangkok to the mouth of the Mekhong River; and the sight of land was not as thrilling an incident as it had often been in the experience of the voyagers, and they were not in condition to appreciate the feelings of Captain Columbus when Watling's Island broke on his vision four hundred years before. It had been smooth sailing all the way; the Gulf of Siam had been as gentle and affectionate as a maiden among the flowers, and the China Sea was scarcely more ruffled.

Mr. Gaskette had finished up his new map of Cochin China, so that it was as creditable to his skill and taste as his former efforts had been; and it was displayed on the frame in Conference Hall, which was the usual sitting apartment of the company, though some of them did a great deal of walking on the promenade deck. The water was deeper inshore than farther out at sea, where several spots were marked at eight fathoms; and the passengers had a view of the land before they were within a hundred miles of the entrance of Saigon River.

"There is a broad opening in the coast, which must be the Cambodia, or Mekhong River," said Morris.

"That is Batac Bay, with a large island in the middle of it," replied Captain Ringgold. "It is one of the mouths of the Mekhong; for there is a Delta here extending about a hundred miles, the Saigon River being the most easterly."

"Mekhong seems to me a new word, though doubtless it was the native name of the great river; but when I went to school we never called it anything but the Cambodia," added Uncle Moses.

"It is now called by both names, and both are usually found on the maps and charts," said the commander.

A couple of hours later he pointed out the mouth of the great river. All the land was very low, and much of it was sometimes under water. Felix had become the owner of an excellent spy-glass, which he had purchased at second-hand at Aden; and he made abundant use of it. It was too large to be worn in a sling at his side, and he always carried it in his hand when the ship was in sight of land. After lunch, in the middle of the afternoon, he stationed himself in front of the pilot-house, and kept a sharp lookout ahead.

"Saigon light!" he shouted, some time before it could be made out without a glass.

The steamer was headed for Cape St. Jacques, near the entrance to the river by which she was to reach the city. The light soon came into view, and a boat was seen pulling out of the mouth. The signal for a pilot had been displayed on the ship, and one of the men in it was believed to be the person desired. The screw was stopped as he approached her, and the ladder lowered for his ascent to the deck. As usual, all the passengers wanted to see him. He was an old man, or at least well along in years.

"Good-day, sir," said Louis, who had gone to the main deck with the third officer to receive him; and he spoke to him in French.

He was conducted to the promenade deck, and presented to the captain. He said that he was born in France, but had been in Cochin China nearly thirty years. He was first sent down to Monsieur Odervie for a lunch after he had given the course, and the ship continued on her way. The cook was very glad to meet a compatriot; and, as he was getting dinner, he had several nice dishes, from which he treated his new friend. But the pilot's services were soon needed in the pilot-house. He spoke a little English, consisting mainly of nautical terms.

He took his place on the starboard side of the wheel, with Quartermaster Bangs on the other side, steering himself; perhaps because he was not willing to trust his English in giving orders. But the quartermaster seconded all his movements, and they steered together in silence. The ship was soon well in the river, and the passengers had enough to do in observing the shores on both sides.

There were many openings in the banks of bayous and cut-offs, and the land was as flat as it had been during the last hundred miles of the voyage. The soil was very rich, and produced abundant crops where it was cultivated. A very few villages were to be seen; but each of them had its temple or pagoda, and the houses hardly differed from those they had seen in Siam.

"I suppose this is all an alluvial soil, Brother Avoirdupois," said Dr. Hawkes, as the ship was passing a rice-field.

"So say the books I have consulted, Brother Adipose Tissue. It is just the right land for rice, and that is the staple product of all this region," replied Uncle Moses.

Both of these gentlemen weighed about two hundred and twenty-six pounds apiece, and they continued to call each other by the appropriate names they had given each other even before the ship left New York on her voyage all over the world.

"What is alluvial soil, Doctor?" asked Mrs. Blossom, who had read very little besides her Bible and denominational newspaper.

"It is the soil or mud which is brought to its location by the action of water; and here it is brought down by the mighty river which spreads itself out into a delta where we are," replied the doctor good-naturedly, and without a smile at the ignorance of the worthy lady; for though her education had been greatly neglected, she was esteemed and respected by all on board, for in sickness she had been the nurse of the patients. "It is just the right soil for rice," he added.

" I have seen so many rice-fields out here, that I should like to know something more about them," suggested the good lady.

" Naturalists class it as a kind of grass; but I will not vex you with any hard words.   Rice is the food of about one-third of all the people on the globe.   It requires heat and moisture for its growth, and it is raised in considerable quantities on the low lands of Georgia and South Carolina and elsewhere in our country.   The plant grows from one to six feet high. I don't know much about the culture of this grain in the East; but in South Carolina they first dig trenches, in the bottom of which the rice is sown in rows eighteen inches apart.   The plantation is prepared so that water can be let in and drawn off as desired.   As soon as the seed is sown, the water is let in till the ground is covered to the depth of several inches.   As soon as the rice comes up, the water is drawn off, and the plant grows in the open air rapidly under the hot sun.   The field is again flooded for a couple of weeks, to kill the weeds, and again when the grain is ripening.   The rice is in a hull, like wheat and other grains; and you have found parts of this covering in the rice when you were cooking it.   It is threshed out by hand or machinery after it is dried, and then it is ready for market. There is a rice-field on your right; and you can see the channels which have been dug to convey the water to the plants, or to draw it off," said the surgeon in conclusion.

"I see them, Dr. Hawkes; and I am very much obliged to you for taking so much pains to instruct an ignorant body like me," replied Mrs. Blossom.

"It is quite impossible for any of us to know everything, and I often find myself entirely ignorant in regard to some things; and I have lived long enough to forget many things that I learned when I was younger," added the doctor with a softening smile.

The villages increased in number and in size as the ship approached the city; though they were about the same thing, except that in the larger ones the temple was a handsomer structure.

"How far is it from the sea to Saigon?" asked Bangs, speaking to the pilot for the first time; but the Frenchman could not understand him, and the quartermaster called Louis in, who repeated the question in French.

"Sixty miles if you go one way; thirty-five by another," Louis translated the reply.

"That may account for the difference in the distance given in the books," said the captain, who was in the pilot-house. "But the information we obtain from what are considered the authorities is so various on the same subject that I don't know where the fault is."

"This is the largest village we have seen," said Louis to the pilot in French.

"Yes, sir; and the next place is Saigon," replied the Frenchman; but he was so much occupied with his duty that he would not talk much, even in his own language.

The city was soon in sight, and the pilot began to feel about for the bell-pull. He spoke to Louis, and the quartermaster was told to ring the speed-bell. A little later, off the town, the gong sounded for the screw to stop. The anchor was all ready, was let go, and the steamer swung round to her cable. The Blanche had not so readily obtained a pilot as her consort, and she was an hour behind her in arriving.

The Guardian-Mother was surrounded by boats as soon as she was at rest, but the boatmen kept their distance till the port physician and the custom-house officials came on board. Both ships passed the ordeal of the examination, and the boats closed up. They were manned by all sorts of people, and they were in all sorts of craft. The captain said that most of them were Chinese sampans, and the boatmen were of the same nation.

"There comes the Blanchita!" exclaimed Felix, who was walking about the deck with his spy-glass under his arm.

"They got her overboard in a very short time," said the captain, who had joined the company on the promenade. "I am glad she is coming, for I desire to see the general."

The gangway had already been rigged out; and the launch came alongside the platform, containing General Noury, his wife, the rajah, Captain and Mrs.

Sharp, Dr. Henderson, the surgeon of the Blanche, and the French maid of the princess. They were warmly greeted on the platform by the commander and Louis, and the ladies were assisted from the boat. They mounted to the deck; and the usual hugging, kissing, and handshaking followed in the boudoir.

"I am glad you have come, General Noury," said Captain Ringgold, after he had shaken hands with everybody. "We have been shut up on shipboard for some time now; and as we have come to a French city, I propose to take my party to a hotel for a day or two. Of course you can do as you please, General."

"I like the idea, Captain, if there is a decent hotel here," replied the pacha. "What do you think, Zuleima?" he asked, turning to his wife.

"I like it very much; and the hotel cannot be any worse than some we have lived in on our yacht voyages," replied the princess.

"Here is the medical officer, and he can tell us something about the hotels," suggested the commander.

The doctor was consulted by the general in French, and he said the Hôtel de l'Europe was very good. The entire party of both ships were invited to go on shore, and remain at the hotel. All of them accepted, including Captain Sharp and his wife. Those on board the Guardian-Mother went below to prepare for the shore, and the Blanchita returned to the Blanche for the same purpose. The gentlemen were on deck again in a few minutes.

"A visitor to see you, Mr. Scott," said a seaman, approaching the third officer as he came from the cabin.

"Captain Rayburn!" exclaimed Scott as soon as he caught sight of the visitor. "I am very glad to see you, Captain;" and the young officer grasped his hand.

"I am quite as pleased to see you, Captain Scott, though I hardly knew you," replied the English captain.

"I am no longer captain, though I am the third officer of this ship; and I did not wear my uniform when I met you at Kuching."

"How are the rest of your party?" inquired the captain of the Delhi.

"Very well, and here they are."

"I am delighted to see you on board of your own ship, Mr. Belgrave," said Captain Rayburn, rushing to the young millionaire as he came on deck with his bag in his hand.

Felix and Morris soon appeared, and gave the captain a hearty greeting. The commander happened to pass near them, and he was approached by Scott.

"Captain Ringgold, allow me to introduce Captain Rayburn, of the steamer Delhi, to whom the Borneo party are greatly indebted for his kindness; and the Blanchita sailed in company of his ship from Kuching to forty miles inside of Point Cambodia."

"Captain Rayburn, I am very happy to meet you; and I am glad of the opportunity to thank you for your kindness to my young men, and especially for standing by the Blanchita during the worst part of her voyage to Bangkok. But we are all going ashore at once to spend a day or two at the Hôtel de l'Europe; and I cordially invite you to be my guest."

After some objections to the plan, he accepted the invitation. He was well dressed, and a gentleman in every sense of the word. He ordered the men in his boat to return to the Delhi, and to bring off certain garments to the hotel. The Blanchita came up to the gangway again, and the party embarked in her.

CHAPTER XXIII

A LIVELY EVENING AT THE HOTEL

The Blanchita had been painted since her return from Borneo, and she had a decidedly holiday appearance. Captain Rayburn had been introduced to all the ladies and gentlemen on board; and in the steam-launch he was presented to General Noury and his wife, and to the others of the Blanche. The port physician went on shore with them, pointed out to them the landing-place, and directed them to the hotel.

The party landed, and found the hotel "good enough," though hardly in the slang sense of the phrase. Apartments were obtained for all, and dinner was ordered. Captain Rayburn had been a couple of days in Saigon, and had learned something about the city. He was the guide of the Nimrods when they took a walk before dinner. They went through the French portion of the place, where they found the streets broad, and ornamented with trees. The houses were seldom more than two stories high.

The governor's palace was a magnificent residence for Cochin China, and the cathedral was also a fine building; but after going half over the world the young voyagers did not find much to attract them.

They were more interested in what the country it-self produced than in what had been brought from France. There was a European garrison in the cita-del; but the natives were enlisted as soldiers, and drilled in French tactics. The promenaders met a squad of the latter. They wore blue blouses, white pants, and a flat cork-lined cap; but they did not wear shoes, and they looked very odd to the visitors in their bare feet.

The walk ended with a visit to the botanical gar-den; but the tropical plants were what they had been seeing for two months, and they were not a novelty to them. The foreign plants and trees were more interesting to them, and they had been set out with a view of ascertaining what were adapted to the soil and climate of the country.

"This place consists really of three towns united," said Captain Rayburn as they walked back to the hotel. "It was formerly but a group of fishing vil-lages, though even then it was the capital. Pingeh is the commercial town, on the west side of the river, and Cholon is the native quarter. The citadel or fortress is in Pingeh, but we have not time to visit either of them to-night."

"You have been here before, Captain?" asked Louis.

"Not in the Delhi. I was for some years the com-mander of one of the P. & O. steamers; but I was taken very sick six months ago, and was obliged to spend three months in Calcutta. When I got well, a merchant there who had been a good friend of mine during my illness, was in a great strait to find a captain for the Delhi in place of one who had died. I agreed to take her for a single voyage; for she is a very small craft for me, as I have been in command of ships of six thousand tons. I shall return to my steamer when she comes to Calcutta in a couple of months."

"I thought you were too big a man to be in command of such a puny vessel as the Delhi," added Scott.

"I took charge of her only to accommodate my friend her owner. I don't find any fault with her, except that she is old and very slow," added the captain as they came to the hotel.

"Ah, Captain Rayburn, how do you do?" exclaimed a gentleman, extending his hand to him. "I was a passenger in your ship to Hong-Kong last year."

"O Monsieur Frôler!" replied Captain Rayburn, grasping the proffered hand. "Of course I remember you very well, for I don't often get so fully acquainted with my passengers as I did with you; and I only wished I could talk French with you. But you speak English as well as I can, so that it made no difference. Do you reside here?"

"I went from Hong-Kong to Canton, and several other Chinese cities, and then to Japan, after we parted, and finally I came here. I like the place, and have been here six months," replied the French gentleman, who was not over thirty years of age. "I live at this hotel; and we have a great American party here, with an English steamer that has a Moorish pacha on board with his wife, who is an Indian princess, so the landlord told me; and I wish to be introduced to them."

"I can assist you to that, Mr. Frôler. Are you in business here?" asked the captain.

"Not at all; my father made my fortune for me, and I do nothing but travel, and when I come to a place I like I stay there as long as I ·please; and I am doing that here."

"Mr. Frôler, allow me to present to you Mr. Louis Belgrave, the owner of the Guardian-Mother, the American steam-yacht in the river," continued Captain Rayburn.

The French gentleman received the young man with the greatest deference and politeness, and introduced him to his companion. A conversation in French followed; for Louis was inclined to use that language when he could, to keep "his tongue in," as he put it. Mr. Frôler told him that he was well acquainted in the city with all the principal men, and was familiar with all the localities. He would be very happy to escort the party wherever they wished to go, and to introduce them to the governor and other officers of the army and officials.

Louis then conducted the Frenchman to the large parlor where the tourists were waiting for dinner, and introduced him to Captain Ringgold, who received him with his usual politeness. While Louis was introducing him to all the members of the party, Captain Rayburn informed the commander that he had first met Mr. Frôler when in command of a P. & O. steamer.

"Were you in command of a P. & O. steamer?" asked Captain Ringgold, opening his eyes very wide.

"I am still in command of one," replied the English captain; and then explained how he happened to be in the Delhi. "Mr. Frôler was really the most agreeable passenger I ever had, and I became very intimate with him. He is very wealthy, and travels all the time, though he sometimes stops a year in a place. He is a high-toned gentleman in every sense of the word. He is acquainted with the principal merchants and all the officials in Saigon, and desires to assist your party in seeing the city and its surroundings."

"I shall certainly be very grateful to him for his services," replied the commander, as Mr. Frôler approached them after making his round of introductions with Louis.

The Frenchman formally tendered his assistance to the party, and they were gratefully accepted by the commander. Of course he was invited to dinner with the party; and the seat of honor on the right of the captain was given to him, while that on the left was appropriated to Captain Rayburn. The princess was placed next to the Frenchman, with the pacha next. The others took seats to suit themselves.

The dinner was excellent, and Dr. Hawkes wondered if Monsieur Odervie had not had a hand in its preparation; and this afterwards proved to be the case. French cooks are very fraternal; and when one of them is to get up a great dinner, his *confrères* generally tender their assistance to him. As no dinner was to be served that day on the steamer, Monsieur Odervie had obtained leave of absence, and called upon the cook of the hotel. His proffered aid was accepted, and the surgeon was confident he had made the sauce for the excellent fish that was served.

It was a lively party at the table, for the guests were desirous of knowing more about the mission of the Guardian-Mother all over the world; and their curiosity was gratified, the pacha telling the Frenchman all about it in the language of the latter. No wine was served, for the reason that none was ordered, doubtless greatly to the regret of the landlord; and the commander made an explanation, though not an apology.

"I am a Frenchman, but I drink no wine," said Mr. Frôler; "for the reason that it does not agree with me. I have great respect for my stomach; for it is very serviceable to me, like my watch, if I keep it in good order. I drank no wine nor liquor in Paris, and still less would I do so in a tropical country."

"I am in the same boat with my friend Mr. Frôler. The P. & O. Company does not encourage its captains to drink anything; and when I entered the service as a fourth officer, I knocked off entirely, afloat or ashore; and I have stuck to my text ever since," added Captain Rayburn.

"Then our teetotal habits do not interfere at all with our guests."

"Not at all," added both of them.

"Did you know that the captain of your consort from Borneo was a commander in the P. & O. service, Mr. Belgrave?" asked Captain Ringgold.

"I did not till this evening; I knew that he was a gentleman, and that was all that I wished to know," replied Louis.

This remark was applauded warmly by the company. The captain then said that he wished to introduce the guests of the occasion over again, though they had been presented individually to all the company. He wished to say that Captain Rayburn was actually the commander of a P. & O. steamer of six thousand tons, on leave of absence on account of sickness. He also told them something more about the Frenchman. He was a gentleman whose father had made his fortune for him, as he expressed himself; he was not engaged in any business, and held no official position. He was travelling only for his own amusement and instruction, and his stay in Saigon had been prolonged to six months.

As the party left the table, Mr. Frôler had a little talk for a few minutes, when he excused himself, and left the hotel, promising to return in half an hour. Conversation was resumed in the parlor;

and presently Mrs. Belgrave started one of the familiar hymns when she found a piano in the room, in which the captain of the Delhi joined with a tremendous bass voice.

While the music was in full blast, Mr. Frôler entered the apartment, accompanied by two ladies and two gentlemen, both of the latter wearing the decoration of the Legion of Honor. It was evident that the visitors were magnates of Saigon; and Mrs. Belgrave rose from the instrument, and the singing was discontinued.

" I have the pleasure of presenting to Your Excellency, Captain Ringgold, commander of the steamer Guardian-Mother, visiting Saigon with the company of tourists here present," said Mr. Frôler, leading up one of the strangers. " Captain Ringgold, I have the honor to introduce to you His Excellency the Governor of French Cochin China."

The two gentlemen then shook hands. Louis Belgrave was then presented, followed by General Noury and his wife; and the pacha then took His excellency to every member of the party, and presented each in due form. While this was in process, Mr. Frôler presented to the commander the other gentleman, who appeared to be about fifty years old, as Monsieur Larousse, merchant of the city; and Louis followed the general in introducing him to the members of the party. The master of ceremonies next led up to Captain Ringgold the two ladies, presenting them as Madame and Mademoiselle Larousse;

and they appeared to be the wife and daughter of the elderly gentleman who had preceded them.

The daughter was a beautiful lady, apparently about twenty-four years old, though it is not always practicable to state the age of a French lady. By this time General Noury had made his round, and the governor was passed over to Mrs. Noury, at his request. The commander made the circuit with Madame Larousse, and the pacha offered his services to conduct Mademoiselle Larousse. He presented her to his wife first, interrupting her *tête-à-tête* with His Excellency for a moment.

"Pretty woman," said Captain Rayburn to Captain Ringgold.

"Very pretty," replied the latter.

"Between you and me, she is the particular reason why Frôler has prolonged his stay here to six months."

"Then I congratulate him," added the commander.

"Her father is not rich; Frôler does not care for that, for he is a multi-millionaire himself, counted in francs. But the prettiest lady here is the sister of Morris, Miss Blanche."

"Madame Noury, you were singing when I came in," said the governor when the introductions had been completed.

"But they were singing American hymns, not adapted to your religion or mine," replied Mrs. Noury.

"I don't care for that," he added; and both spoke

French. "I liked what I heard very much, and I should wish to hear some more of it."

Mrs. Belgrave was called, and the request repeated to her in English by the magnate. And so it happened that the rest of the evening was passed in singing gospel hymns. At a late hour the company separated.

CHAPTER XXIV

TONQUIN AND SIGHTS IN CHOLON

THERE was so little sight-seeing to be done in
Saigon that the tired tourists did not hurry themselves in the morning; for breakfast was not served
till nine o'clock, and they went to the tables at their
own pleasure. The Nimrods had risen at an early
hour, and had taken a long walk before any others
came from their rooms. They were the first to take
the morning meal, and they had earned an appetite
before the regular hour for it. At half-past ten a
number of vehicles had been gathered by the landlord for the use of his guests.

Mr. Frôler was in attendance as soon as breakfast
was ready, and the young men took their meal with
him. He seemed to have taken a fancy to Louis
when he learned that the Guardian-Mother was his
college, and he took pains to inform him in regard
to the affairs of the city and the country.

"How did the French happen to settle here in the
beginning?" asked Louis when they were seated at
the table.

"England, Holland, Spain, and especially France,
began to take an interest in the countries of the East
at a very early date; and France entered the race

for Oriental territory as early as 1787, and agreed to assist Annam in its troubles. Two years later the French Revolution broke out in the destruction of the Bastille, on the fourteenth of July, which is still celebrated. It is our 'Fourth of July,' Mr. Belgrave."

"I was in Paris on that day a few years ago, when I was a smaller boy than I am now, and I wondered that no fire-crackers were let off," replied Louis.

"They are not permitted in Paris. France had her hands full after the Revolution began, and was unable to keep her agreement in full with Annam; but missionaries were sent there, and some commercial relations in a very small way were continued until 1831. Then the king died, and was succeeded by one who did not believe in the missionaries, French and Spanish, settled in Annam, as the whole country east of Siam was then called. The new king wanted to drive away the bearers of the gospel to the natives, and killed or persecuted them.

"Twenty years later, France found it necessary to interfere, which she did by sending a small army to subdue the country. The fortifications which had been built by French engineers held the soldiers back to some extent. When the persecutions of the Christians were believed to be ended, the French soldiers returned home. They were again renewed; and France and Spain sent out a fleet and army, which captured the principal seaport, and continued the war for about four years, when a treaty of peace was concluded. Annam was compelled to pay 25,000,000 francs for the expense of the war, and permit every person to enjoy his own religious belief. The missionaries were to be protected, commercial relations were established, and in 1886 a treaty was ratified at Hué, by which the country was placed under the protection of France, though the native princes were nominally continued in power. This was the beginning of the French dominion in this region."

"If it is not one now, it will eventually become a French colony," suggested Louis.

"Probably it will, for it is largely so now," replied Mr. Frôler.

Captain Ringgold, who had waited for Mrs. Belgrave, finished breakfast about the same time; for they had not listened to a historical talk while they were eating, and they left the room together. At the time appointed for the ride, all the party were in the parlor, and they were loaded into the vehicles. They rode through the principal streets, and to the botanical garden, where all the party walked through the grounds. Then they rode along the banks of the river.

"Those small vessels look like men-of-war," said Louis, who was seated in the first carriage, with Mr. Frôler, the commander, and Mrs. Belgrave.

"They are little gunboats, and the government has about twenty of them," replied the Frenchman. "But I think we had better alight here, and take a general view of the river and the surroundings."

At a given signal the whole party got out of the vehicles.

"But what are those gunboats for, Mr. Frôler?" asked Louis, as the company were looking at them.

"If there should happen to be a riot, or a disturbance of any kind, up the river, which the police could not handle, they would be used for transporting troops; for we have the telegraph here, and could be notified at once. They are also used to beat off pirates, and to see that the laws are obeyed."

"Pirates!" exclaimed Louis. "Are there any about this country?"

"They are not such pirates as we read about in olden times," replied Mr. Frôler with a smile. "But some of these natives may rig up a boat, and go on a predatory excursion among their neighbors, especially in the fishing regions on the Great Lake, over two hundred miles up the river. Their principal plunder is fish, though they take anything they can lay their hands upon."

"I should hardly call them pirates," added Louis.

"But Chinese pirates have been known to capture vessels in the China Sea, off the coast of Tonquin."

"I have heard of such within a few years."

"You can see the citadel, as it is called here, though it would be simply a fort in most places. There are 1,830 French soldiers here, and 2,800 native troops. Only 3,000 of the population are French. The last census gave the country a population of 2,034,453," continued Mr. Frôler, consulting a memorandum book he carried in his pocket. "They are mainly Annamites; but Cambodians, Chinese, savages from the north, and Malays contribute to make up the number. But I don't mean to lecture you, as I am told you are addressed on board your ship by some of your own number."

"But we are an educational institution in part, and we are very glad to hear you," said the commander. "We are supposed to be greedy for information about the countries we visit. I suppose we are about as near Tongking as we shall be, and I am sure my company would like to learn something more about it. We have a nice place here in the shade of this tree to hear a short lecture."

"You use the English name for the region, which is all right; and I have seen it spelled Tonkin, which I think is better yet for your people. The French name is Tonquin," (and he gave the French pronunciation). "It is larger than Cochin China; and we apply this name to what you designate as French Cochin China,—for it has an area of 34,740 square miles, and a population supposed to be about 9,000,000. Its chief town is Hanoï, consisting of a number of villages, with 150,000 inhabitants; and its chief seaport is Hai-Phong. There has been war going on against the people of this country for many years."

"We read something about these operations in American papers, and know very little about Tonquin, which is the reason I asked for more knowledge of the region," added the commander.

"The principal productions of Tonquin,' Mr. Frôler, bowing to the captain, proceeded, "are rice, silk, sugar, pepper, oil, cotton, tobacco, and fruits, with copper and iron in small quantities. The exports are now 13,325,000 francs, which you reduce to dollars by dividing by five. The imports are nearly 28,000,000 francs, only one-fourth from France, with but a small portion of the exports to that country. An expedition was sent out from home, at the instance of Jules Ferry, to open the way by the Songkoi River for the trade of Yun-Nan, a south-western province of China. The experiment was an expensive one, and the difficulty of navigation in the upper waters of the river made it a failure. The troops met with a disaster; and the colonial policy of the statesman here and in Madagascar caused his ruin, and he has since died. Jules Ferry was nicknamed 'le Tonquinais.' But I have talked too long."

"Not at all!" protested several of the company; for they had read in the papers at home something in short paragraphs about the war and other matters in Tonquin, which they did not understand; and they are likely to read much more in the future, which they will comprehend better if they remember the brief account of Mr. Frôler.

The party got into the vehicles again, but stopped soon after at the market, where they alighted. Natives in boats and on foot were bringing in fruits and vegetables in great quantities. All the fruits of the tropics were included, though bananas were the most plentiful. Some came with clumsy carts, loaded with the produce of the surrounding country. The vehicles were very trying to the nerves of the ladies and some of the gentlemen; for they creaked and groaned, and seemed to be screeching for grease, reminding them of the carts of Lisbon, where some of the party had had a similar experience.

"The men here wear tunnels on their heads, after the fashion of the king of Siam," said Morris as they walked through the market, which consisted mainly of an open square, filled with carts, barrows, and baskets.

"The head-covering of the women is more curious," added Scott. "It is about two feet across, and they use them as umbrellas, both sexes."

"I see that you have the yellow dog here, Mr. Frôler, as in Constantinople," said Louis, as the Frenchman came near with the captain and Mrs. Belgrave.

"They are outcast dogs, like those in Constantinople," replied the guide. "Nobody owns them, and they have to pick up their living in the streets. They are no more honest than some of the natives; for some of them will steal a piece of meat, and then comes a fight with all the others in the vicinity."

"Where does the meat used here come from?" asked Louis.

"From Cambodia," replied the Frenchman. "But it is about time for your lunch at the hotel, and I think we had better return. I see that your steam-launch is at the landing-place; and we might go up to Cholon in her, and visit the citadel."

The suggestion was adopted; and on his arrival at the hotel, the commander found a note from the governor, inviting the party to dine with him that day at seven. It was promptly accepted; and after the lunch the party embarked in the Blanchita, and sailed up the river to Cholon, which is the native portion of the city.

" It does not cost much here to build a house," said Mr. Frôler, as the yacht, under the pilotage of the old Frenchman who had brought the Guardian-Mother up the river, worked her way through the multitude of boats that thronged the shore.

But the young men were busy observing the various craft; for they were of all sorts and kinds, from the simple Chinese sampan to the craft fifty feet long, provided with a cabin, and parts of her covered with the leaf awning, something like what they had seen in Borneo.

"Where does this boat come from, Achang?" asked Felix.

The Bornean spoke to a man who seemed to be the captain and a Malay.

"She come from Great Lake," reported Achang. "She bring down dry fish to sell to the poor people of Cholon."

" How much does it cost to build one of these houses, Mr. Frôler?" asked Captain Ringgold, after they had looked over some of them.

" About twenty-five francs."

" It ought not to cost more than that, for they are nothing but shanties," replied the commander. "Some of them are built on floats, as in Bangkok."

" Let us look into one of them; they will not object. This is a Chinaman's abode, and he belongs to the better class here," said the Frenchman as he led the way into the house, followed by the commander, with Mrs. Belgrave on his arm.

Seated at a table was what a sailor would call a kid, or small tub, containing a stew of fish and vegetables; and there was a dish for each individual, which did duty as a plate. There were a man, a woman, and three children at the table.

" These people belong to the aristocracy," said the Frenchman, as they retired, and the family were visited by others of the party. " We will look into another house of a lower grade of people ; " and they went into a hut about six feet square, in which were eight men, women, and children, huddled together around a tub on the floor containing fish and rice. The odor was not agreeable, and they hurried away.

" You noticed the two girls there. If you want them, Captain, you can buy them for thirty dollars apiece of your money."

" I don't want them; and I don't care about staying any longer in this part of the town," replied the commander.

They walked rather hurriedly to the yacht. On the way they met a carriage something like a wheelbarrow, with a single large wheel, and a seat on each side of it, one occupied by a fat Chinaman and the other by a Malay. It was propelled by a native just like an ordinary wheelbarrow.

"That's a big team," said Scott.

"You will see plenty of them in some of the cities of China."

The Blanchita left Mr. Frôler at the landing-place, and then conveyed the passengers to the two ships; for the ladies insisted that they must dress for the dinner at the governor's palace.

CHAPTER XXV

SEVERAL HILARIOUS FROLICS

THE ladies certainly did dress for the occasion; and not only the ladies, but all the gentlemen. The captain put on a new uniform which he had not worn since his ship left Colombo. Scott had a new uniform also; Uncle Moses, the surgeon, Mr. Woolridge, and the professor came out in evening costume, with black dress-coats; and the young men were clothed for their age, in black. The ship's company looked at them with astonishment when they came on deck, for they had never seen them *en grand tenue* before.

The ladies were properly costumed for the dinner, and all of them wore the best they had. When the Blanchita came alongside the ship with the Blanche's party, more surprise was manifested; for Mrs. Noury was dressed as a princess, as she was, with the richest garments of India; General Noury clothed in the full costume of his Moroccan rank, a dress which had not been seen before. Captain Sharp wore his uniform, and his wife proved that no money had been spared on her dress and adornings. The rajah wore his Indian suit, made of the costliest materials and the most brilliant colors, and rubies and diamonds sparkled upon him, as on the pacha. Dr. Henderson was in keeping with his professional brother of the other party.

The seats of the yacht had been overlaid with rugs and other materials, that the rich costumes need not be soiled. The Blanche's barge came soon with the Italian band on board; for the general desired to serenade the governor during the evening. It was an hour too early; for the commander had been so solicitous that the company should not be late, that he had overdone the matter. The landlord was to have the carriages at the landing at half-past six, and there was an hour to wait. But the princess and Mrs. Sharp declined to leave their seats in the launch, for fear of mussing up their dresses; and the general called upon the band to play while they were waiting.

It was near the close of a clear day, and the music was delightful. In a short time not less than a hundred boats surrounded the ship, and three times as many people stood upon the shore. The band had not played before since their arrival. Mr. Frôler, in Parisian evening dress, had come to the landing to receive the party, and when he heard the music, he came off, standing up in a sampan; for he was as careful of his garments as the ladies. The captain had ordered a carpet to be placed on the steps of the gangway, and the polite Frenchman ascended to the deck without peril to his clothing.

" Good-evening, Captain Ringgold," said he, extending his hand. " You have the most ravishing music here."

"It is General Noury's Italian band, and he will take it ashore to serenade the governor," replied the commander.

"I have not seen your steamer before, and she is a magnificent vessel," added the Frenchman.

"I should be happy to show her to you; but we have hardly time to do so now, for I see that the ladies are taking their places in the launch," answered Captain Ringgold; "but I shall ask the governor and such ladies and gentlemen as you will designate to spend the afternoon and evening on board to-morrow, dining in the cabin. I arranged it with the general. Both ships will be visited, the band will play, and we will make a general frolic of it. The next morning we shall sail for Manila."

Both of the gentlemen hastened to the gangway to assist the ladies as soon as the commander saw Mrs. Belgrave moving in that direction. Miss Blanche, conducted by Louis, appeared about the same time. Her costume was very neat, though not showy; but she was as beautiful as a fairy, and the Frenchman clasped his hands in ecstasy when he saw her. In a short time they were all seated in the Blanchita, and the gentlemen then took their places.

Precisely at twenty minutes past six Captain Sharp, prompted by Captain Ringgold, gave the order to cast off. A quartermaster of the Blanche was at the wheel, and in five minutes she was alongside the shore. A platform of clean boards, covered with a carpet, had been laid down by the landlord of the

Hôtel de l'Europe, and the vehicles were in waiting. The ladies were handed from the boat to the carriages without a spot or a splash on their dresses, though the shore was very muddy.

In ten minutes more the head of the procession reached the governor's palace. There they found an awning over the sidewalk, and carpets laid down for the guests to walk upon. The French, English, and American flags were flying on the building. The ladies were conducted to the grand entrance of the palace, and taken by the servants to the apartments set apart for clothing. There were not less than a thousand natives and French people gathered in the vicinity, but they were kept in admirable order by the Malay police. The pacha's band was admitted to the grounds, and Mr. Frôler was acting as chief marshal; he notified them when the party began to descend the stairs, and the music commenced then. They came down in couples, Captain Ringgold and Mrs. Belgrave leading, followed by the pacha and the princess.

His Excellency stood at the head of the large apartment, and received them as they advanced. He was a widower and childless, so that he had no wife nor daughter to present. Louis and Miss Blanche were the next, though the commander had proposed that Louis should come next to him and his mother; but Louis rebelled, and insisted that he should follow the pacha. The rajah came next, and had Mrs. Blossom on his arm, to the no small amusement of the party; but the deposed sovereign prince could find no other lady disengaged.

Possibly Mr. Woolridge and wife were disconcerted to come next; but their daughter had been properly honored, and both were too fond of Blanche to be troubled about the precedence. Mr. Frôler stood by the governor, and announced the names of the members of the party; for His Excellency could hardly be expected to remember them. But he was very cordial to all of them, speaking in his broken English, except to the pacha and Louis. Some of the gentlemen had to present themselves without ladies; but there were at least twenty ladies and gentlemen seated around the room. After all the party from the ships had been received by the governor, they were introduced to the other visitors. Some of the Saigonians could speak English, and some could not; but the conversation soon became general. The commander and Mrs. Belgrave found enough who could speak English. There were seven persons among the tourists who could converse fluently in French, and Mr. Frôler employed these as interpreters for those who could not speak the polite language.

The scene was quite amusing to all; and even the governor laughed heartily as he looked about him, and saw the struggles in the matter of language. The chief marshal proved to be a very potent functionary, and he was omnipresent in the apartment. When the governor spoke to him in praise of Miss Blanche, he immediately sent Louis with her to His

Excellency. The room was the audience chamber of the palace, and the magnate of the occasion invited her to a seat on the dais at his side. She could speak French a little; and it was soon observed that she was enjoying herself very much, and the governor even more.

Mrs. Sharp was passed over to Louis, and he made the grand round with her. The princess was instructed to do the same with Mr. Woolridge, while the professor rendered the same service to Mrs. Woolridge. The rajah escorted Mrs. Blossom around the chamber, and the poor woman was in a flutter all the time. The long robe of the Indian prince bothered her, and she had been nearly tripped up several times; but her new beau was as polite and deferential as though she had been a queen. She had a story to tell the gossips of Von Blonk Park which would last her the rest of her lifetime. It was even a livelier time than that at the hotel, made so by the confusion of tongues, which was not far short of that at the Tower of Babel.

The dinner was announced by the major-domo of the household. Ignoring the houris of the occasion, the polite governor escorted Mrs. Belgrave to the table, and seated her on his right, while the captain of the Guardian-Mother conducted the princess. Those of the gentlemen who could speak French were requested by Mr. Frôler to attend the resident ladies; and the most distinguished was placed in charge of the pacha. The *contretemps* of language were frequent and laughable; and so much amusement was derived from this source that some of the visitors purposely made bulls to keep up the hilarity.

The dinner was a very elegant as well as a very substantial affair. Monsieur Odervie and other French cooks fraternized as usual on this great occasion; and the table was ornamented with many set pieces, and one from the citadel produced a Buddhist temple in sugar, which was the admiration of the guests; and doubtless all these culinary artists would assist the *chef* of the Guardian-Mother for the great dinner of the following day. But it would require a considerable volume to detail all the occurrences of the governor's banquet. A speech was made by His Excellency in French, which was replied to by Captain Ringgold, without knowing much of what had been said; but Louis followed him in a few remarks in French, thanking the governor and the residents of the city for their kindness and hospitality.

The pacha made the speech of the evening in the vernacular of the host, which was violently applauded by the residents, especially by the military officers from the citadel, who had been informed that he was the commander-in-chief of the armies of his country. The Italian band had been brought into the palace, feasted, and stationed in the great hall, where they discoursed their finest music, to the great delight of the guests. Dancing followed, and the governor led Mrs. Noury to the floor. The rajah asked Mrs. Blossom to dance with him; but she did not know a step, and if she ever in her life regretted that she could not dance, it was on this occasion. The commander of the citadel and chief officer of the army of Cochin China led out Mrs. Noury, and the next in rank to His Excellency who could speak English was favored by Miss Blanche.

It was kept up till after midnight; and then the tourists returned to the ships, visiting the hotel the next forenoon to obtain their baggage. All the party at the *fête* of the governor had been invited to the ships; and the Blanchita conveyed them from the landing in two trips, one to the Guardian-Mother, and the other to the Blanche. The guests were shown over both steamers, and they expressed their admiration in both languages. All the officers were kept busy, especially Mr. Gaskette, who spoke French. Every passenger was a host or hostess, and the confusion of tongues created as much merriment as it had at the palace. Captain Ringgold devoted himself especially to the governor. The Italian band played all the time on the deck of the Blanche, which was hardly a ship's length from her consort.

After a light lunch had been served in the cabins of both steamers, the party on board of the Guardian-Mother, with their hosts, were conveyed to the Blanche, where they spent a couple of hours, and had a dance on her promenade deck under an awning. Every part of the ship was visited; and after a stay of two hours, the entire company was conveyed in two trips to the Guardian-Mother. When some of the guests asked how the passengers contrived to amuse themselves on the long voyage, Mrs. Belgrave organized a section of them, and played Blindman's Buff, Turning the Cover, Copenhagen, and other games, to the intense delight of the guests.

At six o'clock dinner was announced. Monsieur Odervie had had the assistance of not less than four *chefs* all day; and several set pieces in varied ingredients, original and artistic, adorned the two tables. The bill of fare had been printed in the city, and of course it was all French. The occasion was much the same as at the palace, with all the confusion of tongues. At the close of the dinner Captain Ringgold made his speech, which the governor could understand, and the chief official of the province responded in his own language. Several others were heard; and when Dr. Hawkes attempted to make a speech in the polite language, he excited bursts of laughter, and it was soon evident that he was speaking for the fun of it. His gestures were more French than his speech, which he interlarded with English and Latin. Uncle Moses made a remark in the latter language, which only the doctor and the professor could understand; but it was as vigorously applauded as though every word had been comprehended.

After dinner the governor called for some singing, and gospel hymns were introduced. Captain Rayburn was one of the guests on board, and his heavy bass was the crowning glory of the music.

The ship had been illuminated, and the band played at times on the deck. The governor wanted some more of Mrs. Belgrave's games, and they were repeated in the music-room. The Cupids, as the two fat gentlemen had been named in Egypt, did their best on this occasion, — rolled on the floor, and were as antic as boys.

It was after midnight when the Blanchita began to convey the guests to the shore; and the adieux were very cordial, with many regrets that the ships must depart so soon. The river was so full of boats that the launch had some difficulty in making her way to the shore; but the Malay police soon made an opening for her.

Mr. Frôler had been invited to sleep on board, as had Captain Rayburn; and both accepted, the former returning to the ship after he had seen his ladies home.

CHAPTER XXVI

THE VOYAGE ACROSS THE CHINA SEA

THE tide was right at six o'clock in the morning, and the order had been given the night before to sail at this hour. Mr. Frôler and Captain Rayburn were on deck before this time; and the latter took a boat to his vessel, after very hearty thanks for the pleasure he had enjoyed.

"I don't feel at all like leaving your steamer, Captain Ringgold, but I suppose I must," said the French gentleman, as the commander took him by the hand in the morning.

"I am as sorry to have you leave as you are to do so," replied the captain. "We have seen the place, and made the acquaintance of quite a number of the people. In fact, you have turned our visit into a general frolic, and I am sure my party have never enjoyed themselves more than during the past two days; and we owe it all to you, Mr. Frôler."

"You praise my feeble efforts to enable you to see the place and some of the people more than they deserve," replied the Frenchman.

"When I meet you in New York, I shall do my best to reciprocate your very kind and hospitable reception, and I am confident all my passengers will do the same. I should be most happy to have you continue on board."

"I should avail myself of your very kind invitation so far as to go to Manila if there were a line of steamers between that port and Saigon. But I should have to go by the way of Singapore. With your permission, I will go down the river with you."

"What is this coming alongside?" asked the captain, as he moved over to the rail.

"It is one of the gunboats, Captain," answered Mr. Frôler. "There is the governor on her deck and two ladies. His Excellency has come off to say good-by to you."

"He is very considerate."

"And there is the landlord of the hotel."

"I paid his bill yesterday afternoon, and for everything up to this morning," said the commander as he hastened down the gangway to receive the governor.

On his way he called Louis, who was on deck early, and directed him to have the stewards call all the passengers, and to inform them that His Excellency was coming on board. The distinguished official was received by the captain, and conducted to the deck. It was a cordial greeting on both sides. The governor declared that he had never enjoyed himself more than on the day before, and he should go down the river for the purpose of saying his adieux to the party.

The gunboat would escort the ships to Cape St.

Jacques, and he would return with it. In ten minutes after the call the passengers began to come on deck, and the governor greeted them as though they had been his friends for years. He was a jolly old fellow, and made himself as familiar with the tourists as though they had been his intimate friends. When Miss Blanche came up he rushed to her, and took her by both hands. Mr. Frôler suggested that the governor had come more to see the beautiful women on board than for any other purpose.

The barge was hastily dropped into the water, and sent for the passengers of the Blanche, the third officer being in charge of the message. The landlord of the hotel said he had come on board to pay his respects to his late guests, and he would go down the river with them. The barge returned after some delay, for none of her party were out of their rooms. They warmly welcomed the governor and the captain of the gunboat, who had been one of the guests the day before.

Both ships got under way at once, for the anchors had been hove short. Mr. Sage and the cook were set to work. The governor divided his attentions between Mrs. Noury and Miss Blanche; and the pacha was not at all disturbed by his old Mohammedan notions about wives. The rajah took Mrs. Blossom on his arm, and promenaded the upper deck with her under the awnings.

"Faix! Oi belayve the ould feller manes to marry her," said Felix.

"Nonsense, Flix! He is a Mohammedan, and she is a Methodist, and neither of them would consent to marry the other," replied Louis.

"He knows she's a fust-rate nuss, and that's what he needs. Oi'll give my free consint to it," added Felix, as Louis was called away.

.The three hours' run to the sea was a continuation of the frolic of the day before, even including the games. At nine o'clock, with the ship in a sheltered bay, breakfast was served; and it was as lively as all the other meals had been. More speeches and a confusion of tongues followed. The two ladies who had come off in the gunboat were the lady who was said to have detained Mr. Frôler so long in Saigon, and her mother; and they were treated with the utmost consideration by all. The band played during the breakfast, having been sent for by the pacha.

Everybody was so happy that Captain Ringgold remained three hours longer than he had intended. Then the time to separate came; and the parting was long and difficult, bringing about another confusion of tongues, but it was over at last. The gunboat received her passengers for up the river; but the craft did not go that way, and accompanied the two steamers about five miles to sea, with the American flag flying at the fore.

As the vessels were to separate finally, the gunboat fired a salute of seven guns, which was returned by both ships; and then they sped on their voyage of eight hundred miles to Manila. The captain gave out the course east by north half-north, and the French flag was hauled down from the topmast. The passengers of the Blanche had been sent on board of her, while those of the Guardian-Mother continued to promenade the deck. The commander noticed that some of them were gaping and yawning, and he remembered that they had had only three or four hours' sleep.

"I advise you all to turn in and finish your night's sleep," said he. "Professor Giroud will give his lecture on the Philippine Islands and Manila to-morrow at half-past nine. There is nothing to do till dinner-time. No lunch will be served to-day in the cabin, for you have but just left the breakfast-table; but any one can ring his bell, and send for whatever is wanted."

The passengers seemed to think favorably of this advice, for they all went below. There was nothing to see; for there was not a single island in the course, and the ship was soon out of sight of land, not to see it again till she made Luban Island, off the entrance to Manila Bay. The wind was almost dead ahead, though it blew very gently; but this circumstance soon attracted the attention of Scott, who had been so busy with the frolics that he had not had time to consult his books and chart.

It was not his watch; and he went to his stateroom, returning very soon with the blue book that goes with the chart of the Indian Ocean. He found that there was an east monsoon which prevailed in the China Sea north of the equator.

"What's the matter, Mr. Scott?" asked the captain when he found him absorbed over his book. "Do you think we are going wrong, or that there is a typhoon within hail?"

"Neither, sir; I was looking to see why the wind was east to-day," replied the third officer.

"You have discovered by this time that there is an east monsoon coming in between those from the north-east and south-west."

"But we did not find it coming up from Sarawak to Bangkok," added the young officer.

"Your course carried you within between one hundred and one hundred and fifty miles of the Malay Peninsula. This and the great island of Sumatra doubtless have some influence on the winds. Both of these bodies of land are very hot; and, as the air from them tends to the cooler atmosphere of the sea, they favor the south-west monsoons. All these bodies of land modify to some extent the prevailing winds."

Scott was satisfied with the explanation, for it conformed with what he found in his book. When he carried his authority back to his room, he turned in and took his nap, in order to be ready for his watch at eight bells in the afternoon watch. In fact, all but the watch on deck were asleep.

The passengers seemed to be rather logy in their movements and heavy of intellect, perhaps because they had slept so well. It was cool at sea in comparison with the shore, and they had by this time become accustomed to extremely hot weather. But they waked up before the meal was finished, and all the talk was about the frolics of the last two days.

"What do you call the place where we go next, Captain Ringgold?" asked Uncle Moses. "I see it spelled in the books with a single *l* and with a double *l*. Which is correct?"

"Both," replied the commander. "If you are writing Spanish, you use one *l*; if you are writing English, you may use two *l's*, though I don't believe in doing so."

"Do the Spaniards ever double the *l?*"

"I will leave the professor to answer that question," replied the captain.

"They never spell Manila with two *l's* when they spell it correctly; for that would make another word of it,—a common noun instead of a proper, and meaning quite another thing," the professor explained.

"Perhaps I am stupid, Professor, and I know next to nothing of the Spanish language," added Uncle Moses, "but I don't quite understand you. If a Spaniard spelled the capital of the Philippine Islands with a double *l* it wouldn't be the capital at all?"

"It would not."

"What would it be?"

"It would be something of which Miss Blanche has a couple in her possession; and I may say the same of every lady at the table," said the professor with a cheerful smile on his face.

"But which no gentleman has?" suggested the worthy trustee.

"I don't say that; for the word means in Spanish a small hand."

There was a general laugh around the table, and all the party held out their paws like dancing bears.

"Then Spaniards must be good spellers," said Dr. Hawkes. "There is very great difference between the capital of the Philippine Islands and Miss Blanche's pretty little hands."

"*Ll*, which we call double *l*, is treated as one letter in Spanish, and it has its own peculiar sound, nearly equivalent to *ly* in English; and therefore Miss Blanche's small hand would be called mah-nil-ya, which is not the capital spoken off. The name of all the islands is spelled in English with double *p*, — Philippine; but that is not Spanish, though the geographers have generally adopted that orthography. The Spanish name is *Las Islas Filipinas.*"

"Thank you, Professor; and I think I understand it now," added Uncle Moses.

"*Quiera V. enseñarme sus manillas, Signorina Blanche?*" said Louis with a laugh. Of course she did not understand him; and he added, "Will you show me your small hands, Miss Blanche?" But she did not do so.

"I should very much like to have all geographical names reduced to a common standard, for I do not believe in translating proper names," said the commander. "I have been sometimes greatly bothered by the difference in names. When I came to Aachen in Belgium, I did not know where I was till I looked in my guide-book, and found it was Aix-la-Chapelle. Vienna has about three or four different names, and people there would not know what you meant if you called it as we do, or Vienne as the French write and spell it."

"I think you are quite right, Mr. Commander," added the professor.

"But I have a few words to say about our voyage; for I find it necessary to repress the ambition of some of my passengers," continued the captain. "Some of them wish to visit all the Philippine Islands, and there are about two thousand of them."

"Oh! oh! oh!" groaned some of the party.

"But the number I gave includes every rock, reef, and shoal that lifts its head above the water. Some call it twelve hundred. We will not stay to count them; but there are many of them big enough to have quite a number of towns on them. I wish to announce that it will not be possible for us to go to any of them except Manila, spelled with one *l*, and make an excursion up the Pasig River, and to the lake. But the ambition of the party is more expansive in regard to China and Japan. As I have told you, we can take only a specimen city in each country we visit. Hong-Kong and Canton in China, with some more northern port or city not yet selected, will be enough to give us an idea of the Central Flowery Nation."

The party left the cabin, and went on deck to study the map of the islands they were to visit.

CHAPTER XXVII

SOME ACCOUNT OF THE PHILIPPINES

THE Guardian-Mother continued on her course without encountering either typhoon or other tempest, and her passengers kept very comfortable under the awnings. The ship was in about 10° of north latitude and 110° of east longitude. She was sailing with the wind nearly dead ahead, and therefore the breeze was good on deck, and even in the cabins.

At the appointed hour the passengers were in their chairs in Conference Hall, two of them occupied by the siamangs, and the baby in the lap of Miss Blanche, who had become very much attached to the little creature. On the frame in front of the orang-outang was a complete map of the Philippine Islands, covering seventeen degrees of latitude, and ten of longitude, with enough of the seas around them to make their position clear to the audience.

Professor Giroud was introduced for this occasion as the speaker; and he was received with more than usual applause, for he had not occupied the rostrum as much as formerly, General Noury having been kept busy since his reappearance off Batavia. It may be said that after the rest of the day before the party were in excellent condition to be instructed.

" We are sailing just now in comparatively shallow water; and just to the south of us there are innumerable shoals, with only from four to ten fathoms of water on them. If the water were entirely drained from the China Sea, the bottom would be like a hilly region; for these numerous shoals would be the tops of various elevations, and the same would be true of a less extent north of us. The portion of the sea over which we are now moving would appear to be a considerable valley. You all have imagination enough to see what I have described.

" All around the Philippines on the east and south the water is from two to four thousand fathoms deep; so that if the seas were dried up around them, these islands would appear like a number of irregular chains of mountains, and the highest peak would be over 10,000 feet above the present surface of the water.

" From north to south these islands extend about a thousand miles, and from east to west about half that distance, with the Sulu or Mindoro Sea four hundred miles across it in either direction, nearly enclosed within them; for the north-east coast of Borneo is part of its boundary on the south. As the commander mentioned at dinner last evening, there are over two thousand islands in the group; and leaving out those rocks and shoals which are not big enough for a man to stand upon, there are twelve hundred of them.

" On a map of the world, or even of Asia, the

Philippine Islands occupy but a small space, and in your school-days you have doubtless regarded them as of but little importance; but several of the islands are larger than any New England State, and two of them are as large as Virginia and Ohio, and nearly as large as New York and Pennsylvania. Luzon and Mindanao," and the professor pointed to them on the map, "the most northerly and the most southerly, have each about 40,000 square miles, and the area of all the islands is 116,000 miles. I think most of you could have no idea from your study of maps of the extent of the Philippines.

"Mindoro, the next island south of Luzon, has 9,000; and the others from 1,200 to 5,500. I shall not mention or describe them separately. We shall visit only Manila and the country near it, and you would not remember even the names of the islands over night. They are all mountainous and volcanic. The highest mountain is Apo, in Mindanao, which is 10,400 feet high, and there are others of 9,000 feet.

"The islands are volcanic, and therefore subject to earthquakes; and an instrument in Manila which indicates vibrations of the earth is said to be shaking about all the time. Several destructive ones are recorded in the past. In 1863 Manila was nearly destroyed by one, and the great southern island is especially liable to them.

"The mountain ranges mostly extend north and south; and there is space between them for some considerable rivers, as the Rio Grande in Luzon has a course of 220 miles. The Agusan in Mindanao is navigable for 60 miles. In this island are several lakes, with rivers flowing from them. In addition to which are many lacustrine basins."

"Spare us, Professor!" exclaimed Uncle Moses.

"The word comes from *lacus*, Latin for lake, and applies here to such lakes as send their overflow to the sea or other lakes by streams made by the rush of water. But I don't use many such words, and I hardly expected a classical scholar to object," replied the professor.

" But I objected in behalf of several here who never studied Latin; and besides the overflow is entirely apart from the root of the word. But I am satisfied, and the commander may invite you to proceed," chuckled Brother Avoirdupois.

"On account of the high mountains and the abundant sea-breezes, though hot and moist, this group is not so unhealthy as most tropical islands and countries. The fevers of hot countries are here of the mild, intermittent kind "—

"What is intermittent, Professor ?" asked Felix. "Is it the kind they don't have in Ireland ?"

"I should say that it was."

"An intermittent fever, Felix, is one that comes and goes, like the old woman's soap," interjected Mrs. Blossom, the nurse; and everybody laughed to hear her say anything.

"The diseases most dreaded in these islands are consumption, dysentery, and anæmia "—

"Mercy, Professor!" cried Mr. Woolridge.

"The reduction in the amount of blood in the system, and the condition resulting from this loss, is anæmia. Dr. Hawkes can explain it more fully," replied the professor.

"Not necessary," added the surgeon.

"As all over the Eastern Archipelago, there are two seasons, the wet and the dry, produced by the monsoons; but the irregularity of the surface variously modifies the result. For the southern and western sides of the mountains the south-west monsoons give the wet season, and the north-east the dry season, and *vice versa*. Manila is subjected by the influence of the south-west winds to rains from June to November, with dry weather the rest of the year.

"The temperature is about the same all the year round. The coolest month is December, when the glass stays at about 77°; and in May, the hottest month, at 86°. Of course there are days, and times of day, when the temperature is lower than the one, and higher than the other. The extremes where we are going vary only about 25° — from 66° to 91°; and we have it hotter than the last in New York. The average rainfall is about seventy inches, varying by months from one-third of an inch in March, to twenty inches in August.

"The flora of the islands is just what you would expect in this climate. Nearly or quite all the plants you have found in the other islands you have visited are to be found here. Particularly plenteous here are the fibrous plants, and abaca forms in its prepared state one of the most important exports of the islands. This is a sort of plantain from which comes the Manila hemp, as it is sometimes called, though it is a misnomer; and with us it is called simply manila, the sailors tell me. It is extensively cultivated here, and grows something like the banana.

"The stalks on which the leaves grow are split into long strips, are threshed, combed, washed, and dried, and then they become manila, of which many of the ropes of this ship are made, though hemp makes the better article. The finest fibres are sometimes fifteen feet long, and from such some very delicate manufactured goods are produced. The coarser parts are used for cordage, which is very serviceable. When we were at Nassau, in the Island of New Providence, last year, we saw fields of *sisal*, which has in late years come into use as a substitute for common hemp and manila, and is said to resist the action of sea-water better than any other material.

"The fauna may seem to be quite limited to the Nimrods of our company, for the large animals we have found in other islands do not exist in the Philippines. The buffalo and the gibbon are the largest in the islands, with a variety of monkeys. The elephant, tiger, rhinoceros, bear, and orang-outang have no home here. The only dangerous animals are the crocodile, serpents, and other reptiles. If the Nimrods wish to hunt they will have to try their hand at the wild buffaloes, though they are not to be found near Manila.

"Birds are numerous and various, and especially the gallinaceous bipeds, such as barnyard fowls, grouse, and pheasants; but the most highly valued here is the 'rooster,' if I may call him by his common American name, for cock-fighting is one of the national amusements of Spain and its dependencies. You will see plenty of it in Manila, if you are so disposed; but it is not an elevating sport, any more than bull-fighting, which may possibly prevail here. Coal and iron are the most common minerals, with others; but mining is too severe work for the enterprise of the people, and I believe most of the mines of Cuba are worked by Americans.

"The original inhabitants of the Philippines were doubtless Negritos; and I hasten to explain the name before I am 'picked up.' It was the word used by the Spaniards to designate, not alone the negroes as we find them in Africa, but those who are similar to them. People of this race formerly inhabited all these islands, but there are scarcely any of them left at the present time. Hindus, Malays, and other natives of the adjacent countries and islands, came here, and the races mingled.

"The people found here at the present time have a variety of names, beginning with the pure Spaniards,

Creoles, Tagals, Chinese, and Mestizoes. The Spaniards and the Tagals need no explanation, for the latter are the pure natives of the islands. Creole, I believe, is variously used in different locations; but it is a Spanish word, coming from *criolla*, which means grown up. They are one thing in the Spanish West Indies, another in Brazil.

"A more general definition is a person born in any country, but not of native blood. In the Philippines, Creoles are the children of Spanish fathers and native mothers. Mestizoes are children of Chinese parents on one side and natives on the other. The last class are usually called 'métis' in Manila and elsewhere. You will doubtless see all of these classes, and with a little practice will be able to identify them.

"The Spaniards of the islands are Catholics, often, I am sorry to say, merely nominally such. Many of the natives are Mohammedan, though the greater portion are Catholic. The Philippines were discovered by Magellan, as we generally call him, though that was not his correct name, in 1521. He was born in Portugal, and his name was Magalhães. He served as a soldier in Malacca and Morocco, and was lamed for life in a battle in the latter. He did not think his services were appreciated by his king, and he offered them to Spain.

"He presented to Charles V. a plan for reaching the Moluccas by sailing to the west; and, his scheme being approved, he was fitted out with a fleet of five ships. He passed through the straits south of Patagonia, which still bear his name, crossed the great ocean, to which he gave the name of Pacific, though it was discovered by Balboa, who called it the South Sea. Succeeding in his enterprise, he reached the Philippines, after putting down a mutiny. He was killed in an expedition he led in the islands. The Victoria, his ship, returned to Spain in charge of one of his subordinates, thus completing the first voyage ever made around the world.

"There were several governments in the islands, and most of them were conquered or conciliated so that they came under Spanish rule; but the Mohammedans of Sulu, the Archipelago north-east of Borneo, and Mindanao retained their independence for a long period, and they still retain their boundaries and government.

"Manila has a population of 270,000, and there are several other considerable towns with 30,000 or more. There is a submarine cable to Hong Kong, 720 miles of telegraph, and 16 miles of railroad out of Manila. The army consists of 4,800 men, with 3,500 gendarmerie, or police, such as ride in pairs all over Spain. It has a navy of two corvettes, six *avisos*, or despatch vessels, sixteen gunboats, with 2,000 sailors and marines. I believe I have told you all that is necessary to know about the Philippine Islands in a general way; and I thank you for your attention through the long talk I have given you," the professor concluded, and retired from the rostrum in the midst of the hearty applause bestowed upon him.

"I think we all know more about the Philippines than we ever knew before, though I have been there; and to-morrow I shall have something to say, very briefly, about the city of Manila," said the commander.

"When shall we get there, Captain?" asked Dr. Hawkes.

"Day after to-morrow morning; but I shall lay off so as not to get there at three in the morning."[1]

[1] On board of a steamer from Colombo, Ceylon, to London, I met an educated Scotch gentleman from Manila, who pronounced the name Philippine, the last *i* long. On the steamer from Liverpool to Boston, I met a lady, also from Manila, and she pronounced it with a long *i* in the last syllable. I conclude this is the fashion among English-speaking people in the Philippine Islands. — O. O.

CHAPTER XXVIII

THE DESCRIPTION OF AN EARTHQUAKY CITY

In the afternoon of the second day out Professor Giroud called his pupils together in the library, which was the schoolroom of the ship, and resumed the lessons which had been interrupted since the arrival at Sarawak. The long intermission had sharpened the intellects of the class, and they were very earnest in their studies. But it could be only for the afternoon and the next day, for the commander was very diligent in the business of sight-seeing.

At half-past nine the next forenoon, the passengers were all assembled in Conference Hall, as the captain had appointed; and the siamangs, who spent much of the time aloft running up and down and along the foreyards, were in their usual places, for chairs had been provided for them; and they looked as grave and attentive as though they understood the whole of the lecture. Captain Ringgold appeared on the rostrum, after he had patted Mr. and Mrs. Mingo on the head, and glanced at Miss Mingo in the lap of Miss Blanche.

"Manila is the capital of all the Spanish possessions in the East, as the professor has informed you; it has a population of 270,000, which is 40,000 greater than Havana," he began. "It is on the south-west coast of Luzon, 650 miles from Hong-Kong, which is a run of about forty-seven hours for the ship. It is located on both sides of the little river Pasig, which is the outlet of Lake Bahia, or the Lake of the Bay. When I was here many years ago, I spoke Spanish enough to get along; but I shall leave the language now to the professor and Mr. Belgrave, for I forget most of it.

"In going to the city we have to pass through Manila Bay, which is really a sea of itself; and, though it is land-locked, it affords little if any protection for vessels in heavy weather, for it is about thirty miles long from north to south, and twenty-five from east to west. A west or south-west wind rakes it about the same as the ocean.

"The city forms a circle, with a piece of it cut off on the bay; and the suburbs are on several islands in the river and bay. To keep a clear channel, the Pasig is extended into the bay between two piers, with a fort at the end of one, and a lighthouse at the end of the other. The anchorage in the bay is good enough so far as holding ground is concerned, except in the south-west monsoon, when vessels of four hundred tons or more have to go to Cavite, ten miles south south-west from the city; and their cargo must be taken to and from them in lighters.

"The oldest part of Manila is on the southern bank of the Pasig, and is strongly fortified; but it has a dilapidated look, for it was founded in 1571.

On the north side of the river is the Binondo suburb, as it is called, which is more populous than the old part. The foreign merchants live here, and it is the more important commercial centre. You would hardly know, if you waked from a sleep there, whether you were in a Spanish or an Oriental city, for you would see something of both. Gloomy-looking churches, awkward towers, and heavily built stone houses are mixed up with pleasant cottages in groves of tropical trees. I believe the people are now inclined to build more of wood than stone on account of the prevalence of earthquakes, which shake down the heavier structures, and crush the occupants under the weight of the material.

"As in Burma and Siam, the cottages I mentioned are built on posts; for the land is sometimes inundated, and the water requires a free passage, or it would do more mischief. In the month of August, nearly two feet of water falls on a level; and it makes bad work in the low places. The streets are wide and not paved; and in the rainy season, with a foot or two of water lying loose around, they become very nearly impassable. The houses are built in Spanish fashion, with a central court-yard. They are generally two stories high; for in an earthquaky country like this, where terra firma becomes terra shaky, the people are not encouraged to erect buildings twenty stories high, as in New York and Chicago.

"An iron suspension bridge connects the old town with Binondo. It was formerly a stone bridge, built more than two hundred years ago, which was thrown down by the earthquake of 1863. A street in the new suburb, called the Escolto, seems to be the Broadway of the city; for it is the great shopping locality, and it is flanked with shops and stalls, filled with people of various races. Beyond this the Chinese, Tagals, and half-castes congregate in numerous occupations, as jewellers, oil and soap dealers, confectioners, painters, and those of other trades. Here you will find plenty of gambling-houses, if you are looking for them.

"As in Singapore, certain sections of the city are given up to particular branches of business. At San Fernando, there are immense cigar manufactories, like the one you saw in Sevilla in Spain, where six thousand women are employed; and probably as many are to be found in some of them here," continued the commander, consulting memoranda he took from his pocket. "At Santo Mesa is a cordage manufactory; at Alcaicerfa the Chinese have a landing-place for their sampans; fishermen and weavers live at Tondo, whose gardens supply the markets with fruit and vegetables; Malate is the resort of the embroiderers; Paco is favored by artists and artisans; and Santa Ana and San Pedro Macati are health resorts."

"McCarty!" exclaimed Felix, as he caught what sounded like an Irish name. "I wondher if he comes from Kilkenny."

"A place, and not a man; and it did not come from Kilkenny. It is a Spanish name, spelled Ma-ca-ti,"

replied tne captain. " I have read off all these names
from my memoranda, not that I expect you to remember them, but to show you how things work
here. All the buildings for public use in a capital
city are found here, and a cathedral, the palaces of
the governor-general and the archbishop, an elegant
town-house, churches, three colleges for young men,
and two for young women (not behind the times,
you see), a large theatre, probably not as large as
that in Barcelona, custom-house, barracks, etc. The
Prado is the largest public square, and is ornamented
with a statue of Charles IV., or Carlos, King of
Spain from 1788 to 1808 ; and I wonder there is not
one of Magellan, who discovered the islands, and lost
his life here.

" The streets of the city are lighted with kerosene-
oil lamps, and not with gas, for the reason that the
earthquakes made bad work of the latter; and the
works were destroyed in a hurricane in 1882, as was
half the city. They do not build houses of brick or
stone now, but of wood, the former being so destructive of human life in an earthquake. The native
dwellings are constructed of bamboo, thatched with
the leaves of the nipa palm.

" Glass windows are not used here; but the flat
shell of a large oyster is substituted for glass, and
the sashes all slide horizontally. Both of these de-
partures from ordinary methods are said to be to
exclude the great heat; but I confess that I cannot
see it. I find among my memoranda that 21,000

women and 1,500 man are employed in making
cigars; which in Sevilla includes the putting up of
tobacco in papers for smoking, and it may be so
here. Before I close I wish to say that authorities
differ in regard to the population of the city; but
I think the professor was about right in putting it
at 270,000. Lippincott gives it with the suburbs at
160,000, and Chambers at nearly 300,000. You have
been patient and longer suffering than I intended you
should be, and I thank you."

The commander made his bow, and descended from
the rostrum. Hearty applause followed, and the
siamangs joined with repeated cries and squeaks.
Miss Mingo had fallen asleep in her comfortable
quarters; but the noise woke her with a start, and
she sprang to the shoulder of Miss Blanche, where
she gave her "Ra! Ra! Ra!" and the squeak
which is the " tiger " at the end of it. As the audience left their chairs for a walk on the deck, Mr.
and Mrs. Mingo sprang into the fore-rigging, climbing the shrouds, and over the futtock-shrouds, dis-
daining to crawl through the lubber-hole to the top.

Miss Mingo looked up at them, and then sprang
into the rigging; for her strength and agility seemed
to have greatly increased since she came on board,
making it probable that the sea-air agreed with her.
But her mamma did not appear to be quite satisfied
with this venture; and she sprang over the futtocks,
and seized her with one arm as she began to mount
them.

Mr. Mingo ran up the topmast rigging, and seated himself on the cross-trees. The anxious mother looked at him a moment, and then darted down to the deck with the baby in her arm. Then, seeing Mrs. Belgrave seated in one of the arm-chairs on the promenade, she carried Miss Mingo to her, placing the infant in her lap. The lady immediately folded the little one in her arms so that she could not escape, caressing her so that she did not offer to follow her mother up the rigging, though she watched her ascent.

Mrs. Mingo ascended to the cross-trees, where she and the gentleman siamang seemed to hold a conference. The latter then sprang up to the topgallant yard, and was closely followed by his mate. They turned somersets, and went through a variety of athletic feats, which greatly interested their audience on deck, who gave them a round of applause. They seemed to understand and appreciate this manifestation of approbation, for they attempted various other feats.

Mrs. Mingo got hold of the topgallant halliards, and finding them loose, swung out over the lee side of the ship. Captain Ringgold was startled at this movement. She swung out as far as she could, the line yielding, and suddenly she dropped into the water. The captain rang the gong to stop the screw, and then to back it. If the siamang could swim at all, she was very clumsy in the water; and the waves, for there was considerable sea on, seemed to bother her.

"Clear away the second cutter, Mr. Gaskette!" shouted the commander as soon as he had rung the gong to stop the screw, and the ship was as nearly at rest as she could be on the billows.

"All the second cutters, on deck!" shouted Biggs, the boatswain, after he had piped his whistle, at the order of the second officer.

The boat was swung out in as much haste as though the cry had been "Man overboard!" and her crew took their places in good order. The cutter was lowered into the water, and the men gave way on a favoring wave and went clear of the ship. They pulled with all their might; and Lanark, the cockswain, steered her for the siamang.

"Stand by, bowmen, to haul in the lady!" called Mr. Gaskette, as the cutter approached the unhappy animal. "In bows!" and the two bowmen tossed their oars, and brought them down in place, the men springing into the fore-sheets to seize hold of the creature. "Way enough!"

It looked to those who were anxiously watching the operations of the men, fearful that Miss Mingo would become an orphan, as though the boat would strike Mrs. Mingo, and kill her by the collision.

"Stern all!" cried Mr. Gaskette with energy.

The order was obeyed, and the cutter came to a stop when near the animal. The bowmen were reaching to get hold of her, when she made a vigorous leap into the fore-sheets, grasping the rail as she did so. She shook herself with all her might as soon as she was in the boat, and a cheer went up from the deck of the ship. The lady then seated herself on the little platform in the bow, and seemed to be as happy as ever, and that was saying a great deal.

"Give way!" said Mr. Gaskette, laughing at the apparent self-possession of Mrs. Mingo when her troubles were over. The cutter came alongside the ship under its davits, the falls were hooked on, and the boat was hoisted up. The lady was the first to leap from her place to the rail of the ship.

The passengers applauded as she moved aft; and she replied with her usual cry, and ended it with a squeak. She went directly to the promenade, which she mounted, and then hastened to Mrs. Belgrave's chair. She looked at her baby as though it had been overboard. Miss Mingo's keeper had taken care that the infant should not see her mother in the water; and the little one could not have told what was the matter if any one had asked her, first because she did not know, and second for an obvious reason.

The ship was going ahead again, and the captain came to the promenade. He took the lady into the sun, and persuaded her to lie down and dry herself. She seemed to understand the matter, and stretched herself out.

"What made her fall overboard, Captain?" asked the lady — meaning Mrs. Belgrave this time, and not the siamang.

SHE MADE A VIGOROUS LEAP INTO THE FORE-SHEETS.

Page 267.

"The fore topgallant halliard was not made fast to the cleat, and when it ran out, it jerked her from it," replied the commander. "It ought not to have been loose, and there is a bit of discipline for some jack-tar."

The ship went along as before; and when the passengers turned out the next morning Manila was in sight, and not five miles distant.

CHAPTER XXIX

GOING ON SHORE IN MANILA

THE ship had slowed down in the afternoon, and reached the entrance of Manila Bay about eight bells, or four o'clock in the morning. At the Boca Grande she had taken a pilot; but she still had twenty-five miles to run. She had come in by the larger of the two passages, formed by a group of islands, both of which are called "mouths" (*bocas*); and the smaller of them is the Boca Chica. The Blanche had followed the example of the Guardian-Mother in slowing down, and had taken a pilot at about the same time.

The passengers had asked the steward on watch in the cabin to call them at half-past five, and they were all on deck as soon as it was light enough for them to see the shore clearly. But the bay is so large that they could make out the shores only ahead of the ship. They could see the mountains in the distance, with a lower stretch of land between them and the low ground of the shore. All that they could observe was tropical verdure, with lofty palms on every hand. The low ground, covered with water in the rainy season, was planted with rice-fields.

The ladies declared that the view was lovely; and certainly it presented variety enough, with the high lands in the background, and the rich and luxuriant growth near the bay. The pilot was a Spaniard who could speak a little English; and the commander ordered him`to bring the ship to anchor at a safe place, as near as convenient off the end of the two piers at the mouth of Pasig. The Blanche took a position abreast of her, off the fort, while the first was off the lighthouse.

The health-officer came on board, and by this time it was after sunrise. He was blandly received by the commander, as every official or visitor was, and the conversation was carried on in English. All the ship's company and the passengers were mustered on the upper deck. The papers, including lists of all the persons on board, were examined, and compared with the number presented, which made it clear that no one was sick in his stateroom or in the fore-castle.

The custom-house officers were not far behind, and the character of the steamer was explained. There was no manifest, for there was no cargo to be invoiced. The principal officer was very minute in his inquiry, and not particularly courteous. He was evidently impressed by his authority; and the captain did not invite him to breakfast, as he would have done if he had been somewhat less conscious of the magnitude of his office.

The duties on merchandise brought into the islands were formerly discriminating in favor of Spanish vessels, which caused other merchantmen to avoid the port to its commercial injury; but about twenty years before a uniform tariff was established, without regard to the flag under which the ship sailed, and all export duties were abolished. The official went over the ship, and the arrangement of her accommodations ought to have been enough to convince the man that the vessel was a pleasure yacht. The self-sufficient officer retreated in good order when he had completed his examination, leaving a subordinate on board to see that no merchandise was landed. The latter was a gentlemanly person, spoke English, and was disposed to make himself agreeable. He was invited to breakfast in the cabin.

The passengers had seated themselves on the promenade during the official examination, observing all the proceedings, and watching the boats in sight, some of which were different from anything they had seen before. They were near enough to the piers to see some distance up the river. Of course the Blanche was subjected to the same examination; but a different set of officials had boarded her, and completed their work in a much shorter time. It could be seen that her crew were putting the steam-launch into the water.

"The Blanchita will be exceedingly serviceable here," said the commander, who had taken a stand near the steps of the promenade. "We can go on shore, and land anywhere we please; for there are quays all along the river."

"Boat coming down the river with the American

flag at the stern, Captain Ringgold," said Mr. Scott, saluting the commander.

"Our consul probably," added the captain. "Would you like to go to a hotel in Manila, ladies?" asked he.

No one answered the question, but three of them glanced at Mrs. Belgrave, as though they expected her to reply; but she made no sign.

"You don't answer, ladies," added the captain.

"We are waiting for Mrs. Belgrave to speak," said Mrs. Woolridge.

"I beg you will excuse me," said that lady, laughing. "I do not know why I am expected to voice the sentiments of the party."

"Because, like the wife of the President of the United States at home, you are the first lady on board," returned the wife of the magnate of the Fifth Avenue. "Your son is the owner of the Guardian-Mother, and you are the mother for whom the ship is named."

"I most respectfully decline to be so regarded; and if I have ever put on any airs, I will repent and reform," replied Mrs. Belgrave, laughing all the while.

"You have never put on airs, or assumed anything at all," protested Mrs. Woolridge.

"I consider my son a very good boy, and an earnest advocate of fair play with others," continued the "first lady" more seriously; and all the party heartily approved the remark. "Louis found that the other members of the 'Big Four' were disposed to rely upon him, and wished to do as he desired. On the Borneo question he took a secret ballot, and would not express his own opinion till the vote was declared, though he voted himself. Every one voted for himself, and could not have been influenced by his desire. I propose to follow my son's example. I wish the commander to be guided by the views of all rather than mine."

All the passengers, gentlemen included, applauded her unselfish stand. The lady tore off a blank leaf from a letter she took from her pocket, and made it into twelve pieces, which she proceeded to distribute among the passengers.

"I think the gentlemen are just as much interested in the question as the ladies; and I invite them to vote, Mr. Scott included. The question is, Shall we go to a hotel in Manila, or live on board of the ship," said the lady. "You will vote yes or no; yes for the hotel, and no for the ship."

"Perhaps I ought to inform you before you vote that there are at least three hotels in Manila, — the Catalana, the Universo, and the Madrid. Of the merits of each I cannot speak; but we can obtain correct information before we go to any one of them, and probably there are more than I have mentioned," interposed the commander, very much amused at the proceedings.

"Please to separate now; and I put you on your honor to be secret, and not consult any person in regard to your vote," Mrs. Belgrave added. "I appoint Mr. Gaskette to collect, sort, and count the ballots. After voting, please return to the promenade."

The passengers went individually to various corners, and wrote their votes. The second officer collected them in his cap, and then went into the pilot-house to make out his return. It required but three minutes to do this, as there was no scattering votes; and he returned to the promenade.

"Whole number of votes, 12; necessary to a choice, 7; Yes, 2, No, 10, and the No's have carried it," read Mr. Gaskette, handing the paper to Mrs. Belgrave, and retiring with a graceful bow.

"Yes means hotel, and no means ship," said the lady. "Mr. Commander, the party have voted to live on board of the ship. I am willing to acknowledge that I cast one of the two yes ballots. But I am infinitely better satisfied than I should have been if I had influenced you the other way. I hope you all consider that the thing has been fairly done."

"Boat coming alongside, sir," reported Mr. Scott to the captain. "Another boat near, flying the English flag, headed for the Blanche."

Captain Ringgold hastened to the gangway to receive the occupant of the boat, whoever he might prove to be. One of the men on the platform brought him a card, on which he found the name of the American consul, who mounted at once to the deck just as the gong sounded for breakfast.

"I am very glad to meet you, Mr. Webb, and to

welcome you to my ship, which is the steam-yacht Guardian-Mother, on a voyage around the world," said the captain, as he grasped the hand of the official. "Captain Ringgold, at your service."

"I am very happy to meet you, Captain, for I have heard of you; and I tender my services for any assistance I may be able to render to you and your party," replied the consul.

"Now I will introduce you to the ladies and gentlemen on board, and you will do us the honor to breakfast with us," added the commander, as he took the arm of his guest, and conducted him to the promenade, where he was duly presented to all the passengers individually.

Louis Belgrave was presented as the owner of the steamer, for the captain never omitted to give him a prominent position. The breakfast was the usual one; but it was always very nice, and Mr. Sage had hailed a boat, and obtained some very fine fish for the meal. Mr. Webb was placed on the right of the commander, Louis's usual place; but he was glad enough always to get the seat next to Miss Blanche. The consul was next to Mrs. Belgrave; and he found her very agreeable, as she never failed to be.

"Now, what are we going to do here, Mr. Commander?" asked the "first lady," as some had actually begun to call her already.

"We are going to see the city, of course," he replied.

"I feel for one as though we had already seen

it, and I can see it all in my mind's eye now," added the lady. "You and the professor have given us such a minute account of the place and its surroundings that it seems to me that I have taken it all in."

"I think most of us have," said Mrs. Woolridge; and several of the company expressed themselves to the same effect.

"We have several books in the library about the city and the islands, and some of us have read them all," suggested Louis.

"What books have you on board, Mr. Belgrave?" asked the consul.

"We have 'Twenty Years in the Philippines' by Monsieur de la Gironière, which some say was written by Alexandre Dumas, but I don't know about that; 'Travels in the Philippines,' by F. Jagor, with an epitome of the work in *Harper's Magazine;* and we have Chambers's Encyclopædia, Lippincott's Gazetteer of the present year, and some other works."

"You seem to be well provided with information, and with the best extant, unless you consult the archives of Spain at Madrid," returned the consul.

"The Blanchita is coming alongside, Captain," said Mr. Scott, to whom a message to this effect had been sent down by the officer of the deck.

The breakfast was nearly finished when the word came; and the party soon went on deck, where they found all the passengers of the Blanche and the British consul. The usual hugging and kissing on the part of the ladies and hand-shaking by the gentlemen followed, and the two consuls were duly presented to all.

"It is time for us to go on shore," said General Noury, looking at his watch. "The Blanchita is at the gangway, and I have engaged a pilot for her. Of course you are all invited to go on shore in her."

The two consuls volunteered to act as guides; and the company took their places in the launch, which was large enough to accommodate double the number. The pilot took her into the river; and if the ears of the tourists had been filled full of Manila, there was plenty for the eyes to take in, and it was not five minutes after they passed the lighthouse before most of the passengers were laughing at some of the queer costumes worn by the people.

They passed a craft which Mr. Webb called a passage-boat. It was a sort of canoe, manned by three men, two of them rowing, and one working a paddle to steer her. Over the after part was an awning, made of the big leaves of the nipa palm; and under it were two men and two women, bound up the river. But a freight-boat interested the young men most. The hull of it looked more like a canal-boat than any other craft they could think of. The planking of the sides extended a little higher up forward and aft than amidships; and the whole was covered with an arched roof woven on hoops, like those of a baggage-wagon, with palm leaves.

The portion at the bow and stern could be removed, as the whole could. The man at the helm was under the stern section of the cover, and it was lifted about a foot to enable him to look ahead.

A wide plank was secured on iron brackets fastened to each side of the craft, on which were two men poling the boat up the stream. It was so far like the mud-scows formerly in use on some of the waters of New England, except that the men who worked her with poles walked on the gunwale of the scow. The boys watched it till it passed out of view astern. The Blanchita made a landing near the bridge, on the Binondo side; and all the passengers went on shore.

CHAPTER XXX.

EXCURSIONS ON SHORE AND UP THE PASIG

THE Pasig flowed from east to west in the city; and landing on the north side of the stream, the tourists soon came to the Escolto, which extended both ways parallel to the river. It was the principal street for shoppers and promenaders, and was exactly what they wished to find, as they had informed Mr. Webb and Mr. Gollan, the two consuls who had brought them there.

The avenue was filled at this hour with a motley variety of people of all the races known in the islands, from the Tagal Indian up to the native-born of Spain. Some of them were disposed to laugh at the strangeness, not to say the absurdity, of some of the costumes which confronted them; but all of them were too well bred to indulge their mirth, or to stare offensively at the subjects of their suppressed merriment. One young man excited their attention especially; and Louis at the side of Miss Blanche, and the rest of the quartet of young Americans, were also interested.

"He is one of the swells of the city," said Scott, looking industriously at the clear blue sky.

"He looks like it," replied Louis, as he and his

female companion each gazed with one eye into a shop window while they fixed the other upon the native, who was sporting a cane . in fantastic twirls, and evidently believing he was worth looking at.

The subject of their mirth, variously concealed, was what would be called a colored man at home, though not a negro; but he was not many removes in complexion from the original Negrito. He was toying with a cigar, and wore a monocule and a "stovepipe" hat. His trousers were a sort of plaid; and his upper works were covered with what looked like a blouse, though it was really his shirt, with a linen bosom, secured with studs. At the base of his figure was a pair of patent-leather shoes, though he did not affect the luxury of stockings.

The party observed his magnificent movements till he was out of sight; but their attention was immediately attracted by a feminine water-carrier, who was standing on the opposite side of the street. On her head was a good-sized earthen jar, which she poised on the summit of her cranium without support from either hand, one of which she employed in coquetting with a banana leaf instead of the national *abanico*, or fan, of the Spanish ladies.

"That girl has a very fine form," said Dr. Hawkes, who was standing near the boys. "She is not a Spanish maiden, but her complexion is quite as fair as any of them."

"She has an abundant crop of dark hair, and

she puts it to a good use; for it is braided and rolled up so that it makes a cushion for the water-jar," said Scott.

"She is much taller than the natives we have been in the habit of seeing," added Louis.

By this time the entire party had halted, and, taking their cue from the surgeon, were looking at the water-bearer. The girl had been observing the strangers before any of them saw her; but as soon as she realized that she was the object of their scrutiny, she smiled, and her pretty face lighted up as though she did not object to being stared at. Her under garment, with long sleeves, was all the covering she wore above the belt; and below it her skirt of uneven length reached just below the knees. She wore neither shoes nor stockings, and her feet looked as though they had been "Trilbied."

"I suppose that man over there is carrying that rooster to market," said Mrs. Belgrave, who was walking between the commander and Mr. Webb.

"Not at all, madam; that is a game-bird. The national amusements of Spain are bull-fighting and cock-fighting," returned Mr. Webb. "I was in Madrid one Sunday, and the programme for the day was a cock-fight at one, a bull-fight at three, and the Italian opera at six; and I went to all of them."

"On Sunday?" queried the lady.

"I was there to see the sights, and learn the

customs of the people; and a bull-fight could be seen only on Sunday, and the cock-fight was patronized on that day by the high admiral of the navy. In Madrid, as in other cities of Continental Europe, Sunday is not regarded as it is in England and the United States; and their failure to observe it as we do is not an evidence that they are irreligious. The next day was All Saints' or All Souls' Day, I forget which; and every shop was closed. The noise and confusion of Sunday and all ordinary days were silenced. The churches were all open and well filled, and the people went to the cemeteries to deposit flowers on the graves of their dead. In Stockholm, which is a Protestant city, people went to church in the forenoon; but at one o'clock the band struck up, and the rest of the day was given up to frolicking."

"I prefer to live in Von Blonk Park," added Mrs. Belgrave, with a smile.

"But cock-fighting is vastly more prevalent here than in Spain, or any other country I have visited. Wealthy people have their games, and all the poor people also," continued the consul. "About every man who can raise money enough to buy one owns a game-cock, and many take them with them when they go out.

"Observe that man and woman approaching us; they are Spanish métis. Both of them wear rather gay colors. On the other side of the street is a pair of Chinese métis; and one couple is not much different from the other, except, if you are an expert, you can see something of the high cheek-bones of the Chinese. Both of the men wear stovepipe hats, which seems to be the fashion among that class. Some of them are quite wealthy."

"Do all these different grades fraternize, Mr. Webb?" asked the commander.

"In business they do, but not socially. The pure Spaniards look down upon all the native and half-caste people; and in turn all the other classes do considerable looking down upon some other grades, till you get to the Tagals, who are so unfortunate as to have no other class to look down upon."

The tourists walked along this Broadway of the city till they were tired, and then turned into a side street to observe some of the dwelling-houses. The first thing that they noticed was that most of the houses were covered on the roof with red tiles, as in Spain and in other countries. They all had very small windows, with sliding sashes; and the panes, of oyster-shells instead of glass, were smaller in proportion than the windows. Most of them had a balcony of some sort, which was an out-door sitting-room, used during leisure hours by the people.

The consuls then conducted the party to a stand for carriages, and enough of them were engaged to accommodate all. They were taken for two hours, with the proviso that the passengers were to be set down at the landing by the bridge.

"You must pay in advance," said Mr. Webb.

Natives preparing tobacco in Manila.

"That is the custom here.   The drivers were cheated so often in some former time, that it became 'no pay, no ride.'   I bargained at five pesetas an hour for each vehicle."

The captain, Mrs. Belgrave, and Mr. Webb occupied the first carriage; and the consul directed the driver where to go.

"Five pesetas," said the lady when they were seated.   "How much is that?"

"About one dollar.   A peseta is the legal unit of the currency, and is of the same value as the French franc and the Italian lira, or nineteen cents, three mills of our money, as estimated by the director of the United States Mint.   The real is a quarter of a peseta, but the escudo of ten reales has been suppressed.   The Spanish dollar, the same as ours, though not on a gold standard, is the usual medium of trade here."

The tourists were driven to the cathedral, the palaces of the governor and the archbishop, and to several of the public squares; but they found little occasion to describe them in their note-books, though they were all worth looking at.   They were taken through some of the streets occupied by the poorer classes and to the great cigar factories.   Then they went a little way into one of these, where thousands of women of all the lower grades of the city were employed, so that they obtained a good idea of the establishment.

They were taken to the landing-place as agreed,

and embarked immediately in the Blanchita for the ship, where all were to lunch, feeling that they had seen all of the city that they wished to visit. The consuls went with them, but all were tired enough to rest during the hour given them for the luncheon.   At the expiration of the hour, the commander remorselessly drove them on board of the steam-yacht for an excursion up the Pasig to *Lago de Bahia*, which is Spanish for Lake of the Bay.

Some of the party were tired; but the captain declared that they could rest in the little steamer, and remain seated all the afternoon if they chose. A skilful pilot for the river and lake had been obtained by Mr. Gollan, who devoted himself especially to the pacha and the princess, for they were the passengers of the English steamer, though he was very kind and polite to all the company. Above the bridge the passengers began to open their eyes, for they had explored the river below this point.

The captain and Mrs. Belgrave (of course), with Miss Blanche, Mr. Webb, and the " Big Four," were all in what had been called the fore cabin in the Borneo cruises.   It was as handsomely and comfortably fitted up as the after cabin, with an awning overhead, and curtains at the side, which were regulated by the relative positions of the boat to the sun. Two of the English sailors, dressed in their white uniforms, were on board to adjust these curtains, and do any other work required of them.

"There's a dead man on a raft!" exclaimed Mrs. Belgrave, pointing ahead.

"The man is not so dead as he might be," replied the consul, laughing. "But the raft is something worth looking at for you. The affair is simply a native going to market with his cocoanuts. Ask the engineer to whistle sharply," he added to one of the sailors; and it was done.

Suddenly the man on the raft sprang to his feet, and looked around him. The launch was stopped to enable the party to see his craft.

"You can see that his boat is a lot of cocoanuts, a hundred or more, strung together with lines. The raft easily floats the man, with the current, down to the city, where he sells his fruit, and then walks back, or rows in a passage-boat for his fare," Mr. Webb explained forward, and Mr. Gollan aft.

Presently they came to a little village where half a dozen dark-colored girls, with their long hair dragging in the water, were swimming in a small bay at the side of the stream like so many nymphs. It was an aquatic frolic, and the Naiads were enjoying themselves to their hearts' content. By the riverside was a house on stilts, with an open door, from which the tourists saw two girls dive into the stream, and swim away as though the water were their natural element. They cut up all sorts of capers, to the great amusement of the party; and then two of them swam to the launch, and held out their hands. They received a couple of pesetas each from the captain and the pacha. Then all the rest of them followed their example, and were rewarded in like manner.

The Blanchita resumed her course up the river at her usual speed; and the voyagers found enough to interest them, and enough in the explanations of the consuls to instruct them. The boat rushed by the barges and passage-boats as though they were at anchor. The villages and the houses reminded them of those they had seen on the Menam in the vicinity of Bangkok.

"Do you notice the horned cattle?" asked Mr. Webb. "They call them buffaloes here."

"They are what we should call broad-horns at home," replied the captain. "I never saw any such wide-spreading and long horns as I see here."

"I am told that you have a quartet of Nimrods in your company; and I am sure they would find plenty of sport in the country beyond the lake, where the wild buffalo is to be found in herds as on our Western prairies formerly. But they are a dangerous beast to hunt; for they will fight like tigers, and not a few hunters have been killed by them."

"We should like to try them; and with rifles good for nine shots, I think we could take care of ourselves," replied Louis.

They found plenty of buffaloes on the shores of the river, but they were as tame as doves. At one place on the bank they saw a naked boy of ten fooling with one of them, jumping over him, and being dragged by his tail. It was but a short trip to the lake for the Blanchita, and the party sailed all around it. They were all delighted with the excursion; and the launch was hurried down the river, and reached the Blanche, where they were to dine at seven o'clock.

CHAPTER XXXI

HALF A LECTURE ON CHINESE SUBJECTS

THE dinner on board of the Blanche was fully up to the standard of the epicureans on board of both steamers; for the cooks of both had been busy all day, and the consuls declared that it was fully equal to the best of which they had partaken in London or Paris. As it was to be the last time the tourists were to meet these excellent and accomplished officials, the occasion was a very jolly affair. Speeches were made by both of them, in which they were lavish in praise of both the dinner and the elegant accommodations of both the steamers.

Captain Ringgold replied, returning the most hearty thanks to both of the official gentlemen for their kindness in acting as the guides of the travellers, and for the interesting and valuable information they had given them. Both of them had declared that the company ought to remain in Manila at least a week; but the commander pleaded the long voyage still before the ships, and repeated what he had so often said before, that, in such a long cruise as they were taking, it was quite impossible to do anything more than obtain a specimen of each country or island they visited.

When they left the table the consuls took leave individually of each of the passengers, and were sent on shore in the barge of the Blanche, for the steam-launch had already been taken upon the deck of the ship. During the day both steamers had taken in a supply of coal, and the chief stewards had procured stores of provisions, ice, and especially fruit. As the party were taking leave of the two agreeable gentlemen, they heard the hissing of steam on the Blanche, which they did not quite understand, as the commander or Captain Sharp "had made no sign." The Guardian-Mother's people were taken on board, after another leave-taking, and conveyed to their ship in their own boats.

"What is going on, Captain Ringgold?" asked Mrs. Belgrave, when she heard the hissing steam on board of the Guardian-Mother.

"Going on to Hong-Kong," replied the commander.

"To-night?"

"To-night."

"But we have been here only one day," suggested the "first lady."

"The anchor is hove short; but if you think of anything more that you wish to see in Manila or its vicinity, I will remain," added the captain.

"I don't know that there is anything more to be seen. I seemed to know the city before I had seen it."

"Very well, then we will go to sea to-night."

By ten o'clock the ships were under way; and in a couple of hours more they were in the China Sea, headed north-west-by-north, for Hong-Kong. The sea was as smooth as glass, for the east monsoon seemed to be interrupted under the lee of the islands. The passengers retired at an early hour, and there was no excuse for not going to sleep at once.

In the morning the ship was a long way out of sight of land. Breakfast had been ordered for an hour later than usual, in order to let the party sleep off the fatigue of the day before. But some of them were on deck at sunrise, and saw the beautiful phenomenon of that orb coming out of the eastern sea. There was not an island or anything else in sight but the broad expanse of water. The air was delightful; and it was not hot in the early morning, and under the awnings it would not be during the day. A gentle sea gave the ship a little motion, but it was a quiet time.

Breakfast was served at the appointed hour; and at this time Mr. Gaskette was busy with his assistants, arranging the frame for a new map, considerably larger than any used before, at the head of Conference Hall. He had been at work upon it for several days, and he intended that it should surpass anything he had done before. The orang-outang, the monkey, and the pheasant had been removed to the library, where there was plenty of room for them.

China was a great country, and the professor thought it would require a long talk to dispose of it; and the conference was called for ten o'clock, and so announced at breakfast time. When the passengers went on deck, the first thing that attracted their attention was the new map; and considering that it was made on board of the ship, it was a beautiful piece of work, for the second officer was an artist. At the appointed hour they were all in their seats.

This map, though correct at the time it was made, did not, of course, include the changes which resulted from the war between Japan and China, and which have not even yet been incorporated in modern history. The pacha had been invited to give the lecture on China; but he declared that it was too difficult a subject for him to undertake, and he begged to be excused, and Professor Giroud had willingly undertaken it. It had required all his time on the voyage from Saigon, and all his spare time at Manila, to prepare himself for the difficult task. With the three siamangs in their usual places, he mounted the platform.

A signal from the Blanche caused him to resume his seat, and the screw was stopped. The barge from the consort dropped into the water; and the general, his wife, the rajah, Mrs. Sharp, and Dr. Henderson came on board, and chairs were provided for them. Miss Blanche gave up the baby to Mrs. Noury, who was very fond of the little creature.

The professor then took his place again on the rostrum, with the pointer in his hand.

"Mr. Commander, ladies and gentlemen," he began. "Before I say a word, I desire to acknowledge my very great obligations to Mr. Gaskette for the elegant map he has prepared and placed before us. You observe that it extends from the Amur River, — which is spelled in older books Amoor; but the latest fashion is to make it Amur, as Hindu and similar words have been changed from oo to u, for both have the same sound in most European and Oriental names, — from the Amur River to Tonquin, about thirty degrees of latitude, with the nineteen provinces of China, with Korea, properly spelled with initial K, with the islands of Formosa and Hainan. It has given the artist a great deal of labor, and he has done his work in a manner to call for your highest commendation."

The audience vigorously applauded this statement; and the siamangs added their "Ra! Ra! Ra!" with a volley of squeaks. Mr. Gaskette bowed his acknowledgments; and the professor handed him the pointer, which looked like a new arrangement.

"The artist is as well or better acquainted with the map than I am, and I have invited him to assist on the platform. Manchuria, and I adopt the most modern spelling of the name," continued the professor, as the artist pointed to the province.

"I thought the subject for to-day was China," interposed Mrs. Belgrave.

"So it is, madam; but the modern history of China begins with Manchuria. On the west of it is Mongolia, which any of the old-fashioned gentlemen may call Chinese Tartary if they prefer, though that designation is not in use now. Manchuria is a province of China; though the latter was a province of the former three hundred and fifty years ago, for then it conquered China, whose present emperor is the descendant of the conquering Manchu monarch. Manchuria has an area of 280,000, and a population of 21,000,000; but not more than one million of the people are Manchus, who wear the costume and speak the language of the Chinese. The rest of the people are emigrants from China or other countries, and are as industrious and prosperous as any other in the vast empire.

"The Manchus are the aristocracy of the country; and ever since they gave China its ruler, their country has been the principal territory for recruiting the Celestial armies; and there are said to be 80,000 of their soldiers in service. And they also furnish China with its magistrates and police. But I will leave their country to take its place with the other provinces of the empire. China is believed by its own chronologists to have been in existence 2637 years before the Christian era, and perhaps from a date still farther back; but these dates are doubtful.

"The people of China do not know their country by the name so familiar to us, or they know it only so far as they have learned it from merchants and travellers. In the matter of names they all seem barbarous to us; I do not attempt to pronounce them; and I don't think you will succeed in doing so any better than I have. I may add that I have never been in China; and what I tell you I did not pick up myself, but must derive it from others who have travelled and lived in the country.

"I have obtained nearly all my information from the very learned and valuable article of Dr. Legge, in Chambers's. He is familiar with the language of the Chinese, has travelled and lived in the country, and is fully acquainted with the manners and customs of the people. In the oldest literature of the empire, it is called *Hwâ Hsiâ*, the first word meaning 'flowery,' and the second is the proper name of the country. Chung Kwo is the Middle Kingdom, which came into being in the feudal period, in the midst of the several states and tribes; and if you wish to know more of China, there is an American edition of Dr. Williams in four volumes, which will tell you all about it. But the name did not mean the middle of the earth, as sometimes claimed, nor is it the foundation of the derisive term applied to China, 'The Central Flowery Nation.'

"Other names have been given to China, though seldom seen or heard; but Cathay, perhaps coming from the Russian name Kitai, is not at all uncommon, especially in poetry. The name we use comes to us from India, when two Buddhist missionaries, who came from 'the land of Chin,' called it China and Chintan.

"As stated before, the native Chinese line of rulers, the Ming dynasty, conquered China in 1644, and placed the first of the Tsing monarchs on the throne. I will not tangle up your intellects by following out the individuals of the succession any farther than to say that the present emperor, or Hwangti, of China is Tsait'ien, who was proclaimed as such in January, 1875. The ruler may name his successor, for the descent is not hereditary to his eldest son; and if he fails to do so, the default is made good by his family. He is the ninth emperor of the Manchu or Tartar dynasty.

"As I said, China has nineteen provinces, including the island of Formosa, all of which are represented on the map before you. The divisions of the country are immensely populous; though the average of the whole to the square mile is less than that of Belgium by nearly one-half, several of whose provinces are more densely peopled than any in China. It is also less than the State of Rhode Island, and but a little above that of Massachusetts, — the two States the most densely inhabited in our own country.

"Many say that the population of China has been exaggerated; and it is variously given at from 282,000,000 to 413,000,000, a very great difference, and you suit yourselves with the figures if you can. Dr. Legge thinks that 400,000,000 is not an overestimate. The area of the eighteen provinces is

1,336,841 square miles, to which about 15,000 may be added for Formosa; but the area of the whole Chinese empire is 4,218,401, while that of the United States, including Alaska, is 3,501,409.

"If you look at the map, you will see that there are numerous chains of mountains in the countries lying west of China, especially in Tibet, while China proper has but few of them. The land generally slopes from the several ranges to the sea, but I will not perplex you with the names of them. The rivers, of course, flow from the mountains, and you can see that they have space for a long course. They are generally called *ho* in the north, and *chiang* or *kiang* in the south. The Ho, Hoang-ho, or Yellow River, and the Chiang, known to us as the Yang-tsze Chiang, must be over three thousand miles long. I will not follow them from source to mouth. Canton, or *Choo-Chiang* River, which means Pearl River, is also a very large stream. All these waterways, you notice on the map, have a general course from west to east. All of them are navigable, though the Hoang-ho is less so than the Yang-tsze Chiang, the 'most beloved' of the Chinese; for its counterpart in the north is a turbid stream, so tricky that it changed its course in 1853 so that its mouth is now about two hundred and fifty miles north of where it was before that date."

Mr. Gaskette pointed out the former course, which he had indicated by double dotted lines, and that of the present course to the Gulf of Pe-chi-li.

"Chinese history begins twenty-four hundred years before our era, when the first human kings of Egypt were on the throne, with the narrative of a tremendous inundation, which some have identified as that of the Flood in the Old Testament. But the floods did not cease with that event, for several others have followed. As late as 1887, only half a dozen years ago, the treacherous Hoang-ho broke loose, and poured its waters into the populous province of Honan, tearing everything to pieces and destroying millions of lives. There have been so many of these floods that they have given the great river the name of 'China's Sorrow.' But the Manchu rulers are repairing damages, and providing against such disasters in the future.

"I have to speak next about the Grand Canal and the Great Wall; but I will defer it for half an hour for a recess, for I think you must be tired of the dry details I have been giving you," said the professor, as he stepped down from the rostrum.

The company then promenaded the deck for the time indicated.

CHAPTER XXXII

THE CONTINUATION OF THE LECTURE

A WALK of half an hour had freshened up the minds and bodies of the passengers, and they took their places on the promenade for the continuation of the lecture. The professor had been to his stateroom, and returned with additional notes.

"Dr. Legge quotes Marco Polo, the greatest traveller of the Middle Ages, who visited China in the thirteenth century," the speaker began, taking a paper from the table, and reading as follows in regard to the Grand Canal: " 'Kublâi caused a water communication to be made in the shape of a wide and deep channel dug between stream and stream, between lake and lake, forming as it were a great river on which large vessels can ply.' Kublâi was the first sovereign of one of the old dynasties.

"The canal extended from Peking, the capital, in the north, to the south of the empire, a distance of six hundred miles; and it was in use all the way in former times. The Chinese were not distinguished as navigators; but in modern times steamers ply between Canton and the ports of the Gulf of Pe-chi-li, so that the canal is less necessary, and much of it is in bad condition.

"The Great Wall is better known to all the world than the Grand Canal as a peculiarly Chinese wonder, and every school boy and girl has heard of it. It was built as a defence against the raids of the northern tribes, though for this purpose it was a failure; but it still stands, though some of the English newspapers only a few years ago treated it as a myth; yet there is no doubt whatever of its existence, for it has been visited by many reliable English and American travellers. It was begun two hundred and fourteen years before the Christian era.

"Our artist has indicated the wall on the map;" and Mr. Gaskette pointed it out on the west shore of the Gulf of Liau-tung, properly a part of the Gulf of Pe-chi-li, and traced it some distance to the west. "Its length, following its numerous twists and bends, through valleys and over mountains, is fifteen hundred miles. It is twenty-five feet wide at the base, and fifteen at the top. It is formed by two walls of brick, different from those we use, weighing from forty to sixty pounds; and the space between them is filled with earth and stones. It varies in height from fifteen to thirty feet.

"The top of the wall is paved with brick, but is now overgrown with grass. Along the wall, and not on it, are towers of brick at intervals. You observe that at Peking the wall makes a sweep to the north, perhaps thirty miles or more, enclosing a square of land of this extent outside of the general

course of the structure. I met an American gentleman who had been to the capital of China, and he
told me he had been to the Great Wall. Dr. Legge
may take the conceit out of some travellers when
he says: 'What foreigners go to visit from Peking
is merely a loop-wall of later formation, enclosing
portions of Chih-li and Shan-hsî.'

"Leaving the Grand Canal and the Great Wall,
we will pass on to the lakes of China. They are
not on a large scale, like the rivers; and they are
insignificant compared with those of our own country.
The Tung-ting Hû appears to be the largest, mostly
in the province of Hunan, which is sixty-five or
seventy miles long. The others are Po-yang Hû,
in Chiang-hsî, and the Tai Hû, which is noted for
its romantic scenery and numerous islets.

"The temperature of the various provinces is on
the average lower than any other country in the
same latitude. There is every variety of climate
in the vast territory of China. The natives consider
the three southern provinces, including the island
of Hainan, less healthy than the other portions of
the country; but foreigners find no difficulty in residing in them. In a region taking in over twenty
degrees of latitude, the productions vary from those
of the tropics to those in the latitude of central
New York, from bananas and pineapples in the south
to wheat and Indian corn in the north.

"About all the common grains are raised in the
north, and rice is the staple product of the south.

All sorts of vegetables and herbs, ginger, and various condiments, are produced and largely used; though I believe the people are not so hot, gastronomically, in their taste as we found them in Batavia and some other places in the islands. They raise the cane and make sugar in Formosa and the southern provinces. All the fruits of our own country, including Florida and Louisiana, are grown in different parts of China. Opium, which formerly came into the country only from India, is now produced even in Manchuria.

"The Chinese are pre-eminently agriculturists, and farming is their occupation above anything else. In the spring the emperor turns over a few furrows in a sacred field, introducing the work of the season; and the chief official in every province does the same, keeping the importance of farming pursuits always before the people. The tools they use are very primitive; the hoe being the principal hand-tool, and the plough of ancient use for animal power. There is an extensive application of irrigation, which is found to be so necessary in some of our extreme Western States. In the north wells are used; and various simple machinery is employed to raise water when the canal or river is below the level of the field where it is needed, which you may have an opportunity to see.

"No kind of fertilizer is wasted, and some are used which are often neglected in other countries. A great deal of fun and sarcasm is applied to the food of the Chinese, but most of us rather approved the dishes set before us by our host of the Flowery Nation in Singapore. In some articles used for culinary purposes, Parisians go beyond the Chinese, as in the use of horse-beef. I have been in a provision store in Paris where nothing else was sold ; and every part of the animal was economized, including the liver, kidneys, and tongue, and sausages of this meat were on view and for sale to epicures in this flesh. But I believe the Chinese do not eat the horse, unless it be in a season of famine ; and they had to eat cats in Paris during the siege of 1870.

"When you go into the markets you may see whole dogs dressed for food, or cut up into pieces ready for cooking. These are not common yellow dogs, such as you saw in the capital of the Turkish empire; but they are the peculiar Chinese breed, sleek and hairless, which are carefully fatted, and prepared for market. I have no doubt that your stomachs revolt at the very idea of eating dog; but I cannot see that it is any worse than eating pork and fowls, which feed more or less on animal food. However, I do not hanker after dog-meat.

"The Buddhist religion prevails to a great extent here, which diminishes the quantity of beef used, though not so much as the kindly feeling towards the creature that is so useful in tilling the soil. Pork is the most common in use for meat, and the number of pigs raised is enormous. Geese and ducks are abundant, artificially hatched as in ancient Egypt, and to a considerable extent in America, and are largely used for food.

"The sea, rivers, and lakes supply fish in all needed quantities. They are taken in nets, and also by a novel method of fishing with which you cannot be familiar. A boat goes out with a number of cormorants trained for the purpose, which are fishers by nature. The birds dive and bring up the fish, which they deposit in the hand-nets of the boatman.

"Dr. Legge says the Chinese are not gross feeders, as generally represented, except the very poor, and that a Chinese dinner of twenty-seven courses 'may hold its own with the most luxurious tables.' He adds that the famous bird's-nest soup is a misnomer; but he admits that nests from the Indian Archipelago are sliced into other soups, in his opinion without improving the flavor.

"For a drink, tea has superseded every other beverage, and is taken without sugar or milk. It was not used at all in ancient times, but its use is universal at the present time. The plant is not grown in the north. Black tea comes from the central provinces, and green from two eastern mainly. Next to silk, if not equal to it, tea is the principal article of export. The doctor says that tea-drinking promotes the temperance of the people more than any other influence. Alcoholic liquors are distilled from rice and millet.

"From the twelfth century B.C. the literature of

the nation abounds in temperance lectures, warning the people against the injury of strong drinks; but tea has done vastly more to prevent their use than anything else. As a people at home the Chinese make little use of liquors, though that is not always the case with those who live in New York. They do not sit down to tea as we do, but keep it at hand at all times, and treat their visitors with it. Tea is written in the vernacular of the natives *ch'â*. When it was first imported into England it was called *t'ay;* but those who gave it the name were doubtless Irishmen, and they still stick to it.

"There is no doubt that silk was first produced in China; and silk, linen, and cotton form the clothing of the people. A ceremony like that with the plough is performed by the emperor over the silkworms and mulberry-trees, whose leaves are the food of the worm. From before the twenty-third century B.C., the care of the silkworm, and the spinning and weaving of the thread from the cocoon, has been the particular labor of the women. The mulberry-tree grows everywhere in the country, and silk is manufactured in greater or less quantities in every province.

"The cotton-plant has been propagated in China; and the cloth is largely used there, though not equal in finish to the imported article, but is heavier and more lasting in wear. Nankeen comes from Nanking. There are no fireplaces in the houses; and the people keep warm, if they can, by increasing their clothing. Woollen goods are not manufactured to any great extent.

"I will not describe the pagodas, pavilions, bridges, and palaces; for you will see them for yourselves. The streets of the cities in the south and some in the north are no better than mere lanes; and the crowds of people hustling through them fill them about full, and make you think the place is vastly more populous than it really is. As a set-off to this idea, you will wonder what has become of the women, for you rarely meet any of them.

"The streets are paved with stone slabs, badly drained, and abounding in bad odors, and you are not likely to enjoy your walks through them; but they have magnificent names, which you will not read at the corners, such as the street of Benevolence, Righteousness, etc. When you go into the house of a tolerably well-to-do family, you will find the quantity of furniture rather scanty, and not luxurious. The floor may be covered with matting, but you will find no carpets or rugs. A table and some straight-backed chairs are the principal pieces. On the walls you may find Chinese pictures, which will not challenge your admiration, though they may be artistic in China. Some jars and specimens of fine porcelain may adorn the room, with writings on the walls expressing moral sentiments. There may be a couch, or more of them, of bamboo and rattan.

"The bamboo is quite as important a production in China as we have found it in India and the islands;

and it is used for all the purposes here, and more in addition than have been mentioned to you before. The bastinado of the magistrate and the schoolmaster's instrument of torture are both bamboos.

"Our Nimrods would not find much sport here; for the country is too densely populated to afford hiding-places for wild animals, though a bear or a tiger may sometimes appear, and is quickly killed. There are elephants, rhinoceroses, and tapirs in the forests of Yun-nan; and the emperor has tame elephants at Peking for state purposes. The brown and the black bear are found in certain localities, as well as varieties of deer.

"The domestic four-footed animals are small horses and small cattle, which have not been improved. The donkey is a livelier beast than in England or America. About the capital there are very fine mules, which are fashionable there as they are in some parts of Spain. Birds of prey are common, and magpies are sacred birds which the Nimrods must not shoot. The people are very fond of songbirds and flowers, which proves their good taste.

"There are vast quantities of minerals beneath the soil of the country, yet little had been done in mining; though, since the government has steamers of its own, they are doing more to develop the mines. The currency of the country is nowhere; for the only coin that is legally current is the copper *cash*, of which it takes ten to make our cent. Large payments are made in silver by weight, and the housekeeper has to keep a pair of scales handy to ascertain the value of the silver she receives or expends.

"But I know, my friends, that I have wearied you; and though I have something more to say about this very interesting country, I shall defer it till such time as the commander shall appoint."

The professor bowed and retired; but, as an offset to his last remark, the applause was more prolonged and vigorous than usual.

CHAPTER XXXIII

THE CONCLUSION OF THE LECTURE

AT lunch the passengers talked about the lecture that was not yet finished; and all of them who said anything declared that they were very much pleased with it, and they hoped the remainder of it would be given in the afternoon. Of course all of them had read more or less about China; and while there was much that was new to them, they were glad to have their knowledge of the country revived.

"I have been in Hong-Kong, Canton, and Shang-hai, and I have heard no lecture on board that pleased me more than that to which we listened this forenoon; and I appoint this afternoon at three o'clock for the conclusion of it," said the commander.

At this hour all the company, including the passengers from the Blanche, were in their places; and the speaker mounted the rostrum, apparently as fresh as ever. He was received with as much and as earnest applause as had been given at the end of the second part of his lecture; and with this pleasant approval of his work, he continued his discourse.

"According to the accounts of all recent travellers, the roads of China are in a villanously bad condition, and there are no railroads worth mentioning," he began. "And yet the necessity of good common roads was apparent to the ruler, even before the building of the Great Wall, and twenty thousand of them have been constructed; but the Chinese, having finished a great work, do not meddle with it again. The roads have never been repaired thoroughly, and that accounts for their present condition. The rivers and canals furnish the principal means of communication, though the roads are still used.

"The dress of the poorer classes is very much the same for both sexes. It is regulated by sumptuary laws for all classes; but it is varied by the wealthy in the use of costly material, and the ornaments they add to it. You have all seen Chinamen enough in the streets of New York and other cities, and the dress they wear is about the same as that worn in their native land. The queue is the most notable thing about them. This was not the ancient custom of wearing the hair, but was introduced and enforced by the Manchu rulers over three hundred years ago, when it was considered a degrading edict; though now the Chinaman sticks to his queue with as much tenacity as he does to his very life.

"The small feet of the women, even of the highest class, is quite as notable as the queues. This species of deformity was not required by the Manchus, for they wore their feet as God gave them; and it is not an ancient custom, for it has prevailed only from the sixth century of our era. Nature's growth is checked by tightly bandaging the feet in early childhood, subjecting the victim to severe pain and discomfort. But you will see the women for yourselves, and can judge of the effect upon them. The very poor and those in menial conditions are not necessarily subjected to the torture, but fashion carries even many of this class into the custom. Small but natural feet are the pride of our young ladies, and some of them complain that when the feet were given out they got more than their share.

"The sexes are kept apart until marriage; and this has been a social feature from the earliest time. Girls and boys in the family did not occupy the same mat or eat together from the age of seven, and when the former were ten they ceased to appear outside of the women's apartments. Girls were taught manners therein, to handle the cocoons, to do all the work appertaining to the manufacture of silk and the details of Chinese housekeeping. This was in the feudal time; and the females were not instructed in book-learning, and are not now, though they pick up something of an education, and learned women are not unknown, even those who have written books.

"In regard to marriage, the parents have entire control, and professional match-makers are an institution. It is to a great extent a matter of horoscopes. Usually the bride and groom have not seen each other till the marriage ceremony, and of course they lose all that delightful period which precedes the event. But they appear to take to each other when brought together, and to be happy as man and wife. Though the man has one legal wife, there is no law or custom to prevent him from taking half a dozen more secondary wives.

"There are seven lawful grounds for divorcing a wife from her husband, — disobedience to her husband's parents; failure to give birth to a son; dissolute conduct; jealousy of her man, especially in regard to the *other* wives; talkativeness; thieving; and leprosy. I will leave the ladies to make their own comments. There are three considerations which may set aside these reasons for divorce, — that her parents are no longer living; that she has passed with her spouse through the years of mourning for his parents; and that he has become rich after being poor. The children are often affianced in childhood, and probably this fact furnishes many of the grounds for proceedings in the divorce court.

"Infanticide is not an uncommon crime in China, female children being almost always the victims. Probably its prevalence is somewhat exaggerated. It is among the poorest class that this atrocity prevails, the universal desire for male children, in connection with the ancestral worship of the people, being the root of the evil. Public opinion is against the practice, though not as decidedly as might be wished.

"The complexion of the Chinese is yellowish, as you have seen in our streets; and from the extreme north to the Island of Hainan, they all have long black hair, almond or oblique eyes, high cheek-bones, and round faces. They are greatly addicted to opium and gambling wherever you find them. Dr. Legge says that the longer one lives among them the better he likes them, and the better he thinks of them; but we are not likely to be able to test the correctness of this remark.

"The Chinese bury their dead in graves in the form of a horseshoe, and with an almost infinite variety of ceremonies and sacrifices. Where the friends are able to pay the expense, the last rites are ostentatious and very costly. You may chance to see something of them before you leave the country. When a very rich Chinaman travels, he takes his coffin with him.

"They have no day in the week corresponding to our Sunday, but they have an annual universal holiday at New Year's. It is a season of rejoicing and festivity all over the country. Stores are closed for several days, and the government offices are shut up for a month. The people 'dress up,' and the temples are visited, the gambling resorts are in full blast, and crackers and other fireworks make Fourth of July of the season.

"There is some sort of a festival every month, such as the 'Feast of Lanterns,' on the full moon, of the tombs, 'Dragon Boats,' and 'All Souls,' in honor of departed relatives, when the supposed hungry spirits from the other side of the Styx are fed at the cemeteries. The people are extravagantly fond of theatricals; and a kind of bamboo tent is erected for the performance, which is usually of inordinate length. Females, as in India, do not appear on the stage.

"It would be quite impossible for me to follow the consecutive history of China from 2637 B.C. down to the present time; it would be an infliction upon you, and I shall only mention some of the principal events. Our authority in these remarks numbers the Chinese army at three hundred and fifty thousand; the Year Book makes it double this number. Judged by a European standard, it does not amount to much outside of mere numbers; though in addition to it there is a sort of militia, camped in the several provinces, more in the nature of police than soldiers, of twice as many men as the imperial army.

"The first great war in China was the Tâi-Ping rebellion, which the older of you can remember. It began in 1851, and was continued for nearly twenty years. Its leader was Hung, a poor student, who studied up a new religion, which was certainly an improvement upon those of the people, for it recognized the Great God, and Christ as the Elder Brother. A strict morality and the keeping of the Sabbath were required of its adherents, and idolatry and the use of opium were forbidden.

"Hung incited the rebellion; and its object was to overturn the ruling dynasty of the Manchus, and place himself on the throne. It was at first very successful in its progress, and it looked as, though the imperial cause was doomed. In 1855 the rebels, for the want of sufficient re-enforcements in an attempt to capture Pekin, were compelled to retreat to Nanking, and then the decline of the insurrection began. A body of foreigners under an American by the name of Ward joined the imperialists, and rendered important service; but he was killed in battle in 1862. He was succeeded by one of the subordinates, who became General Burgevine; and he was quite as successful as General Ward had been. The new general fell out with the government, and retired. By the influence of British residents at Shanghai, who had organized an effective army, General Charles George Gordon, of whom you heard in Egypt, was placed in command. He captured Nanking, and the rebellion was suppressed in 1865.

"You have been informed of the movements of the Portuguese, English, French, Dutch, and Spaniards to obtain territory in the East from 1497, when Vasco da Gama doubled the Cape of Good Hope. All of them established colonies; and in 1516 they began to send their ships to China, whose people did not receive them kindly. This was in the early days of the Manchu rulers, who claimed to be superior to all other monarchs on the face of the earth; they would not acknowledge the visitors as their equals, and regarded them as vassals.

"When the Chinese ruler learned of the conquests

of those from the West he tried to prevent their approach to his dominions.   But trade had been established; and the opium traffic had its birth, and the people were crazy to procure and smoke it.   This was the cause of the wars between China and England and France, with the vassal question.   In 1800 an edict of the emperor prohibited the importation of opium into his dominions.

"England before this had entered upon the task of making a treaty to settle the relations between the two countries; but no treaty was made, and the smuggling of opium continued for many years.   In 1816 another embassy went to Pekin; but it was summarily and contemptuously dismissed because the ambassador refused to go through the ceremony of repeatedly prostrating himself before the emperor, and acknowledging his own sovereign as a vassal of the emperor.

"The trade went on after India passed to the government of England.   China was still obstinate, insisted upon the vassalship of the Western nation, and was confident in her power to repress the opium trade.   The merchants pressed vigorously for the enlargement of their trade with China, which did not seem to be aware of its weakness before a European power.   A famous mandarin was appointed governor-general of the Kwang provinces to bring the barbarians to their senses.   He proceeded in earnest, and England declared war against the country in 1840.   The result was evident from the first, and the war ended with the peace of Nanking in 1842. The items were the ceding of Hong-Kong to the victor, the opening of five ports to the trade and residence of the British. Correspondence was established between the officials of the two nations; but not a word was said about opium, and the smuggling went on as before.

"In 1857, after some troubles in Canton in which the English were at fault, and the refusal of the governor-general to meet an agent of the British government, the latter declared war again, with France as an ally. Canton was captured the same year; and Yeh, the governor, was taken prisoner, and sent to Calcutta. There was little fighting in this war; and Canton being in possession of the allies, a joint commission, attended by representatives of the United States and Russia, proceeded to Pekin to make their demands upon the emperor. A treaty was made at Tien-tsin, confirming the former, and with many important articles. One provided for the appointment of ambassadors by each nation, another for the protection of Christian missionaries, and several others of less moment.

"It looked as though the Chinese emperor had been sufficiently humiliated; but the treaty 'slipped up,' for its last clause provided that the treaty should be ratified at Pekin within one year. The emperor could not abide the idea of permitting the ambassadors to enter the sacred capital, and he looked about him for the means of escaping the issue. The forts between the capital and the Gulf of Pe-chi-li had been rebuilt and were well armed. The Chinese officials urged the signing at Tien-tsin, and this was done by several of the embassy; but France and England insisted that it must be signed in Pekin, as provided in the instrument itself.

"They started for the sacred city with several men-of-war, but they found the mouth of the river closed to them by the forts. A severe engagement followed, in which the allies were beaten, the only battle gained by the Chinese. At the end of a year another expedition with twenty thousand men went with the ambassadors, the forts were all taken, and the officials went to Tien-tsin. The force marched on Pekin; and the emperor fled, leaving his brother Prince Kung to meet the embassy. The north-east gate of the city was surrendered, and the treaty was duly signed at Pekin.

"In 1861 the emperor died, having named his son, six years old, as his successor. A dozen years later he took possession of the throne, the regency expiring then. He died two years later, and a nephew of Prince Kung was appointed to the succession by the imperial family. He was a child of four years of age then, and reigned under a regency till 1887, when he took possession of the government at the age of sixteen.

"I should have said before that a change of the tariff in 1842 made the importation of opium legal in the empire. The country has in recent years employed foreign officers in its army and navy, and foreign mechanics in its workshops. China is represented at five of the principal nations of the world by ambassadors. It has built up a very respectable navy, mostly at the shipyards of Great Britain; and foreign officers have greatly improved the condition of the army.

"Telegraphic communication has been extensively established, and a railroad eighty-one miles long has been built. Educational institutions have been founded, and schools opened for the instruction of young men in several foreign languages. The increasing consumption of opium, which seems to have been placed in the way of the people by the action on the part of England, is a cause for great regret among the friends of China. I have said too much already, and I know you must be very tired. I thank you for bearing with me so long; and I will promise not to do so again, at least so far as China is concerned. China is at peace with all the world, and I leave her so."

The professor retired with even greater applause than in the forenoon. Since he spoke, China has been engaged in a great war with Japan; and possibly his account of the country will assist those who are yet to read the history of the conflict.

CHAPTER XXXIV

SIGHT-SEEING IN HONG-KONG AND CANTON

AFTER the conclusion of the lecture in the afternoon, the passengers of the two ships had another frolic, as Captain Ringgold called it, and then dined in the cabin; after which those from the Blanche "went home," as the ladies termed it.

Towards the close of the following day, while the passengers of the Guardian-Mother were seated on the promenade, the lookout forward shouted, "Land, ho!" The announcement caused a sensation, as usual, though it was an old story. It was reported off the port bow; and the captain said it was Lema Island, a considerable distance from Hong Kong.

"The Chinese name of Hong-Kong is Hiang-Kiang, which means 'sweet waters,'" said the commander. "It is a ridge of rocks, the highest point of which is over eighteen hundred feet above the water. It is ninety miles south by east of Canton. The island has an area of twenty-nine square miles, and is not more than half a mile from the main shore. It is a barren rock, and you will hardly see a speck of vegetation on the whole of it. In the south-west corner of the island is the city of Victoria, with a population of two hundred and twenty-one thousand; and it is one of the great centres of trade with Western nations. The principal import is opium, and the principal exports are tea and silk. We shall anchor soon in its splendid harbor."

An English pilot was taken; and at sunset the ship was at anchor, and the party had abundant occupation in observing the rugged shores, the shipping that filled the harbor, and especially the Chinese boats, in charge of boat-women generally. A few junks were in sight; and they had seen several of them among the islands which form an archipelago at the mouth of Canton River, extending some distance up the stream.

"There are a number of hotels here with English names," said the captain at dinner; "but I shall not trouble you to take a vote on the question of going to one of them, for we shall not remain here long, not more than one day. Our steamers can go up to Canton; but I think we had better go up in one of the regular steamers, not Chinese."

After breakfast the next morning, the first thing in order was to ascend the promontory for the view it would afford. But they could not walk up, it was so difficult and tiresome. Before they left the ship the American consul visited her, and proffered his assistance to the tourists; for he had read about the ships in the papers of some of the ports they had visited.

This gentleman was very kind and very polite, and

while he was on board the party from the Blanche came to the ship in the steam-launch. He was introduced to everybody, and advised the travellers to take Chinese sampans for their visit to the shore, for the novelty of the thing. The water around the ship was covered with them, and a sufficient number of them were taken to accommodate the party. "The colonel," as the consul was generally called, talked "pidgin" English, which is practically a dialect in itself, to the boat-women.

The captain, Mrs. Belgrave, the colonel, and a few others went in the first sampan, and the lady was pleased with the women in charge of the craft; and several children were in a coop at the stern. The price of the craft was ten cents for half an hour. In a few minutes they were landed at the town; and then a crowd of coolies, as the laborers are called here, surrounded the party with sedans and rickshaws, and all were anxious for a job. The passengers waited till all the company had landed, and then took sedans or rickshaws for the Hong-Kong Hotel.

It required twenty of them to accommodate the party. The commander and the consul went into the hotel; and a lunch, or tiffin as it is called here as in India, was ordered for the tourists at one o'clock. Then the colonel instructed the coolies where to go, and the procession started for a round in the city. The buildings are constructed of granite, which is the material of the surrounding heights, the dwellings with verandas.

"How is the weather here, Colonel?" asked the captain, when they stopped to examine a locality.

"The average temperature is seventy-five; and that, of course, gives us some hot days in summer, which is a rainy season. Thunder-storms come often; and once in a while a typhoon breaks in upon us, sometimes doing an immense amount of damage," replied the consul. "But the climate is not unhealthy. If the town had been built around the corner of the island, it would have been cooler, though we could not have had this magnificent harbor."

The company had all descended when a stop was made; and most of them insisted upon walking along Queen's Road in order to have a better opportunity to look into the stores, and see the street traders, for most of the Chinese pursue their business in the open air. The stores were filled with the curious goods peculiar to the East, such as China crapes, porcelain vases, and other wares, and camphor-wood boxes, proof against moths. The shop people were well dressed and extremely polite. Several stores were visited, those indicated by the colonel.

One man, who appeared to be the "boss," sat at a desk with a little brush, or camel's-hair pencil, for the natives do not write with pens, and made a tea-chest character in a kind of book for every article sold. The salesmen were very skilful in handling the goods, and showing them in the most tempting manner. Mrs. Belgrave bought some things that she fancied; and then came up the question as to how to pay for them, for they had no Chinese money. The colonel helped them out by giving cards, like bank-checks, payable by the steward of the Hong merchants.

Continuing the walk, they came to a money-changer. The commander put down two English sovereigns, for which he received a bag full of the current coins, which were not the native *cash*, but the pieces made for Hong-Kong, as they are made for the island of Jamaica, where an English penny will not pass. The smallest was of the value of a cash, or one mill. A cent was about the size of our old copper one, and a ten-cent piece was a little larger than our dime. The value was given in Chinese as well as English for the benefit of the natives; and the cash piece had a square hole in the centre, for the natives keep them on strings or wires.

The captain gave about a half a dollar's worth of this money to each person, so that none need be bothered about paying for small articles. The boys invested a portion of their wealth for a quantity of Swatow oranges, about the size of heavy bullets. They could not understand the native seller, and permitted him to take his pay out of a handful of coins; but he took next to nothing, and they were confident they were not cheated, for he took the same coins from the hands of all.

Among the pedlers all sorts of vegetables were for sale, and the groper-fish, shark-fin soup, meats minced with herbs and onions, poultry cut up and sold in pieces, stewed goose, bird's-nest soup, rose-leaf soup with garlic — heaven with the other place, Scott called it — and scores of other eatables for native palates, and some of them would suit the taste of Americans.

Taking their places in the vehicles, the tourists were borne through the principal streets. There are only five or six thousand English in the city, and Hong-Kong is substantially Chinese. At about eleven, the coolies toted the sedans to the top of the peak, where an observatory is located, following a zigzag path. The approach of every vessel of any consequence is signalled from this elevation by flags. The ascent is difficult, it is so steep; and the bearers of the sedans had to stop and rest occasionally. The view is magnificent, and the consul pointed out the objects of interest.

It was easier to get down the steep than to get up, and the party reached the hotel at the appointed time. The lunch was ready, though it was hardly first-class. When the captain asked about the expense of living for Europeans in China, the colonel said that the price per day at the best hotels was from four to six dollars, and that one could not keep house for less than four thousand dollars a year. In summer the people live in bungalows on the peaks, where quite a town has grown up. The captain paid the bill in English gold. In the afternoon the company made an excursion by a regular steamer to Macao, on the other side of the river, forty miles distant.   It has been a Portuguese settlement since 1557; but it had little interest for the tourists, and they returned by the same steamer, and went on board of the ship.

The colonel dined on board, and the captain announced his intention to go to Canton the following day.   The next morning the tourists were on board of the steamer for that city.   The colonel could not go with them; but he procured a couple of English guides to attend them, one of whom was Mr. Inch and the other Mr. Larch.

"Kwang-tung is the native name of the city to which we are going, and from this the English had made Canton," said Mr. Larch, as the boat left the shore; and he proceeded to name the islands in sight, and point out all objects of interest, as he did all the way up the river.

The city is on the north side of the Choo-Chiang, or Pearl River, ninety miles from Hong-Kong.   They saw nothing of especial interest except a temple on the shore, and a fort with a three-story pagoda rising from the centre of it.   On the arrival of the steamer off the city, she was surrounded by boats as at Hong-Kong.   The captain of the boat recommended one he called Tommy, though it was a woman; and her craft was engaged, with as many more as were needed, indicated by her.

At the landing-place Mr. Seymour, the American consul, to whom the colonel had telegraphed, was waiting for them.   He introduced himself, and was soon on the best of terms with all the tourists. He advised them to go to the International Hotel, and they went there. A score of sedans and rickshaws were at once engaged; and Tommy and the other women carried the valises and bags for them, each attended by the owner. They were to remain three days in Canton. Dinner was the first ceremony they performed after they went to the hotel, and the consul joined the party by invitation.

"Canton is a city with a population estimated at a million and a half, including the people that live in boats from one year's end to the other, and doubtless you noticed their aquatic dwellings as you came up the river," said the consul, who had been invited to tell the company something about the place. "It is surrounded by a wall nine miles in length, built of brick and sandstone, twenty-five to forty feet high, and twenty feet thick, and divided by a partition wall into two unequal parts. There are twelve outer gates, and also gates in the partition wall. The names of these are curious, as Great Peace Gate, Eternal Rest Gate, and others like them. There are more than six hundred streets, lanes you will call them; for they are not often more than eight feet wide, very crooked, and very dirty. This is the general idea of the city, and the details you will see for yourselves."

After breakfast the next morning the party was organized for sight-seeing, and the sedans they had used the day before were ready for them. The two

TEMPLE AND GARDEN IN CHINA.

Page 329.

guides insisted upon going on foot, the better to discharge their duties. They rode through some of the principal streets, looked into the shops, and observed the pedlers; but all was about the same as in Hong-Kong, except that the streets were wider in the latter. The same goods were for sale. They looked into a tea saloon; and the gentlemen entered an opium den, which nearly made some of them sick.

"This is called the Plain pagoda," said Mr. Inch, when they came to it. "It was built a thousand years ago, and is one hundred and sixty feet high."

They were taken to a couple of Joss-houses, or temples. A sort of tower attracted their attention; and they were told that the one before them, and hundreds of others, were occupied each by a watchman at night to call out the hours of the night, and give the alarm in case of fire. They halted before the nine-story pagoda, the most interesting structure they had seen, and the most peculiarly Chinese.

"It is one hundred and seventy feet high, and was built thirteen hundred years ago," Mr. Larch explained. "Brick, covered with marble or glazed tile, is the material used. Each story is smaller than the one below it, and each has a balcony around it."

"Now we come to the Temple of Honam, which is one of the largest in China," said Mr. Inch, as they halted before its gates, after the party got out of the sedans. "With its grounds it covers seven acres, and one hundred and seventy-five priests are employed in it."

"What is the religion of these people?" asked Mrs. Woolridge.

"The priests and nuns of Canton number more than two thousand, and nine-tenths of them are Buddhists. The Temple of Five Hundred Genii contains that number of statues, various in size, and was erected in honor of Buddha and his disciples."

At the usual hour the party went to lunch, and were tired, though they had done but little walking. The sedans were dismissed till the next morning; the afternoon was devoted to an excursion on the river, and Tommy had been directed to provide the boats. They moved through the wilderness of floating dwelling-places, and looked them over with wonder and surprise. Many of the sampans were made of three planks; and the people on board of them, mostly women, were exceedingly amusing.

Large junks, some of them from five hundred to sixteen hundred tons burden, were to be seen, and long, broad, flat Chinese men-of-war, with twenty to forty guns; but the latter are out of fashion now, and modern-built vessels take their places. They have two great painted eyes on the bow to enable them, as the Chinese say, to find their way over the sea. But the most beautiful sight was the flower-boats, having galleries decorated with flowers, and arranged in most fantastic designs. Each of these floating gardens contains one large apartment and a number of cabinets. The walls are hung with mirrors and graceful draperies of silk, and glass chandeliers and colored lanterns are suspended from the ceiling. Elegant little baskets of flowers are hung in various places. It seems very like fairy-land on these boats. They are stationary, and dinners are given on board by the Chinese who can afford them. They are also places of amusement by day and night, and plays, ballets, and conjuring take place at them; but no respectable females frequent them.

During the next two days the tourists continued to wander on foot and in sedans over the city with the guides. One day they went to the great examination hall, 1330 feet long by 583 wide, covering sixteen acres, and containing 8653 cells, in which students are placed so that there shall be no stealing others' work.

When a member of the party asked the meaning of certain tall buildings, he was told that they were pawnbrokers' offices; for the Chinese have a mania for pawning their clothes, or whatever they have, even if not in need of the money, to save the trouble of taking care of the articles. Before the third day of the stay in Canton was over, some of the party had seen enough, and preferred to remain at the hotel while others were out with the guides. The next day they returned to Hong-Kong, and were glad to be once more on board the ships, for sight-seeing is the most tiresome work in the world.

CHAPTER XXXV

SHANG-HAI AND THE YANG-TSZE-CHIANG

THE passengers of the Guardian-Mother were on deck at an early hour the next morning, and the smoke was rising from the funnel as though it was the intention of the commander that she should sail soon; and some of them began to wonder if they were to see anything more of China than could be seen from the deck of the ship.

"Well, ladies and gentlemen, have you seen all you wish of China?" said Captain Ringgold, as he seated himself at the head of the table at breakfast.

"We can put it to vote," suggested Mrs. Belgrave.

"I don't think it is necessary," replied the commander, laughing. "We shall sail this forenoon for Shang-hai, for I suppose that some of you who keep hens wish to see the home of the famous rooster that bears that name."

"I thought yesterday afternoon that I had seen enough of China to last me the rest of my lifetime; but I feel a little different this morning since I got rested," said Mrs. Woolridge.

"It is said that travellers enjoy their visits to foreign countries more after they get home, and think over what they have seen, than they do while going from place to place," added Mrs. Belgrave. "I think of a hundred things I saw in Canton, and did not understand, that I shall recall when I read about China, as I intend to do when I get home."

"That is just my idea!" exclaimed Mrs. Woolridge. "It will take me three years, at least, after I get home to read up what I have seen on this voyage."

Much more in the same general direction was said by others. When they went on deck they found the pilot who had brought the ship into port walking back and forth. He had brought off the *China Mail*, and three other newspapers in English, and a pile of others in Chinese to be kept as curiosities by the party. The captain had obtained his clearance and other papers the day before, as soon as he arrived from Canton, with the assistance of the colonel, who had come off with the pilot to make his adieux. In less than half an hour the ship was under way again, with the Blanche following her.

"How far is it to Shang-hai?" asked Mrs. Belgrave, as she met the captain in front of the pilot-house.

"It is eight hundred and seventy miles, and the voyage will require two days and fourteen hours," he replied. "I shall keep well to the eastward, and if you are up by six to-morrow morning you will see the island of Formosa. Then we shall be about on the Tropic of Cancer, when we shall pass out of the Torrid Zone — out of the tropics."

This information was circulated by the lady among all the passengers. Before noon the ship was out of sight of land, and the voyage was just about the same as it had been in smooth seas and pleasant weather. All the party were seated on the promenade at six o'clock the next morning.

"But there is land on both sides of us, Captain Ringgold," said Mrs. Belgrave. "Which is Formosa?"

"That on your right. We are going through the Formosa Channel; and the islands on the port side are the Pescadores, about twenty miles from Formosa."

After breakfast, when the ship had passed the smaller islands, and the passengers were seated on the promenade, the commander opened upon them with a talk about Formosa: "The name of the island in Chinese is Taiwan; and it is off the province of Fu-chien, and from ninety to two hundred and twenty miles from it. It has an area of 14,978 square miles, or about the size of the States of Massachusetts, Rhode Island, and Connecticut put together. It has a chain of mountains through it, the highest peak of which " —and the speaker looked at his memoranda — "is 12,847 feet high.

"The number of inhabitants is estimated at about 2,000,000, mostly immigrants from China, with the original natives. The island is exceedingly rich in its vegetation, and the plants are about the same as those of the main land. Rice paper is made of the pith of a tree found only in Formosa. In the south sugar and turmeric are the staples. The latter is a plant whose root is bright yellow, used in dyeing silk. Formosa tea has become well known at home as of excellent quality. Other productions are about the same as in southern China.

"There are plenty of birds there, but no wild animals of any consequence that are game for the Nimrods. A great deal more might be said about the island, but you have more now than you are likely to remember. You can see many junks now, and the trade with China is mostly carried on in them; and some of them are pirates in these seas, even to the south of Hainan, for a trading-junk turns into a pirate when her captain can make some money by it."

After lunch the Blanche's people came on board, and all hands had the usual frolic during the afternoon and evening. The next morning the captain told his passengers that they had passed out of the China Sea the day before, and that they were on the Tung-hai, or Eastern Sea, outside of which was the broad Pacific Ocean. On the third morning from Hong-Kong, when the company came on deck, they found the Guardian-Mother at anchor, but just getting under way with an English pilot on board, who had been taken late the evening before.

"Where are we now, Captain Ringgold?" asked Mr. Woolridge, when the party had seated themselves on the promenade to see what was to be seen.

"We are at the mouth of the great river Yang-tsze-Chiang; but we shall soon pass into a branch of it called the Woo-Sung, and find Shang-hai, for it is correctly written with a hyphen between the syllables," replied the commander. "But the tide is right; and we can go over the bar without any delay, the pilot says. It is about twelve miles up the river to the town; and, as you can see, the country is low and flat. The city has 250,000 inhabitants, and is the principal central port of China for foreign trade."

The channel of the river was crowded with junks, and there are sometimes as many as three thousand of them between the town and the sea; but they were careful to keep out of the track of steamers, even though they had the right of way. The two steamers picked their way through the native boats, and they were at anchor off the city in season for the late breakfast ordered.

"Shang-hai stands on low ground; and cholera, dysentery, and fevers prevail here in summer," said the commander when they were all seated at the table. "The English, French, and American quarters are in the suburb north of the native city, and they have broad and clean streets; but in the city proper, they are narrow and filthy, not unlike those of Canton. It is enclosed by a wall five miles in extent. What else there is here you can see for yourselves."

The captain decided, after the pacha came on

board in his barge with the rest of his party, to lunch and dine at the Astor House, perhaps because the name sounded like home; but he found that the hotel "was a horse of another color." They went on shore in some of the native boats that crowded around the ship; and their first care was to secure six guides, all that offered their services on the quay. The next was to procure a supply of the money current in the city, which was accomplished with the aid of the principal guide, all of whom were English, who could speak Chinese and pidgin.

The company were then divided into six parties, who had suggested this plan when they found that this number of guides could be obtained. The " Big Four " went together, and the rest of the company were in parties of three. The conveyances were found to be small, low broughams, pony gigs, palanquins, jinrickishas, and wheelbarrows, the last such as the party had seen in Cholan. The boys decided to walk first, and try the vehicles later. They went into a shop where Louis saw something in a window he wanted, and the guide asked the price for him. The dealer refused to show the article, or to name a price, unless Louis would agree to buy if he did so.

They were not like the Hong-Kong salesmen; for there were several of them, and they were impolite enough to make fun of the tourists. Scott doubled his fists, and was inclined to pitch into the one who refused to show any goods till they were practically sold; but Louis begged him to desist. They next went into a tea saloon in the middle of a dirty pond of water, which would have just suited the taste of a Dutchman at home.

The tea was given to them in the cups, and they poured in hot water. The keeper swindled them in asking about five times the price, and the guide remonstrated; but the fellow was saucy, and the charge was paid to avoid trouble. The guide said the other fellow would have cheated them in the same ratio, if Louis had agreed, as he required, to buy. Then they looked into an opium joint, where the smokers were reclining on broad benches. The pipe was a tube with the bowl on the top. The drug is boiled till it is of the consistency of honey. Something like a knitting-needle is then taken by the smoker, the end of which is dipped in the jar; the needle is then turned till the opium becomes a ball as big as a pea. It is then held in a flame till it is partially lighted, when it is dropped into the bowl of a pipe. The amount used is counted in pipes, some being satiated with two or three of them, while the hard cases require twenty. In either case he goes to sleep, and has pleasant dreams. The habit is very deleterious to those who practise it, and death results from excessive use of the drug.

"There is a sedan with a Chinese magnate in it, with four bearers," said the guide; "but it is not so common here as in Hong-Kong and Canton."

The barrow excited the attention of the boys more than the other vehicles. At the door of the shop they saw a native reading a paper, wearing a pair of spectacles whose eyes were almost as big as saucers. After walking through the streets of Hong-Kong and Canton, the boys saw very little that was new to them.

" Is there a cemetery in the town ? " asked Louis, after they had become somewhat tired, not to say disgusted, with the dirty streets, and the crowd in them.

" Nothing that you Americans would call by that name," replied the guide. " There are some small burial-grounds; but the Chinese generally bury their dead in private grounds, outside of the cities. They have a reverence for their dead which is not equalled by any people on the face of the earth. The graves of the rich and noted are very carefully selected, and are decorated with great care and taste. Some of the finest gardens in the country are those enclosed in a private burial-place.

" A rich Chinaman thinks more of his coffin than he does of his house. He often buys it years before he has occasion to use it, and keeps it, taking better care of it than he does of his female children. Wherever a Chinaman dies, he must be sent home to be buried; and many of them come here from America, taken up from the earth even a year or more after death."

At this point the party came to an open place where there were all the different vehicles used in the city waiting to be employed; and as it was nearly time for the lunch, they decided to ride to the hotel. Louis took a rickshaw, as it is called here; Scott and Morris preferred a wheelbarrow, and Felix took another, balanced by the guide. They were novel conveyances to the boys, and they enjoyed the ride very much. The rest of the parties returned to the hotel about the same time. There were Chinese dishes on the table; and those who had tried some of them before ordered them, especially the bird's-nest soups. The hams were very nice, and the captain hoped that Mr. Sage had procured some of them for the ship.

The afternoon was spent as the forenoon had been, but the party found little to interest them. The next day the tourists made an excursion up the Yang-tsze-Chiang, and enjoyed it very much. They saw a little of the farming operations, as a man ploughing with a buffalo, which looked more like a deer than a bovine; others carrying bundles of grain, one at each end of a pole on their shoulders; another threshing by beating a bunch of the stalks on a frame like a ladder or clothes-horse; but what pleased them most were the fishermen. One had a net several feet square, suspended at the end of a pole. It was sunk in the water, and then hauled up. Any fish that happened to be over it then was brought up with it; but Scott declared that this device was an old story, and they were used in the United States, though an iron hoop was the frame of the net.

They were more interested in the fishing with cormorants. A man with a dip-net in his hand stood on a bamboo raft, on which was a basket like those the snake-charmers use in India, to receive his fish. The birds were about the size of geese. They dived into the water, and brought up a fish every time. They have a ring or cord on their necks so that they cannot swallow their prizes, and they drop them into the dip-net.

They went up as far as Taiping, where they took a returning steamer, and that night slept on board the ships. On the following morning the steamers went down the river; and then the question where they were to go next came up, and the commander soon settled it by announcing that the ship was bound to Tien-tsin, on the way to Pekin.

CHAPTER XXXVI

THE WALLS AND TEMPLES OF PEKIN

THE company had hardly expected that Captain Ringgold would go to the capital, for it was off the course to Japan, which was the next country to be visited; but their curiosity had been greatly excited, and he was disposed to gratify it.

"Pekin is not on navigable water, and we cannot go there in the ship," said he. "We go to Tien-tsin, which is the seaport of Pekin, about eighty miles distant from it. It is a treaty port, and is said to have a population of six hundred thousand; the number can doubtless be considerably discounted. The next thing is to get to Pekin; though we can go most of the way by boat to Tung-chow, thirteen miles from the capital. Some go all the way on horseback or by cart. We will decide that question when we get to Tien-tsin."

"How long will it take us to go there?" asked Uncle Moses.

"About two days; we are off Woo-Sung now. We have the pilot on board, and we shall go to sea at once," replied the commander.

Nothing of especial interest occurred on the voyage; and before noon on the second day out the two ships were off the mouth of the Pei-ho River, and a Chinese pilot was taken. As they went up the river they saw the Taku forts, where the Celestial soldiers won their only victory over the English, but were badly beaten the following year. On the rising tide the ships got up the river, and anchored off the town.

The place was like any other Chinese city, and was quite as dirty as the dirtiest of them. Two of the guides from Shang-hai, who were couriers for travellers, had been brought, one in each ship; and both of them were intelligent men. The Blanchita had been put into the water as soon as the anchors were buried in the mud; and the party went on shore in her, to the great disgust of the boat-people.

The American consul came on board with the Chinese officials; and the commander took him into the cabin for a conference in regard to getting to Pekin, while the tourists were on shore with the guides. Mr. Smithers had seen the steam-launch, and the question was whether the party could go up Pekin River in her. The consul could see no difficulty in the way, any more than there would be in the ships' barges. He thought he could put them in the way of making the trip securely, and they went on shore together in the barge.

Mr. Smithers knew a couple of high officials who were going to the capital the next day, and the commander was introduced to them. They were very polite, and both of them spoke English. One had been educated at Yale College in New Haven. They were invited to go with the party to Pekin in the Blanchita, and accepted. The arrangements were completed for the trip. They went on board of the Guardian-Mother, and were treated with the most distinguished consideration, shown over the ship, and invited to lunch.

When the launch came off with the party at noon, all the ladies and gentlemen were presented to them by the commander. The pacha, the rajah, and the princess were clothed in their elegant robes; and they evidently made a profound impression. The plan for the journey to the capital was announced to the passengers, and they could not help being delighted with it. Mr. Sage had been directed to spread himself on the lunch, and he did so. Monsieur Odervie even prepared a few Chinese dishes, the art of doing which he had learned from a native cook in Hong-Kong.

In the afternoon the party went on shore again, under the escort of Mr. Psi-ning and Mr. Ying-chau, visiting the temple in which the treaties had been signed, and several others, and then walked through the street of "Everlasting Prosperity," as the Chinese gentlemen explained it. The prosperity seemed to consist mainly in the sale of eel-pies with baked potatoes, the former kept hot at a small charcoal fire. Live fish in shallow bowls with a little water in them were common, and cook-shops for more elaborate Chinese dishes were abundant.

Both the native gentlemen were mandarans of different orders, and they were received with the most profound deference by the common people. The tourists saw everything in the town that was worth seeing; and early in the afternoon they returned to the Guardian-Mother, where the consul and the native gentlemen were to dine. The latter were invited to sleep on board in order to be in readiness for an early start the next day, and they had ordered their baggage to be sent to the ship. Mr. Psi-ning said he had telegraphed to an official at Tung-chow to have conveyances ready for the party at that place, which was as far as the boat could go, thirteen miles from Pekin.

Mr. Smithers was exceedingly kind, and did far more than could be expected of a consul. The commander expressed his obligations to him in the most earnest terms for all he had done, and especially for introducing the distinguished Chinese gentlemen. The dinner was the most elaborate the steward and the cook could provide, and it was one of those hilarious affairs which have several times been described during the voyage. In the evening there were Mrs. Belgrave's games, music, and dancing with the assistance of the Italian band, and finally the singing of the Gospel Hymns.

The Blanchita was prepared for her voyage as soon as she came off from the shore, coaled for the round trip, supplied with cooked provisions, though the galley was available, and with everything that could possibly be needed. She was put in about the same trim as when she went up the rivers of Borneo. Felipe was to be the engineer, Pitts the cook, and four sailors were detailed for deck-hands. The excursion had been arranged for five days; and the bags, valises, and other impedimenta of the voyagers, were on deck at an early hour. Breakfast was ready at half-past six; and at half-past seven the Blanchita got under way with a native pilot for the river, who could speak pidgin English.

The party were in a frolicsome mood; and they went off singing a song, to the great astonishment of the native boat-people. Mr. Psi-ning joined with them; for he had learned the tunes in the United States, where he had travelled extensively. Tien-tsin is the terminus of the Grand Canal in the north, and they passed through a small portion of it into the river. The trip was through a low country. The road to the capital was in sight, and they saw various vehicles moving upon it. The first that attracted their attention was one of the barrows, with a native between the handles, supporting them with a band over his shoulders. On one side of the large wheel was a passenger; and behind him was a lofty sail, like those depending from the yards of a ship, but about three times as high in proportion to its width. It had five ribs of wood in it below the upper yard to keep it spread out. The boys thought the craft would be inclined to heel over with all the cargo on the starboard side.

They saw a rickshaw rigged with a sail in this manner. A man on a farm was working with an ordinary wheelbarrow sailing in this way. There were no end of men riding ponies, or in the two-wheeled passenger-carts having a cover over them which extended out over the horse. Farther up they observed a couple of coolies irrigating the land with a machine which had four paddles for moving the water, with four more each side of the stream, under a frame to which two men were holding on, and working treadmill fashion, with their feet on each of the four arms. They noticed mixed teams of horses and bullocks, such as one sees in Naples. The most curious was a mule-litter, which was simply a sedan between two animals.

Felipe drove the launch at a nine-knot speed, and at half-past three in the afternoon the boat arrived at Tung-chow. Contrary to their expectation, the passengers had greatly enjoyed the trip; but it was out of their own hilarity rather than their surroundings. Pitts had arranged the lunch in a very tasty manner on the tables in what the boys had called the fore and after cabins. They found all the variety of vehicles they had seen on the road, and in three hours they came to the great gate of Pekin. They were conveyed to the small German hotel, which they more than filled; and other lodgings were provided for some of the gentlemen, though the meals were to be taken at the public-house.

The Chinese gentlemen had to leave them to

attend to their own affairs, but after dinner the professor told them something about Pekin: "The city is in about the same latitude as New York, and the climate is about the same. It is situated on a sandy plain, and the suburbs are comparatively few. The town consists of two cities, the Manchu and the Chinese, separated by a wall; and the whole is surrounded by high walls, with towers and pagodas on them, as you have already seen. The Manchu wall is fifty feet high, sixty feet wide at the bottom, and forty at the top. Without the cross-walls, there are twenty-one miles of outer wall, enclosing twenty-six square miles of ground.

"There are sixteen gates, each with a tower a hundred feet high on it. Your first impression must have been that Pekin is the greatest city in the world. You came in by a street two hundred feet wide, with shops on each side; but when you have seen more of it, you will find dilapidation and decay, and about the same filth you have observed in other Chinese cities. But it is one of the most ancient cities in the world, for this or another city stood here twelve hundred years before Christ. Kublai, a grandson of Genghis Khan, the great conqueror of the Moguls, made Pekin the capital of all China. When the Manchus came into power the city was all ready for them, and for a time they kept it in repair; but for more than a hundred years it has been going to ruin.

"The Manchu, or inner city, is divided into three

parts, the largest of which is the real city. In the middle of it are two walled enclosures, one within the other. The outer one seems to be the guard-room of the inner, to which entrance is forbidden to all foreigners, and even to Manchus and Chinese not connected with the court. This last is called the Purple Forbidden City, two and a quarter miles around it, and is the actual imperial residence. It includes the palaces of the emperor and empress and other members of the family. It contains other palaces and halls of reception.

"The 'Hall of Grand Harmony' is built on a terrace twenty feet high, and is of marble, one hundred and ten feet high. Its chief apartment is two hundred feet long by ninety wide, and contains a throne for the emperor, who holds his receptions here on New Year's Day, his birthday, and on other great occasions. The 'Palace of Heavenly Purity' is where the monarch meets his cabinet at dawn for business; and you see that he must be an early riser. Within these enclosures are temples, parks, an artificial lake a mile long, a great temple in which the imperial family worship their ancestors, and many other grand palaces, temples, and statues, which I have not time to mention.

"The outer, or Chinese, city, is thinly populated, and a considerable portion of it is under cultivation. The principal streets are over a hundred feet wide; but those at the sides of them, like Canton and other cities, are nothing but lanes. None of the streets are paved, and mud and dust reign supreme. As with other Eastern cities, the population of Pekin is exaggerated, being estimated by some as high as two millions; but Dr. Legge thought it was less than one million.

"The charge of infanticide seems not to be applicable to Pekin or the surrounding country, and is said to be almost unknown there. A dead-cart passes through the streets at early morning to pick up the bodies of children dying from ordinary causes whose parents are too poor to bury them. There are foundling hospitals, to which the mothers prefer to take their female children rather than sacrifice them. In fact, infanticide is said to be known only in four or five provinces. I have nothing more to say, and I leave you to see the rest for yourselves," said the professor, as he resumed his seat.

The next morning Mr. Psi-ning presented himself at the hotel, before which were gathered vehicles enough to accommodate the entire party. The rickshaw had recently been introduced from Japan, and several of them were included in the number; but the carts and the barrows were generally preferred. The company selected what they pleased. Mr. Psi-ning led the way through the principal street, and through some of the lanes; but the scenes in them were so much like what they had seen in three other cities that the novelty of them had worn off. The residences of the ambassadors of foreign countries were pointed out to them, including that of the Hon.

C. Denby, before which they halted; and the Chinese gentleman conducted them all into it, where they were presented in due form to His Excellency, who received them very pleasantly.

They then went to the Temple of Heaven, which was quite a curious building, somewhat in pagoda style. It began on the ground at a round structure, with an overhanging roof. The second story was smaller, with the same kind of a roof; and the third was the same, but with a roof coming to a point, like a cone. It was almost a hundred feet high. The tiles were of blue porcelain, in imitation of a clear sky.

In the afternoon the tourists were conveyed to the office of the Board of Punishments, and Mr. Psi-ning explained the criminal processes and sentences. The latter are very severe, including torture, which makes one think that he is reading Foxe's "Book of Martyrs." The party declined to witness any of the punishments. Some culprits are treated to twenty or more blows-with a bamboo. Men suspected are tortured to make them confess. They are put in all sorts of painful positions.

Capital punishment is inflicted by placing the victim on his knees, with his arms bound behind him, and his head is severed from his body by the stroke of a heavy knife or sword.

The next day the mandarin conducted the tourists to the gate of the Forbidden City; for he had obtained a permit for the admission of the whole of them in a body. The professor had described the principal structures within the enclosure; and it would be only a repetition to report what the mandarin said of them, though he added considerable to what had come from the books. The third gateway was especially noted as one of the finest pieces of Chinese architecture the party had seen.

The " Abode of Heavenly Calmness " was the noblest, richest, and most luxuriously furnished in the great palace; for it is the private apartment of the emperor. The Great Union Saloon, where His Imperial Majesty receives the high-class mandarins, was elegant enough for any royal apartment.

The tourists walked about among the Chinese glories till they were tired out. The two Cupids were completely "blown;" and when they found a place, they seated themselves, and let the rest of the company finish the survey of the Forbidden City. The palace of one prince of the imperial house was so large that three thousand men could be quartered in the out-buildings, and doubtless as many more could be accommodated in the main structure. The Cupids were picked up on the return; but there was more to be seen, and they went to the beautiful temple of Fo, containing a gilded bronze statue of the god, sixty feet high, with one hundred arms, and Scott remarked that he was like a big man-of-war, well armed.

They came again to the Temple of Heaven; but the mandarin had not obtained a permit, which was exceedingly difficult to procure in recent years. Mr. Psi-ning told them that the interior, in its chief hall, represented the heavens. It was a circular apartment surrounded by twenty-two pillars, and everything was painted sky-blue. A portion of this temple is the "Penitential Retreat" of the emperor, where he keeps three days of fasting, meditating over his own sins and those of the government, previous to offering up his sacrifice. Connected with the temple was a band of five hundred musicians, who reside there; but the commander was thankful that the party were not compelled to listen to their performance.

The tourists were very glad to get back to the hotel in the street of the legations, and they did not go out again that day. The question of visiting the Great Wall then came up for discussion. Brother Avoirdupois and Brother Adipose Tissue declared in the beginning that they would not go; and the mandarin laughed heartily when these names were applied to them, and still more when they were called the Cupids.

"It is forty-five miles to the loop-wall which travellers generally visit from Pekin," said Mr. Psi-ning. "You would have to go in mule-litters, or on horseback, or by the carts you have used; and it would take you a day to get there, and as long to return. Then it would be only the loop-wall, and not the Great Wall, which cannot be reached without going over a hundred miles. I can say for myself that I have never been to either, just as I heard a man in Boston say that he had lived there over sixty years, and had never been to Bunker Hill Monument."

"The wall is an old story to you, I suppose," said the princess.

"You have seen the walls of Pekin, and they are a good specimen of the Great Wall; at any rate, they satisfied me," replied the mandarin.

But the "Big Four" and Professor Giroud decided to visit the loop-wall, and the Chinese gentleman advised them to start immediately after lunch. One of the guides, who had been there several times before, was to accompany them, and was sure they could reach their destination by sunset; and they started as soon as they had lunched. Mr. Psi procured for them six fine horses and a mule-litter. The road was paved with solid granite slabs, ten feet long, all the way.

The attentive mandarin kept the rest of the tourists very busy the next two days; and they visited everything that was worth seeing in the capital, and they dined with him one day in his palace. The party from the wall returned before night the next day, and said they had had a good time, though the wall did not amount to much more than that seen at Pekin.

"I have a government mission in Tokyo next week, and I have to go to Japan," said Mr. Psi-ning, while they were dining together at the German Hotel. "I shall probably meet you there."

"If you are going to Japan, permit me to offer you a stateroom on board of the Guardian-Mother," interposed the commander eagerly. "You are practically an American after a five years' residence in the United States, and are familiar with our way of living; though I will add that Monsieur Odervie, our French cook, has learned to make a few Chinese dishes, and we will endeavor to make you comfortable."

"Your living will suit me perfectly, for I am used to it; and having dined with you on board, I know that your bill of fare is better than any hotel in the States. But when do you sail?"

"Whenever you are ready, my dear sir."

"I have to spend a day in Tien-tsin, and then I was to take a steamer to Shang-hai, and thence a P. & O. to Yokohama."

"But that is out of the way; and we go direct to Yokohama, or we will go there first if you honor us with your company," said the captain, glancing at General Noury.

"By all means!" exclaimed the pacha. "Mrs. Noury and myself will be delighted to have you with us, Mr. Psi-ning."

"Then I shall be too happy to accept your cordial invitation," replied the mandarin. That matter was settled; and the new passenger went to his palace to prepare for his journey, though he did not forget to send one of his people to Tung-chow to arrange for the reception of the party the next day.

The horses the young men rode, the mule-litters, wheelbarrows, and jinrikishas were at the door of the hotel early in the morning; and the mandarin, with his valet, were on time. The company reached Tung-chow before noon; and a Chinese lunch was ready for them, ordered by the new passenger. The Blanchita was all ready for them to step on board when they had partaken of roast goose, duck, and chicken at the inn. The passage down the river was a frolic all the way, and the guest told them more about China than they had learned before in regard to matters not generally known.

Felipe hurried the steamer, and she was alongside the Guardian-Mother before five in the afternoon. Mr. Psi-ning had several pieces of baggage, including despatch-bags, which were placed in the finest state-room on board. The commander had telegraphed for dinner at the usual hour. Mr. Smithers came on board before it was ready, and was invited to join the company. From him they learned that Mr. Psi-ning was in the diplomatic service of the government, and that he would be of great assistance to them in Japan.

The ships had to wait only one day for him; and on Wednesday, May 10, at six in the morning, they sailed for Tokyo, though the commander's original intention had been to go first to Nagasaki. The Blanche's party went on board of the Guardian-Mother before she sailed, with the Italian band. They played to the great delight of the boatmen around the ship, as well as of those on board. The consul went to the mouth of the river, and took a tug home. It was a frolic all day and till midnight, when the Blanche's passengers returned to her.

It was a smooth sea all the four days of the voyage, even on the Pacific shores; and the Guardian-Mother's people spent the next day on board of the consort. On the third day there was a lecture on Japan in Conference Hall, given by Mr. Psi-ning, who was as familiar with that country as with China. But his discourse must be reported in another volume.

Those who are disposed to follow the tourists through Japan, and then on their long voyage of two thousand miles to Australia, New Zealand, and the Sandwich Islands, will be enabled to do so in "PACIFIC SHORES; OR, ADVENTURES IN EASTERN SEAS."

OLIVER OPTIC'S BOOKS

Army and Navy Stories. By OLIVER OPTIC. Six volumes. Illustrated. Any volume sold separately. Price per volume, $1.25.

1. The Soldier Boy; OR, TOM SOMERS IN THE ARMY.
2. The Sailor Boy; OR, JACK SOMERS IN THE NAVY.
3. The Young Lieutenant; OR, ADVENTURES OF AN ARMY OFFICER.
4. The Yankee Middy; OR, ADVENTURES OF A NAVY OFFICER.
5. Fighting Joe; OR, THE FORTUNES OF A STAFF OFFICER.
6. Brave Old Salt; OR, LIFE ON THE QUARTER DECK.

"This series of six volumes recounts the adventures of two brothers, Tom and Jack Somers, one in the army, the other in the navy, in the great Civil War. The romantic narratives of the fortunes and exploits of the brothers are thrilling in the extreme. Historical accuracy in the recital of the great events of that period is strictly followed, and the result is, not only a library of entertaining volumes, but also the best history of the Civil War for young people ever written."

Boat Builders Series. By OLIVER OPTIC. In six volumes. Illustrated. Any volume sold separately. Price per volume, $1.25.

1. All Adrift; OR, THE GOLDWING CLUB.
2. Snug Harbor; OR, THE CHAMPLAIN MECHANICS.
3. Square and Compasses; OR, BUILDING THE HOUSE.
4. Stem to Stern; OR, BUILDING THE BOAT.
5. All Taut; OR, RIGGING THE BOAT.
6. Ready About; OR, SAILING THE BOAT.

"The series includes in six successive volumes the whole art of boat building, boat rigging, boat managing, and practical hints to make the ownership of a boat pay. A great deal of useful information is given in this Boat Builders Series, and in each book a very interesting story is interwoven with the information. Every reader will be interested at once in Dory, the hero of 'All Adrift,' and one of the characters retained in the subsequent volumes of the series. His friends will not want to lose sight of him, and every boy who makes his acquaintance in 'All Adrift' will become his friend."

Riverdale Story Books. By OLIVER OPTIC. Twelve volumes. Illustrated. Illuminated covers. Price: cloth, per set, $3.60; per volume, 30 cents; paper, per set, $2.00.

1. Little Merchant.
2. Young Voyagers.
3. Christmas Gift.
4. Dolly and I.
5. Uncle Ben.
6. Birthday Party.
7. Proud and Lazy.
8. Careless Kate.
9. Robinson Crusoe, Jr.
10. The Picnic Party.
11. The Gold Thimble.
12. The Do-Somethings.

Riverdale Story Books. By OLIVER OPTIC. Six volumes. Illustrated. Fancy cloth and colors. Price per volume, 30 cents.

1. Little Merchant.
2. Proud and Lazy.
3. Young Voyagers.
4. Careless Kate.
5. Dolly and I.
6. Robinson Crusoe, Jr.

Flora Lee Library. By OLIVER OPTIC. Six volumes. Illustrated. Fancy cloth and colors. Price per volume, 30 cents.

1. The Picnic Party.
2. The Gold Thimble.
3. The Do-Somethings.
4. Christmas Gift.
5. Uncle Ben.
6. Birthday Party.

These are bright short stories for younger children who are unable to comprehend the Starry Flag Series or the Army and Navy Series. But they all display the author's talent for pleasing and interesting the little folks. They are all fresh and original, preaching no sermons, but inculcating good lessons.

The Way of the World. By OLIVER OPTIC. Illustrated. $1.50.

"One of the most interesting American novels we have ever read." — *Philadelphia City Item.*

"This story treats of a fortune of three million dollars left a youthful heir. The volume bears evidence in every chapter of the fresh, original, and fascinating style which has always enlivened Mr. ADAMS' productions. We have the same felicitous manner of working out the plot by conversation, the same quaint wit and humor, and a class of characters which stand out boldly, pen photographs of living beings.

"The book furnishes a most romantic and withal a most instructive illustration of the way of the world in its false estimate of money."

Living too Fast; OR, THE CONFESSIONS OF A BANK OFFICER. By OLIVER OPTIC. Illustrated. $1.50.

This story records the experience of a bank officer in the downward career of crime. The career ought, perhaps, to have ended in the State's prison; but the author chose to represent the defaulter as sharply punished in another way. The book contains a most valuable lesson; and shows, in another leading character, the true life which a young business man ought to lead.

In Doors and Out; OR, VIEWS FROM A CHIMNEY CORNER. By OLIVER OPTIC. Illustrated. $1.50.

"Many who have not time and patience to wade through a long story will find here many pithy and sprightly tales, each sharply hitting some social absurdity or social vice. We recommend the book heartily after having read the three chapters on 'Taking a Newspaper.' If all the rest are as sensible and interesting as these, and doubtless they are, the book is well worthy of patronage." — *Vermont Record.*

"As a writer of domestic stories, Mr. WILLIAM T. ADAMS (OLIVER OPTIC) made his mark even before he became so immensely popular through his splendid books for the young. In the volume before us are given several of these tales, and they comprise a book which will give them a popularity greater than they have ever before enjoyed. They are written in a spirited style, impart valuable practical lessons, and are of the most lively interest."—*Boston Home Journal.*

Our Standard Bearer. A Life of Gen. U. S. Grant. By OLIVER OPTIC. Illustrated by THOMAS NAST. Illuminated covers, $1.50.

It has long been out of print, but now comes out in a new edition, with a narrative of the civil career of the General as President for two terms, his remarkable journey abroad, his life in New York, and his sickness, death, and burial. Perhaps the reader will remember that the narrative is told by "Captain Galligasken" after a style that is certainly not common or tiresome, but, rather, in a direct, simple, picturesque, and inspiring way that wins the heart of the young reader. For the boy who wants to read the life of General Grant, this book is the best that has been published,—perhaps the only one that is worth any consideration.

Just His Luck. By OLIVER OPTIC. Illustrated. $1.00.

"It deals with real flesh and blood boys; with boys who possess many noble qualities of mind; with boys of generous impulses and large hearts; with boys who delight in playing pranks, and who are ever ready for any sort of mischief; and with boys in whom human nature is strongly engrafted. They are boys, as many of us have been; boys in the true, unvarnished sense of the word; boys with hopes, ideas, and inspirations, but lacking in judgment, self-control, and discipline. And the book contains an appropriate moral, teaches many a lesson, and presents many a precept worthy of being followed. It is a capital book for boys."

J. T. TROWBRIDGE'S BOOKS

THE SILVER MEDAL STORIES. 6 volumes.

The Silver Medal, AND OTHER STORIES. By J. T. TROWBRIDGE. Illustrated. $1.25.

There were some schoolboys who had turned housebreakers, and among their plunder was a silver medal that had been given to one John Harrison by the Humane Society for rescuing from drowning a certain Benton Barry. Now Benton Barry was one of the wretched housebreakers. This is the summary of the opening chapter. The story is intensely interesting in its serious as well as its humorous parts.

His Own Master. By J. T. TROWBRIDGE. Illustrated. $1.25.

"This is a book after the typical boy's own heart. Its hero is a plucky young fellow, who, seeing no chance for himself at home, determines to make his own way in the world. . . . He sets out accordingly, trudges to the far West, and finds the road to fortune an unpleasantly rough one." — *Philadelphia Inquirer.*

"We class this as one of the best stories for boys we ever read. The tone is perfectly healthy, and the interest is kept up to the end." — *Boston Home Journal.*

Bound in Honor. By J. T. TROWBRIDGE. Illustrated. $1.25.

This story is of a lad, who, though not guilty of any bad action, had been an eye-witness of the conduct of his comrades, and felt "Bound in Honor" not to tell.

"The glimpses we get of New England character are free from any distortion, and their humorous phases are always entertaining. Mr. TROWBRIDGE'S brilliant descriptive faculty is shown to great advantage in the opening chapter of the book by a vivid picture of a village fire, and is manifested elsewhere with equally telling effect." — *Boston Courier.*

The Pocket Rifle. By J. T. TROWBRIDGE. Illustrated. $1.25.

"A boy's story which will be read with avidity, as it ought to be, it is so brightly and frankly written, and with such evident knowledge of the temperaments and habits, the friendships and enmities of schoolboys." — *New York Mail.*

"This is a capital story for boys. TROWBRIDGE never tells a story poorly. It teaches honesty, integrity, and friendship, and how best they can be promoted. It shows the danger of hasty judgment and circumstantial evidence; that right-doing pays, and dishonesty never." — *Chicago Inter-Ocean.*

The Jolly Rover. By J. T. TROWBRIDGE. Illustrated. $1.25.

"This book will help to neutralize the ill effects of any poison which children may have swallowed in the way of sham-adventurous stories and wildly fictitious tales. 'The Jolly Rover' runs away from home, and meets life as it is, till he is glad enough to seek again his father's house. Mr. TROWBRIDGE has the power of making an instructive story absorbing in its interest, and of covering a moral so that it is easy to take." — *Christian Intelligencer.*

Young Joe, AND OTHER BOYS. By J. T. TROWBRIDGE. Illustrated. $1.25.

"Young Joe," who lived at Bass Cove, where he shot wild ducks, took some to town for sale, and attracted the attention of a portly gentleman fond of shooting. This gentleman went duck shooting with Joe, and their adventures were more amusing to the boy than to the amateur sportsman.

There are thirteen other short stories in the book which will be sure to please the young folks.

The Vagabonds: AN ILLUSTRATED POEM. By J. T. TROWBRIDGE. Cloth. $1.50.

"The Vagabonds" are a strolling fiddler and his dog. The fiddler has been ruined by drink, and his monologue is one of the most pathetic and effective pieces in our literature.

J. T. TROWBRIDGE'S BOOKS

THE TIDE-MILL STORIES. 6 volumes.

Phil and His Friends. By J. T. TROWBRIDGE. Illustrated. $1.25.

The hero is the son of a man who from drink got into debt, and, after having given a paper to a creditor authorizing him to keep the son as a security for his claim, ran away, leaving poor Phil a bond slave. The story involves a great many unexpected incidents, some of which are painful, and some comic. Phil manfully works for a year, cancelling his father's debt, and then escapes. The characters are strongly drawn, and the story is absorbingly interesting.

The Tinkham Brothers' Tide-Mill. By J. T. TROWBRIDGE. Illustrated. $1.25.

"The Tinkham Brothers" were the devoted sons of an invalid mother. The story tells how they purchased a tide-mill, which afterwards, by the ill-will and obstinacy of neighbors, became a source of much trouble to them. It tells also how, by discretion and the exercise of a peaceable spirit, they at last overcame all difficulties.

"Mr. TROWBRIDGE's humor, his fidelity to nature, and story-telling power lose nothing with years; and he stands at the head of those who are furnishing a literature for the young, clean and sweet in tone, and always of interest and value." — *The Continent.*

The Satin-wood Box. By J. T. TROWBRIDGE. Illustrated. $1.25.

"Mr. TROWBRIDGE has always a purpose in his writings, and this time he has undertaken to show how very near an innocent boy can come to the guilty edge and yet be able by fortunate circumstances to rid himself of all suspicion of evil. There is something winsome about the hero; but he has a singular way of falling into bad luck, although the careful reader will never feel the least disposed to doubt his honesty. . . . It is the pain and perplexity which impart to the story its intense interest." — *Syracuse Standard.*

The Little Master. By J. T. TROWBRIDGE. Illustrated. $1.25.

This is the story of a schoolmaster, his trials, disappointments, and final victory. It will recall to many a man his experience in teaching pupils, and in managing their opinionated and self-willed parents. The story has the charm which is always found in Mr. TROWBRIDGE's works.

"Many a teacher could profit by reading of this plucky little schoolmaster." — *Journal of Education.*

His One Fault. By J. T. TROWBRIDGE. Illustrated. $1.25.

"As for the hero of this story, 'His One Fault' was absent-mindedness. He forgot to lock his uncle's stable door, and the horse was stolen. In seeking to recover the stolen horse, he unintentionally stole another. In trying to restore the wrong horse to his rightful owner, he was himself arrested. After no end of comic and dolorous adventures, he surmounted all his misfortunes by downright pluck and genuine good feeling. It is a noble contribution to juvenile literature." — *Woman's Journal.*

Peter Budstone. By J. T. TROWBRIDGE. Illustrated. $1.25.

"TROWBRIDGE's other books have been admirable and deservedly popular, but this one, in our opinion, is the best yet. It is a story at once spirited and touching, with a certain dramatic and artistic quality that appeals to the literary sense as well as to the story-loving appetite. In it Mr. TROWBRIDGE has not lectured or moralized or remonstrated; he has simply shown boys what they are doing when they contemplate hazing. By a good artistic impulse we are not shown the hazing at all; when the story begins, the hazing is already over, and we are introduced immediately to the results. It is an artistic touch also that the boy injured is not hurt because he is a fellow of delicate nerves, but because of his very strength, and the power with which he resisted until overcome by numbers, and subjected to treatment which left him insane. His insanity takes the form of harmless delusion, and the absurdity of his ways and talk enables the author to lighten the sombreness without weakening the moral, in a way that ought to win all boys to his side." — *The Critic.*

J. T. TROWBRIDGE'S BOOKS

THE TOBY TRAFFORD SERIES. 3 volumes.

The Fortunes of Toby Trafford. By J. T. TROWBRIDGE. Illustrated. $1.25.

"If to make children's stories as true to nature as the stories which the masters of fiction write for children of a larger growth be an uncommon achievement, and one that is worthy of wide recognition, that recognition should be given to Mr. J. T. TROWBRIDGE for his many achievements in this difficult walk of literary art. Mr. TROWBRIDGE has a good perception of character, which he draws with skill; he has abundance of invention, which he never abuses; and he has, what so many American writers have not, an easy, graceful style, which can be humorous, or pathetic, or poetic." — *R. H. Stoddard in New York Mail.*

Father Brighthopes: AN OLD CLERGYMAN'S VACATION. By J. T. TROWBRIDGE. Illustrated. $1.25.

This book was published in the early fifties by Phillips, Sampson & Co., of which firm Mr. Lee (of Lee and Shepard) was then a member. It was very favorably received, and was followed by other stories, — a long series of them, — still lengthening, and which, it is hoped, may be prolonged indefinitely. Recently a new edition has appeared, and for a preface the author has related with touching simplicity the account of his first experience in authorship.

It is well known that Mr. TROWBRIDGE is primarily a poet. Some beautiful poems of his were printed in the early numbers of the *Atlantic Monthly* (in company with poems by LONGFELLOW, EMERSON, LOWELL, and HOLMES), and were well received. "At Sea" is a gem that has become classic. The poetic faculty has not been without use to the story-writer. The perception of beauty in nature and in human nature is always evident even in his realistic prose. But his poetic gift never leads him into sentimentality, and his characters are true children of men, with natural faults as well as natural gifts and graces. His stories are intensely *human*, with a solid basis, and with an instinctive dramatic action. He has never written an uninteresting book.

Woodie Thorpe's Pilgrimage, AND OTHER STORIES. By J. T. TROWBRIDGE. Illustrated. $1.25.

"The scenes are full of human interest and lifelikeness, and will please many an old reader, as well as the younger folks for whose delectation it is intended. As in all the books of this author the spirit is manly, sincere, and in the best sense moral There is no 'goody' talk and no cant, but principles of truthfulness, integrity, and self-reliance are quietly inculcated by example. It is safe to say that any boy will be the better for reading books like this." — *St. Botolph.*

Neighbors' Wives. By J. T. TROWBRIDGE. Cloth. $1.50.

As a novelty, the following acrostic is presented. The praise from the different newspapers is brief, but to the point.

N ot in the least tiresome. — *Troy Press.*
E xquisite touches of character. — *Salem Observer.*
I ntroducing strong scenes with rare skill. — *Gloucester Telegraph.*
G roups well certain phases of character. — *New Bedford Standard.*
H appy sprightliness of style and vivacity which fascinates — *Dover Legion.*
B y many considered the author's best. — *Journal.*
O ne of the best of TROWBRIDGE's stories. — *Commonwealth.*
R eader finds it difficult to close the book. — *Hearth and Home.*
S toryall alive with adventures and incidents striking and vivid. — *Dover Star.*

W hich is one of TROWBRIDGE's brightest and best. — *Boston Transcript.*
I s destined to be enjoyed mightily. — *Salem Observer.*
V ery pleasant reading. — *New York Leader.*
E xcels any of the author's former books. — *Montana American.*
S tory is in the author's best vein. — *New Haven Register.*

LEE AND SHEPARD, BOSTON, SEND THEIR COMPLETE CATALOGUE FREE.